THE CONCORDAT

THE
CONCORDAT

SEAN HEARY

Matador
9 Priory Business Park,
Wistow Road, Kibworth Beauchamp,
Leicestershire. LE8 0RX
Tel: 0116 279 2299
Email: books@troubador.co.uk
Web: www.troubador.co.uk/matador
Twitter: @matadorbooks

ISBN 978 1789013 443

British Library Cataloguing in Publication Data.
A catalogue record for this book is available from the British Library.

Printed and bound in Great Britain by 4edge Limited
Typeset in 11pt Minion Pro by Troubador Publishing Ltd, Leicester, UK

Matador is an imprint of Troubador Publishing Ltd

For Oksana, William and Tess

PROLOGUE

Late evening on the Hellersdorf housing estate in Berlin. A hollow-faced old man shuffled through the slush towards his Soviet-era apartment. He took a swig from his flask, then steadied himself as he stepped onto the quiet cul-de-sac. Through the gusting sleet he discerned the dim distant lights of an approaching vehicle. The saloon was upon him sooner than he thought. But he showed no urgency as the road was wide and well lit.

"What the hell?" he murmured to himself.

No blast on the horn, no screech of tyres. Only the sickening thud of the saloon striking his frail body. The driver studied his victim in the rear-view mirror. Certain he was dead, he slammed his foot on the accelerator and sped off.

Out of the shadows came a tall, lean man wearing a black overcoat. He pulled his green flat cap down low over his eyes as he moved cat-like towards the victim. Hunched over the body, he checked the carotid artery for a pulse. There was none.

"What happened?" bellowed a bearded man, jogging up from behind.

The capped stranger didn't react. Nervelessly he ran his searching fingers over the victim's body.

"That looks painful," a youth called out, joining in from the side.

As the two men drew nearer their gaze locked on to the smashed face of the toothless man. The distraction provided the capped stranger the few seconds he needed to deftly slide his hand into the victim's trouser pocket and remove something unnoticed.

"He's dead," the stranger proclaimed, rising to his feet. As the crowd swelled around their reclusive neighbour, the man in the green flat cap slipped away and faded into the darkness.

From the apartment block opposite a hastily dressed, rotund woman waddled onto the street. "I've phoned the police," she announced with verve.

"No surprise there," mocked a voice from the pack.

Sirens echoed off the estate's prefabricated concrete towers. Then all heads swung south as flashing blue lights appeared between buildings on the ring road encircling the estate.

The crowd had grown to over thirty. Two teenage boys laughed as they dreamt up captions to accompany selfies with the old man's contorted body as the backdrop.

"Damn it! I said beam me down. Not drop me on my head," one of the youths howled, thumbing the text into his post.

Sarcastic applause and cheers greeted the orange-red ambulance as it turned cautiously into the icy cul-de-sac.

"Full house," the driver said.

The paramedic nodded. "You sure we've got the right address? Looks more like a street party."

But it wasn't. Instead of warming themselves round a blazing bonfire, the neighbours stood shuffling their feet, gazing down at a mangled corpse.

"Bet you a tenner it's a transport only," the driver said, glimpsing the victim as he pulled the ambulance to a stop short of the mob.

Undeterred, the paramedic grabbed his bag and hurried towards the old man.

"Move back," came an amplified voice from a police car that had just drawn up.

"He got what he deserved," one onlooker called out as two officers climbed from the vehicle. "We should've strung him up years ago," came another. "Leave him for the dogs," said a third.

"Show some respect," Senior Constable Hoffman said, frowning.

Nothing more was said as the two policemen elbowed their way to centre stage.

"What we got, Hans?" Hoffman enquired.

The paramedic glanced up from next to the body. "Massive head trauma incompatible with life. Hit-and-run."

"An unlikely place," Hoffman said, scratching the back of his fat neck as he glanced up and down the street.

1

The Vatican was an extraordinary city. Her secrets cloaked in mystery, her residents quaint and queer. Enemies eternally at the gate. And sometimes within her walls. Sitting naked on the edge of his empty bathtub, Inspector General Lorenzo Rossi took a long sip of his Scotch. Through a partly open window he gazed vacantly at the lonely soldier of the Swiss Guard protecting the Porta Sant'Anna border entrance. It was Thursday night, eight o'clock. Barring incident, Rossi had finished for the day. He closed the toilet lid and set his glass on top.

"Not now," Rossi murmured, picking up his phone. "Mama, can I call you back? I'm shaving my legs."

"Enzo," she said with a tut. "Why do you tell me such things?"

"It's for cycling, Mama," Rossi said, ending the call.

Rossi smiled wistfully as he applied shaving gel to his right leg. His mother's call had reminded him of why he was here.

Rossi joined the Vatican Gendarmerie on his twenty-third birthday, nineteen years ago, as a compromise to his parents. The youngest of six brothers he grew up in a sprawling farmhouse nestled amongst vineyards and olive groves in Siena, Tuscany. His father, determined that one of his sons would join the priesthood, had nurtured young Lorenzo with the Church in mind. His mother was having none of it. She insisted he was far too popular with the village girls to consider such mad folly. Besides, little Enzo was her favourite. Grandchildren were what she expected. To further complicate matters, Rossi from an early age had dreamt of becoming a soldier. To resolve the three-way tug-of-war, Rossi joined the Vatican Corpo della Gendarmeria – an accommodation he never regretted.

"What the hell?" Rossi said, dropping his shaver. He sprang to his feet and dashed out of the bathroom, only to return seconds later with a pair of binoculars.

He flung open the window and focused on the small secluded churchyard to the right of the border crossing. Nothing. He watched for a few minutes more, but whatever he had seen was gone.

Rossi draped a towel round his shoulders and sat back down, his gaze constantly drawn to the open window as he lathered his other leg.

"Gotcha," he said, knocking over his empty glass as he grabbed for the binoculars.

Despite the unsavoury sight of a nun bent over a tombstone with her lily-white arse in the air, and a trouserless priest readying himself nearby, Rossi didn't overreact. Inside the Vatican he had seen it all. The Church was a magnet for those lacking a normal moral compass. He reached for his phone.

"You guys asleep?... Someone's shooting a porno film in the garden of Sant'Anna," Rossi said in a gruff tone.

He leant out of the window for a better view. Instantly he realised he should have been more instructive. "Discretion," he bellowed down, but it was too late. He bit his lip as he watched the naked nun and the well-hung priest escape back into Rome. The tourists on Via di Porta Angelica hooted in delight. The film cameraman was not so lucky. He had been taken into custody by two red-faced gendarmes who refused to look up.

"Just perfect," Rossi yelled out to no one in particular.

The phone rang. Rossi glanced at the screen. *Bad news travels fast.* "Good evening, Monsignor."

"Inspector General, sorry to interrupt your evening but Cardinal Capelli requires your immediate presence."

Rossi looked down at his one shaved leg and rolled his sea-green eyes. "I'm on my way."

2

Rossi hated surprises. Top of the list were unscheduled meetings with Cardinal Santo Capelli, the Dean of the Sacred College of Cardinals. To be called urgently to the cardinal's office so late in the evening was highly unusual. *Something's gone wrong*, he thought, bustling down the stone-floored corridor that led to the prelate's office.

Rossi skidded to a halt in front of a partly opened door. Inside he saw Cardinal Capelli's executive assistant, Monsignor Polak, working at his desk. The cardinal's apricot-coloured pug lay asleep at his feet. Rossi ran his fingers through his thick black hair and straightened his jacket, then entered.

"I trust it's nothing serious?" Rossi enquired in a respectful tone.

"His Eminence is expecting you," Monsignor Polak said. Exactly the response Rossi foresaw.

Monsignor Polak moved past Rossi and knocked sharply. He turned the handle and the tall wooden door opened silently. Rossi waited in the doorway as the short, fat monsignor announced his arrival.

"Come in, Inspector General," the elderly cardinal said, looking up from behind his large mahogany desk.

"I came the moment I received your message," Rossi said, sensing tension in the room. "There was a disturbance on Piazza San Pietro. A young Dutchman decided to climb the Egyptian Obelisk…"

"I have invited Commandant Waldmann to join us."

Christian Waldmann, the Commandant of the Corps of the Pontifical Swiss Guard, rose and greeted Rossi warmly. Waldmann, a willowy man with slicked-back blond hair, had only been in the job for three weeks. Recruited from outside the force, Rossi had been assigned to mentor him on Vatican politics and protocol.

"I have another engagement in thirty minutes," the cardinal said in a soft, but urgent voice. "So let us begin."

As they took their seats in front of the desk, the cardinal handed them a copy of an agreement between Pope Pius XII and Hitler.

A chill ran through Rossi's bones as he read the date. "1 June 1939."

"Three months before the Nazis invaded Poland," Waldmann added, "marking the beginning of World War II in Europe."

The bespectacled cardinal tapped his pen on the burgundy leather inlay of his desk as he waited for them to finish reading.

"What is the concern?" Waldmann said, his hooded blue eyes darting between Rossi and the cardinal as he spoke. "It's a forgery."

The cardinal blew out a long breath and raised his overgrown eyebrows to the heavens.

"To the Church's enemies it's irrelevant," Rossi said, still studying the document.

"But what's written isn't remotely credible," Waldmann protested, pointing to the preamble. "The notion that Pope Pius would partner with Hitler is farcical."

"Where'd it come from?" Rossi asked.

The white-haired prelate reached for his notes. "Maximilian Wolf, a history teacher from Bonn, Germany. Not one of us, unfortunately."

"A Protestant?" Rossi said.

"Worse – an agnostic."

Waldmann sneered. "A fence-sitter."

"He claims to have found it while cleaning out his late father's apartment in Berlin."

Rossi put the document aside. "What does he want?"

"That's what I need you to find out," the cardinal said, looking at Rossi. "Bishop Muellenbach, the Church's leading scholar on World War II documents, will meet Wolf tomorrow evening at the Münster Basilica in Bonn. I would like you to join him."

"With pleasure," Rossi said in a low, vengeful tone.

"Inspector General, this is an extremely sensitive matter. You are to go gently. We want none of this getting out."

Rossi nodded. Having worked at the Vatican for all his adult life, he didn't have to ask why.

"But, Your Eminence," Waldmann said, looking at Rossi. "The Church collaborating with Hitler? Who in their right mind would believe such a thing?"

Cardinal Capelli glanced at his watch. "For those who despise the Church, the truth is of little consequence."

"You're right, of course, Your Eminence," Rossi said, turning his gaze towards Waldmann.

The cardinal leant forward, resting his forearms on the table. "It's obvious the Concordat was created to coincide with a very dark and uncertain period of European history. And its similarity to the 1933 Nazi Reichskonkordat is uncanny. God help us."

Rossi understood the cardinal's apprehension. There was no shortage of historical context for such a document. The Vatican had signed numerous treaties over the years with the aim of safeguarding the Church's interest.

With Germany, Rossi could recall close to fifteen. All relatively harmless, notwithstanding the fact that some now may fall short of today's secular values. But not the 1933 Reichskonkordat, it was different.

Rossi was well acquainted with its text. Two years ago he had participated in a Vatican workshop on 'developing strategies for communicating the benefits of concordats in the twenty-first century', or some long, convoluted title like that.

The working group consisted of a cross section of the Church's elite. To be invited to such a prestigious event was a privilege and an honour. But there was a downside. Rossi found himself on the wrong side of the debate; playing devil's advocate against his omnipotent employer.

The first morning passed without drama, best remembered for a long, lifeless speech by a tired-looking Cardinal Capelli. But proceedings abruptly changed pace after lunch, when Michael Dempsey, the Professor of Moral Theology and Ethics from Notre Dame University, spoke.

The professor's unkempt, long brown hair and scruffy beard gave Rossi the impression he had just woken up. But if he had, it was on the wrong side of the bed. No hint of apology, the professor bravely berated the Church for executing concordats with Hitler, Franco, Salazar and Mussolini.

"The moral recognition given to these dictators by the Church, through the execution of such treaties, was undeniable," the professor proclaimed.

"Undeniable?" Cardinal Capelli huffed. "How did you arrive at such an erroneous conclusion?"

To make his point, the professor suggested they discuss one of the more problematic of the Church's twentieth-century treaties – the so-called 1933 Nazi Reichskonkordat.

Surprised by the confident American's persistence, Cardinal Capelli mumbled something that the professor liberally interpreted as "proceed".

Rossi stared, as the sixty-something professor rose from his chair and moved slowly around the large oval conference table leaning heavily on his walking stick. He fought back a smile as Professor Dempsey paused deliberately behind each of the prelates while chastising the Church's leadership for executing such an ill-conceived document.

"It is my view, and that of many distinguished historians," the professor said in an oratorical tone, "that the 1933 Reichskonkordat helped legitimise Hitler. And in doing so helped the Nazis consolidate their position in Germany."

At that moment, the sun appeared between the buildings. Golden rays poured in through a small high window onto the professor's face, temporarily blinding him. *A lightning bolt to follow*, Rossi remembered thinking.

Cardinal Capelli refused to be provoked. He calmly stood, to present the Church's position. "Distinguished Professor, like my Church's enemies, you have forgotten half the story."

The professor smirked and raised his shoulders.

The cardinal explained that the Church had pursued the Reichskonkordat to redress the discriminatory Kulturkampf policies of Chancellor Otto von Bismarck, policies which focused on bringing the Roman Catholic Church under state control.

"And don't forget, Professor, the Reichskonkordat was signed a full six years before the start of the war," an Opus Dei participant added.

"The Nazi Party was simply the elected German government of the day," Cardinal Capelli continued. "Furthermore, support of the Nazis was considered a legitimate means of preventing the spread of Russian communism throughout Europe."

To Rossi's disappointment, when the bell sounded for the next round, the professor remained seated, no doubt influenced by whatever Cardinal Capelli had whispered in his ear on the way back to his seat. *Too much truth for one day.*

"So then, Inspector General," Cardinal Capelli said, jolting Rossi back to the present, "you will travel to Bonn tomorrow afternoon and examine the document together with Bishop Muellenbach. If, in the opinion of the bishop, the document is of the highest quality then you are to acquire it."

"That's clear, Your Eminence."

"Inspector General, remember, whatever happens do not allow this unholy forgery to fall into the hands of the Church's enemies," Cardinal Capelli said in a firm tone. He then stood as if to signal the end of the meeting.

Rossi walked to the door. His leather-soled shoes slid on the polished wooden floor as he turned back to face the cardinal. "Your Eminence, I promise you by tomorrow night the forgery will be secure in my possession destined for the Vatican archives."

"Is there any possibility the Concordat is genuine?" Waldmann asked as they headed back to their offices.

"Good Lord, Christian, this is the Roman Catholic Church with all its mysteries. Anything's possible. But as loyal servants of the Church we must suppose the document is a forgery," Rossi said with a wink.

3

Oksana Koroleva felt content. Today was the fifth anniversary of her arrival in Paris. Hidden away in the private sanctum of her third-floor apartment, alone and unloved. She wouldn't have it any other way.

A petite woman in her early thirties with fair skin, long, dark auburn hair and hypnotic amber eyes, love was not an emotion she believed in. 'Cold heart, clear mind' was the creed by which she lived.

From the kitchen island, she stood barefoot in a white cotton bathrobe, gazing dreamily out at the rain falling on the street below. The lavish ceiling to floor wisteria-coloured curtains that framed the tall panelled windows were never closed. Oksana adored the colour and the bustle of the street. If it meant that occasionally a peeping Tom got an eyeful of her nakedness, then so be it. For her, Paris was far too beguiling to worry about what the neighbours might

11

see. Besides, in all the time she had lived at 17 Rue Clément Marot in the 8th arrondissement, she had never seen a single soul at the windows opposite, not even a cleaner.

As she opened a bottle of her favourite Krug Rose Brut champagne, she heard the faint muffled sound of 'Bitter Sweet Symphony'. "Where's my mobile phone?" she murmured, turning her head in the direction of the string loop.

Ordinarily she refused to take calls at home, as she had no true friends. Only acquaintances and colleagues. Tonight was one of the rare exceptions – this was a call she had to take.

"*Salut*," Oksana said in a rushed voice, fearing she had taken too long to answer.

"Your assignment has been sent," a man said in Russian.

"*Yasna*," Oksana said ringing off; grateful she had never met her handler, who she imagined was as unpleasant as the missions he assigned her.

Oksana dropped her mobile phone into her bathrobe pocket and moved purposely towards the entrance hall. "It pays the bills," she rationalised, removing an iPad from her canvas messenger bag, which was hanging next to her damp trench coat.

Oksana looked edgy as she sat down at the small writing desk hidden away in an alcove near the kitchen. She opened the encrypted message and read it.

Clean and Recover.
The Presbytery, Münster Basilica, Bonn, Germany (site plan attached).

Tomorrow 20.00.
Secure Nazi Concordat dated 1939.
2 persons: Maximilian Wolf & Bishop Muellenbach (photos attached).
Full service.

"Not very subtle," Oksana sighed, opening the attachments.

She took a mental snapshot of each of the images before deleting the email. Then, faithful to her training, she ran a program the geeks from the office had installed on her iPad that wiped any trace of her activity.

Sliding the iPad towards the back of the desk, Oksana gazed momentarily at the bare wall in front of her. With a shake of the head she rose and returned to the kitchen, and to her glass of pink champagne.

4

"But it's your father's seventy-fifth birthday."

"Mama," Rossi said, removing Wolf's document from inside his jacket. "I just can't get down this week. I have to fly to Bonn tomorrow afternoon and I'm staying the night."

"What on earth for?"

"To thwart a blackmailer."

Rossi's mama let out a soft sob and blew her nose. "Couldn't they send someone else? Surely you're far too important to the Pope to be running errands?"

"I'm not too sure I'd call this an errand. Besides, Cardinal Capelli wouldn't have asked if it wasn't important."

"He'll be so disappointed."

"Who?"

"Your father of course."

"I'll be home for Christmas."

"Hopefully he hasn't passed by then."

"Passed what?"

A slight snigger. "Passed away – gone to God."

"Stop it, Mama."

"And where are my grandchildren? A forty-two-year-old bachelor. Who's ever heard of such a thing? Your brothers were all married by the time they were thirty. It's not as though there's a shortage of…"

"Mama, I've got to go. There's someone at the door. Love you."

"Love you too, Enzo. Don't forget to call him."

"I won't," Rossi said as he rang off.

Naturally there was no one at the door. Rossi, who had just walked in, was keen to prove his hypothesis. He fetched a dilapidated suitcase from on top of the wardrobe in his bedroom and emptied the entire contents onto the Oriental rug that covered the wooden floor. Rifling through the papers, he quickly found what he was looking for – a copy of the 1933 Nazi Reichskonkordat, which he had used in his research two years earlier. He laid it on the table next to the newly discovered document.

Rossi looked up as heavy rain pelted against the window. Normally he wouldn't have noticed, but he was flying tomorrow, and he hated flying in bad weather.

He poured himself a large Scotch then set to work. Rossi's suspicions were immediately confirmed. Except for the wording, the two treaties were identical. The language and the terminology were the same. As were the format and style. It was as though they were written by the same person, albeit six years apart. To Rossi it was clear. The earlier document had been used by the forger as a template for the newly discovered treaty. But to the enemies of the Church, the consistency in style would be regarded as further proof that the document was genuine.

Rossi's Vatican apartment was small and comfortable. Other than a poster of a dripping wet Sophia Loren hanging on the toilet door and an impressive LP collection, there was nothing to suggest it was the abode of one of Rome's most eligible bachelors.

Rossi poured himself another Scotch and sat down on the sofa. Staring blankly at the crucifix hanging on the wall in front of him, he drifted into deep thought. On the surface the task was straightforward. Still, something deep down worried him. The document had a purpose. He wondered whether it was recent. Was it part of an existing plot, or a relic left over from the Cold War that could be acquired and forgotten about? Let's hope the latter.

Running his eyes once more over the document, Rossi's gaze rested on the phrase 'including the Soviet Union when annexed'. The words seemed so unnecessary. The document was dated three months before the war had even started, so why single out the USSR? It was as though it was created to anger Stalin. But why?

Rossi glanced at his watch. It was late and he was tired, but he knew there was no point in trying to sleep. His mind was racing – full of espionage and intrigue. Resigned to a long night, Rossi poured himself another Scotch and turned on the stereo. Bocelli was already on the turntable so he let it play. Still dressed for the office, Rossi lay down on the sofa and tried to clear his mind.

Within minutes he was asleep.

5

A loose corner of an old canvas concert banner cracked in the icy Moscow wind as a dirty white GAZelle rolled up to the barrier controlling vehicle access to the Olympisky construction yard.

Built for the 1980 Olympics, the weary giant was still one of the largest covered sporting facilities in Europe.

Four years ago, Olympisky was given a new lease of life. As part of a winning bid to host the World Judo Championships, the mayor of Moscow committed $200 million of taxpayers' funds to modernise the arena. A blatant exercise in self-promotion that seemed to pay off, or at least until last month when the International Judo Federation voiced grave concerns about the venue's readiness.

To head off a political firestorm, Mayor Levin opened the city's coffers wider. He demanded work be carried out around the clock. As word got out, Russia's ruling elite began circling the trough. Contractors turned up daily with busloads of unregistered Gastarbeiter from the Central Asian republics. Men in expensive suits came and went. For the poorly trained security personnel it was never clear whom to grant access to and whom to refuse.

"Documents," a short bull-necked security guard ordered through the GAZelle's partly opened window.

Pavel Greshnechov handed over his site pass without saying a word.

"Open the back."

Pavel furrowed his brow. "Are you serious? We've been here every day this week."

"Every vehicle is checked."

"Wait here," Pavel said to his hollowed-eyed passenger.

"Where did you serve?" the guard asked, as he followed Pavel to the back.

Pavel's short-cropped hair and stiff upright gait, acquired while serving in the Russian military as an ordnance officer, were unmistakable. "Middle East."

"Artillery?"

"Catering Corps."

Snigger. "Why so late? It's almost midnight."

"We got a call an hour ago to finish Box 7. The carpet goes down tomorrow."

The guard shone his torch into the back of the van. "What's in the cardboard boxes?"

"Exactly what it says. Air conditioning parts."

"Open them."

"Stop wasting my time."

The guard blew out a soft dismissive breath. "I've got all night."

"Have it your way," Pavel said, clambering up onto the cargo tray. Grabbing the closest of the three boxes, he slashed open the seal and tipped the contents wildly onto the bare metal floor. "Satisfied?"

"And the other two?"

"Go to hell," Pavel said, his voice full of rage.

The guard took a step back. "Just doing my job."

"Well, you've done it. So open the boom gate." Pavel jumped down and slammed the van door. "Otherwise I'm leaving and you can explain to the mayor why there's been another delay."

"These are dangerous times," the guard said with an unapologetic shrug. Then, without another word, he turned and ambled back to the guardhouse.

It was not until the boom gate started to rise that Pavel realised the watchman had capitulated.

"What was that all about?" Oleg asked, as Pavel jumped back behind the wheel and fired up the engine.

"You tell me."

"He didn't like you?"

Pavel drove slowly past the guardhouse. Through the large curtainless window he could see clearly inside. The bull-necked guard was now sitting in front of the video surveillance system. A second guard with spiky red hair was dozing in an armchair. "There should be a third."

"He's probably still on patrol," Oleg said, glancing at his watch.

Pavel pulled the GAZelle up in an unlit part of the loading area. With great care, they transferred the two remaining unopened boxes onto a platform trolley they had brought with them.

In the distance a metal door slammed. Oleg grabbed the binoculars from inside the GAZelle and focused them on a uniformed man hurrying across the construction yard towards the guardhouse. "That's him. We've got fifteen minutes."

Oleg, a small man with a crooked back, scurried ahead. He entered the arena through an access gate located next to a towering roller shutter door. Running the torch beam along the door frame, he located the control panel. He held his thumb on the green button until the shutter rose to head height.

"I'm good," Pavel said, appearing from outside. "Go check we're alone."

Oleg jogged with an odd, uneven stride to the centre of the staging area. The arena was dark, aside from intermittent ribbons of dim, yellow low-voltage lighting that ran along the corridors and stairways. He turned slowly in place, scanning the stands. Everything was still.

By the time Oleg returned, Pavel had already called the service lift. "All clear."

They rode the mechanical dinosaur up to level three. "To the right," Pavel said, as the doors shuddered open.

Thirty metres along the dark, curving corridor stood a door different from the rest. Scrawled above it, in white chalk, '7'.

Oleg pushed open the concrete-filled steel door and switched on the light. He found himself inside an enormous room overlooking the events area. It was empty, except for a ladder standing in front of a private bathroom at the back. The raised floor was tiered at the front to accommodate seating, which was yet to be installed. A small flight of stairs ran down the centre for access. And mounted high on the far wall was a signal amplifier and antenna.

"Find a place to breach the floor," Pavel said, pushing the trolley out of the way.

While Oleg crawled about on the ground, Pavel carefully removed an aluminium transport case from the larger of the two boxes and laid it on the floor. Inside were fifteen one-kilogram blocks of Semtex plastic explosive, surrounded by ball bearings and nails. The Semtex had been covertly manufactured in a Russian military plant by a deep-cover sympathiser. It contained no taggant, which would make it virtually undetectable once hidden under the raised floor.

Pavel had designed the IED to inflict maximum damage, a task made easier by the characteristics of the room. The reinforced concrete walls were 120 centimetres thick and the viewing window, constructed of seven panels of blast-proof laminated glass, was set deep into a rebated steel frame. By placing the bomb inside the room, the energy released during the explosion would have nowhere to go. Anyone caught inside Box 7 would be reduced to DNA.

"What'd you find?"

"The floor's glued. But the stair treads and risers look clean. I'll see whether I can remove them?"

"No. Leave it to me," Pavel said, without looking up. "You go keep an eye out for the watchman."

***

"I'm telling you, I sense something," Bulldog said. "This guy's ex-military."

Ginger yawned and stretched his arms high in the air. "Every second person in Russia is ex-military. They've got to end up somewhere."

"I'm not talking about your run-of-the-mill conscripts. This guy's hardcore," Bulldog insisted, turning his head from the surveillance screens.

"You checked the vehicle, didn't you?" Ginger said in a sleepy mumble.

"I guess so."

"And you found nothing – right?"

"Yeah, but…"

"So shut the fuck up."

"And there's another thing. He lied about being in the Catering Corps. His face was badly scarred, and he was missing a couple of fingers on his left hand. You don't get that from peeling potatoes."

Ginger's florid complexion brightened. "Don't be such an asshole."

"I thought they called you Bulldog because you've got no neck," the senior guard said, joining in. "You're like a dog gnawing at a bone."

"A dry, meatless bone," Ginger added.

"Come on, I'm serious. These two guys are working

unsupervised in the Presidential Box. Shouldn't we at least check what they're up to?"

"And Ginger will," the senior guard said, glancing at his watch.

"Yes, I will," Ginger mocked, zipping up his M4 military parka. "I know you fancy yourself as a bit of a Sherlock Holmes, Bulldog. But you're nothing more than a poorly paid nightwatchman providing security to inanimate objects – you mustn't forget that."

"Piss off, rust boy."

"Enough already, ladies," the senior guard said, pouring himself a mug of coffee from his vacuum flask. "Ginger, to appease your industrious colleague, start your patrol at Box 7."

Ginger shrugged. "It makes no difference to me."

"In the unlikely event Bulldog is right, call it in," the senior guard said, throwing Ginger a wink. "Remember, you're unarmed. Equipped to handle trespassers and vandals – not 'hard-core' military."

"If I'm not back in forty-five minutes – send in the troops," Ginger said over his shoulder, as he stepped out into the cold night air.

***

Down on all fours, Pavel peered through the dismantled steps into the dark space under the raised floor. The distant whine of the service lift signalled he was no longer alone.

Seconds later, Oleg burst into the box. "He's coming this way."

"Close the door and block the entrance."

Oleg grabbed the ladder, stood it in front of the door, and climbed up.

"Take this," Pavel said, holding up a cordless drill.

Oleg pushed aside a couple of tiles and stuck his head above the drop ceiling.

With the door temporarily secured, Pavel manoeuvred the primed IED through the opening in the stairs, and placed it carefully on the concrete floor.

Sensing the watchman was nearby, Oleg let fly with the drill. The screaming pulse of the masonry bit thumping against the ceiling penetrated the whole arena.

"Oi," bellowed Ginger, banging his fist on the massive, vault-like door.

Nothing could be heard above the shriek of the drill.

"Oi," the guard repeated, this time pushing on the door.

Oleg removed his finger from the trigger switch. "Careful."

"Get down off the ladder," the guard ordered.

"Give me a minute, brother."

The guard gave the door another nudge.

"You crazy?" Oleg protested, wrapping his free arm around one of the ceiling brackets. "The air conditioning ducting is hanging by a thread. If it collapses you'll be responsible."

"Sorry. My colleague's got me all worked up."

Oleg peered down through the opening at the top of the door. "You mean the neckless wonder at the boom gate. He's not normal if you ask me."

"He reckons you're up to no good."

"Did you hear that, Pavel? The stormtrooper thinks we're up to no good."

"He's paranoid. I told you already," Pavel said, frantically replacing the treads and risers.

"Give me a minute to secure the ducting," Oleg said to the watchman.

Ginger casually nodded, then stepped back from the door and lit up a cigarette.

A few minutes later, Pavel gave the thumbs up.

"That should do it," Oleg said, climbing down and opening the door.

"It seems like your colleague has taken a strong dislike to me," Pavel said flippantly.

"He does that sometimes."

"So, how can we help you?"

Ginger leant forward, and with a feigned steely gaze whispered, "I need to check you're not planting a bomb."

Pavel sniggered. "In the ceiling?"

"It's a security requirement for work being carried out in the Presidential Box."

"Presidential Box?" Pavel said, sounding suitably surprised. "That would account for the size."

"Twice as big as my apartment," Ginger said.

"Help yourself. But there's not much to see."

Ginger poked about in the boxes on the trolley. "What's up there?" he said, motioning with a slight flick of the head.

Pavel placed the ladder back under the opening in the ceiling. "Be my guest."

"Don't forget to turn off the lights," Ginger said, declining the offer.

***

Kneeling on the bare wooden floor of his apartment, Father Arkady anxiously thumbed his prayer rope. "Lord Jesus Christ, Son of God, have mercy on me, the sinner."

Father Arkady had taken the sacrament of Holy Orders as a young man because of his love of God, which had been gifted to him by his late mother. Growing up in Moscow, it was only natural that he would embrace the Russian Orthodox Church.

In the fifteen years since his ordination, he has never once doubted the existence of God, or for that matter, his chosen vocation. The same cannot be said about his attitude towards the Church's leadership. Almost from day one, Father Arkady had surreptitiously sought out other like-minded clerics with the naive view to tackling the cancer head-on. Thankfully, before his treachery was discovered, he was recruited by Revealing Light – an ultra-secret society established inside the Russian Church during the time of Peter the Great. The purpose of the society is to emancipate the Church and Russian Christians from the control of the state.

Five years ago, frustrated by the society's spectacular lack of success, Father Arkady pushed for new leadership and a new strategy. A secret ballot was called, and, not surprisingly, Father Arkady emerged triumphantly as the new Shepherd of Revealing Light.

Father Arkady, a strong fit man in his early forties, liked to rise early and run before breakfast. So he's normally asleep by ten. Tonight was a rare exception.

He glanced at the old Slava mechanical clock. It was well past one. "What's taking so long?" he murmured, rising to his feet and pouring himself a glass of water from the pitcher on the bedside table.

The faint sound of voices wafting up from the street below brought Father Arkady to the window. He gazed down at two heavily armed policemen standing in front of a guardhouse harassing a young lady who had chosen the wrong way home.

"Finally!" he said, putting his phone to his ear.

The policemen, attracted by the movement in the lit window, glanced up.

"Hello," Father Arkady said. A subtle smile came to his face as he listened. "Thank God... now stay out of sight until you're needed... God be with you."

6

Cutting across the Cortile della Pigna on his way to meet with Commandant Waldmann, Rossi spotted a familiar face in the crowd milling around Arnaldo Pomodoro's *Sphere Within Sphere.*

"*Ciao* Professor Moretti. How's the wife?" Rossi called out as he strode past.

"*Formidabile*, Inspector General," the professor said, partly obscured by his tour group.

The retired academic's shock of wild silver hair and intelligent face reminded Rossi of his father. A sharp twinge of guilt. When he first joined the Corps of Gendarmerie of Vatican City, he managed to get home every other week. After all, it was only a three-hour drive to Siena from Rome. Later, as he rose steadily through the ranks and his responsibilities grew, trips home became less frequent. And now as Inspector General and the Pope's personal bodyguard, even going home at Christmas was a challenge.

He wondered how his life had reached this point; comfortable missing his father's seventy-fifth birthday celebration. Not so long ago the thought would have been unimaginable. The very idea he desperately wanted to be there made him feel better. And the notion he was doing it for the Church helped ease his conscience. The Church always came first.

As he rushed to beat the downpour, images of past family gatherings flashed through his mind. Rossi mused about his brothers. How at Christmas they sat round the table reminiscing. They teased him about his childhood aspirations of becoming a soldier. And how they worked like slaves in the heat of the sun picking olives while he fought the Soviets in the shade. "Rightful privileges of the youngest child," Rossi would plead. Then his father would chime in: "Big-shot policeman in a country no bigger than a municipal park." But Rossi always got the last word. He would make much of the fact that his Vatican Gendarmerie, together with the soldiers of the Pontifical Swiss Guard, protected the head of a Church with 1.3 billion members. "By any measure, a huge responsibility," he would say. Sooner or later the goading always ended the same way, with the entire family telling him how proud they were of their little Enzo.

Turning left onto Via del Pellegrino, Rossi glanced up at the black sky and opened his umbrella. "*Pessimo!*" he mumbled to himself as the rain pelted down. The forecast was for thunderstorms and strong winds. Unfortunately, the *Servizio Meteorologico* was right. Momentarily, the idea of driving to Bonn flashed into his mind, but Rossi knew it was impractical.

"Commandant Waldmann is waiting for you, sir," a guard said, holding open the door to the barracks.

Rossi glanced at his watch as he entered. Although it was tempting, he didn't want to miss his flight. He couldn't say why, just a strong sense that something bad was going to happen. *Blackmail's a dirty business*, he thought, hurrying along the corridor.

"I heard you're looking for me," Rossi said, dropping his umbrella into a metal bucket by Waldmann's door.

"I thought we'd better catch up before you disappear."

"*Naturalmente,*" Rossi said, sitting down in front of Waldmann's desk.

"I read the file you sent me."

"Did it help?"

"It's not pretty," Waldmann said, shaking his head. "In fact it's downright distasteful. For the German bishops to support the constitutional changes that gave Hitler dictatorial powers was reckless, to say the least. And in return for what? The 1933 Reichskonkordat – unless you bow to the most improbable coincidence."

"Now you understand why Cardinal Capelli is keen to remove the threat."

"By paying hush money?"

"By managing the risk. Hush money implies guilt."

"Last night you didn't seem so sure."

"Oh I'm sure," Rossi said with a wink.

A long silence before Waldmann spoke. "I was

wondering – shouldn't we be doing something more proactive?"

"Like what?"

"Investigating Wolf."

"No police," Rossi said firmly. "If I do my job well, no one will know the document ever existed."

"I've been checking the internet," Waldmann said, gazing down at his desk. "There was a hit-and-run accident in Berlin a few days ago. The victim's name was Wolf – a pensioner about the right age."

Rossi looked at Waldmann for a long while then asked, "Anything on the blackmailer?"

"If it's the same guy, then he's prone to overreacting."

"Same guy?" Rossi said, furrowing his brow.

"Eighteen months ago, a high school teacher named Maximilian Wolf attracted the attention of the regional German newspapers."

Rossi sat forward. "For counterfeiting football tickets?"

"For wearing a T-shirt with 'Fat People are Harder to Kidnap' printed on the front."

"I've seen worse."

"He got his bottom smacked by the school director."

"Must have been a slow news day if that made the papers."

"After returning to class, Wolf got creative. In front of his students, he removed the offending T-shirt, set it alight and tossed it into the wastebasket."

"Not so clever."

"Then when the flames started lapping at his desk, he extinguished the fire by urinating on it."

Rossi laughed. "I hope he doesn't try that on me tonight."

"Police investigation, followed by a school board enquiry. Both inconclusive. In the end Wolf was saved by the Teachers' Union, who attributed his breakdown to low wages and poor working conditions. After three months' therapy, he was allowed to resume teaching."

"Working a second job as an extortionist," Rossi quipped.

"Listen, I have a friend in the German Federal Police," Waldmann said. "Perhaps I could make some discreet enquiries? Surely it would be useful to know whether Maximilian Wolf has done anything like this before?"

"I'll keep it in mind," Rossi said politely.

"Well I'm here if you need me. By the way, have you seen the weather? Better you than me."

"Thanks. I hadn't noticed."

7

The Aeroflot flight from Berlin arrived at Moscow's Sheremetyevo Airport well behind schedule. A heavy snowstorm had forced the pilot to circle the city of twelve million for more than forty minutes while the runways were cleared.

Four-thirty in the afternoon, but already dark. Foreign Intelligence Service (SVR) agents Yuri Kutin and Mikhail Rudoi walked briskly along the jet bridge pulling their carry-on bags.

Behind them, two dozen rowdy football fanatics chanted "Lokomotiv, Lokomotiv" in full voice.

"Welcome back to Moscow," a sharp-dressed man said, stepping in front of them as they entered the terminal building. "My name is Timur. Colonel Demchenko sent me – I'm your driver."

Kutin removed his hat and ran his hand over his bald head. "Finally, some recognition."

"Twenty years of foreign service, and this is the first time I've been met at the airport," Rudoi added.

"How was the flight?"

"Kept bumping my knees against my ears," Rudoi said.

"You'd think with all that oil money the office could afford a little more legroom for guys your size."

Kutin huffed. "That wasn't the problem."

"Dry flight," Rudoi explained, motioning towards the loutish thugs. "Captain's orders."

"This way."

"Passport control?" Rudoi asked as Timur ushered them away from the other passengers.

"No need."

They followed Timur through a deliberately confusing maze of narrow passageways, and then along a dimly lit corridor to an unmarked door. Timur waved his proximity card over the access control reader and the electromagnetic lock released. The door opened onto the icy second-floor landing of a steel-grated stairway. Hand on the railing, they descended to a small private car park.

"This is highly unusual," Rudoi said.

"I've taken many agents out this way. Mostly operatives returning from missions like Red Dove."

"Can we stop on the way?" Kutin asked. "I need to buy flowers."

"Unless they're for Demchenko, I wouldn't bother."

"What does that mean?"

"My orders are to drive you directly to Gosdacha 17."

"Please tell me you're joking," Kutin said, trying to light a cigarette in the wind.

"Someone high up in Lubyanka wants you out of sight for a while."

"I'm calling Demchenko."

"Do what you like. But I'm waiting in the Jeep."

Kutin rang. No answer.

Motioning for a cigarette, Rudoi approached Kutin. "How the *fuck* does he know about Red Dove? Berlin was strictly need-to-know."

Kutin shrugged. "You know how it is at Lubyanka. Spend enough time around the coffee machine, you can find out anything."

"He's a driver, for God's sake."

Kutin's mobile phone pulsed. Throwing his cigarette to the ground, he read the message. "It's Demchenko. He's waiting for us at the dacha."

"Odd. I thought he was in top level meetings all week."

"Apparently not."

It took them two hours to travel to Dmitrov. As the bottle-green Jeep Cherokee turned into the heavily wooded forest surrounding Gosdacha 17, Rudoi and Kutin were still napping. An eye on his passengers, Timur set his mobile phone alarm to go off in two minutes.

"We're almost there," he said, glancing over his shoulder.

Kutin woke sluggishly. Groaning, he stretched his strong limbs. In the distance, through the broad-leaf birch and spruce trees he could see the dacha. It had stopped snowing, and the wind had dropped. The only sound was the crackling of the Jeep's studded winter tyres on the forest track.

The driver's phone broke the peace. He killed the alarm and put it to his ear. "Yes, Colonel… due north from the blue boat shed," he said, as though he was repeating an instruction.

Kutin cleared his throat. "Demchenko?"

"He's waiting for you on the lake. Sounds half-cut."

Timur drove slowly past the two-storey dacha, searching for the track running down to the lake. "This must be it," he said, swinging the Cherokee sharply right.

As the SUV swayed and bounced along the narrowing forest track, Rudoi woke. He looked back over his shoulder at Gosdacha 17; no lights or smoke coming from the chimneys. "What's happening?"

"While you were asleep, Demchenko called," Kutin laughed. "We're going ice fishing."

"Just perfect."

Suddenly the track opened onto a white expanse. Timur glimpsed the boat shed perched high on top of a small rise. He drove to the water's edge, pulling the Jeep up next to a rustic log table and bench.

"Stay here. I'll grab the gear." Leaving the engine running, Timur jumped out and headed up the slope.

Rudoi sprang to life. "Don't you smell it?"

"Sorry! I'll wind down the window."

"I'm deadly serious, Misha. What the fuck are we doing all the way out here?"

"Keeping our heads down," Kutin said, feigning a yawn of disinterest.

"That's crap. We'd be just as safe in Moscow."

"To be eliminated then. Is *that* what you want me to say?"

"Think about it…"

"Don't flatter yourself, Misha. We're not worth the bullet," Kutin scoffed. "We're legmen."

A few minutes later, Timur returned carrying several sets of Arctic gear. "Help yourself, gents," he hollered, dumping the kit onto the picnic table.

Kutin climbed out first. Showing no enthusiasm, Rudoi followed. As they layered up, Timur fetched a bulging plastic grocery bag from the back of the Cherokee, and laid the contents on the table: one bottle of Smirnoff; one loaf of black rye bread; one slab of pork salo.

"To your success," Timur said, handing each of them a tumbler full of vodka.

"You're not joining us?" Rudoi asked.

"I've got another pick-up tonight," Timur said, slicing up the salo with a long-bladed hunting knife, also from the grocery bag.

"Then it's just you and me, Misha."

"And Demchenko, supposedly," Rudoi added, discreetly tossing the vodka over his shoulder.

Timur refilled the tumblers. "Another one?"

"What a question," Kutin scoffed. "There's nothing worse than being sober when Demchenko's *bukhoy*."

Every time the driver topped up their glasses, Rudoi found a new and inventive way of disposing of the brain-numbing potion without being noticed.

An hour had passed before Timur switched off the headlights and shut down the engine. Bottle laid waste, Rudoi and Kutin staggered arm-in-arm down the embankment onto the frozen lake.

"How much further?" Rudoi called out over his shoulder.

"There," Timur bellowed, pointing his torch towards the faint glow of an ice-shelter in the distance.

As they drew near, Rudoi's dark eyes darted about. He urgently needed a plan, in case he was right. He glanced at the snow sled next to the illuminated canvas shelter. Fishing tackle and not much more. Ten metres to the right a dozen blocks of ice scattered around an ominously large fishing hole. Nearby, three fold-up chairs. Then, something more promising. A wry smile came to Rudoi's face. Against the horizon, a heavy-duty chisel planted in the ice like an explorer's flag.

"Where the hell's Demchenko?" Kutin asked.

"Gone for a piss," Timur called out from inside the ice-shelter.

"He's known for his modesty," Rudoi scoffed almost to himself.

"Take these," Timur said, handing Kutin the gas lantern and another bottle of vodka. "I'll get the rods."

As Timur fossicked about in the sled, Rudoi grabbed Kutin firmly by the arm and steered him towards the fishing hole. "Listen to me, Yuri," Rudoi said frantically. "This is not a fishing hole. It's massively too big. That shit plans to drown us in it."

"Then we'd better hurry up and finish the bottle," Kutin said in a drunken slur, breaking free.

"That's right, drink up," Timur said, dropping the fishing tackle at their feet.

Picking up one of the rods, Rudoi lowered himself lumberingly onto the stool next to Kutin. "Demchenko's not here."

Timur turned and inspected the fishing hole. A thick layer of ice had formed over the opening. "Seems that way."

"Let's call it a night," Rudoi said. "Demchenko's fooling with us. He's probably in the dacha by the fire." A smokeless fire in an unlit house.

Kutin wobbled to his feet. "Not till I catch dinner."

"A man's got to eat," Timur said.

Rudoi looked on anxiously as Kutin zigzagged his way to the far side of the fishing hole and pulled the chisel out of the ice.

"I'd better give him a hand," Timur said. "We don't want him falling in."

Rudoi half rose to follow, but sat down again. He watched on helplessly as Timur threaded Kutin's hand through the chisel's wrist strap and twisted it tight.

"I've got this," Kutin said, pushing Timur away.

"If you say so."

Kutin raised the two-metre-long chisel high above his head, and let out a roar as he plunged the blade into the hole. The chisel's sharp chipping head shot through the ice cover like a bullet, pulling him down with the momentum. Gasping for air, Kutin floated in the frozen water, buoyed by the air trapped in his clothes.

"Grab my hand," Rudoi yelled, throwing himself forward onto the ice.

Producing a Grach pistol from his jacket, Timur trained it on Rudoi. "Move away from the edge."

"What ya doing?" Rudoi shrieked, stumbling to his feet.

Timur sneered. "Isn't it obvious?"

"Erasing the trail back to Moscow."

"The Motherland thanks you for your service."

The two adversaries fell silent. Their attention turned to Kutin, who was thrashing about wildly in the water.

"Hyperventilation," Timur said.

Too drunk to think and too cold to fight, Kutin surrendered to his fate. Weighed down by the ice chisel, he sank peacefully to the bottom.

Pistol raised, Timur moved closer.

Rudoi held up one of the foldable chairs. "If this looks anything more than a fishing accident, Demchenko will have your balls."

"Too late. I lost those years ago," Timur said, knocking the chair out of Rudoi's hand.

Rudoi looked ridiculous, holding up his fists. "Come on, let's have you then."

Timur couldn't help but laugh. But it didn't stop him from whacking Rudoi across the head with the Grach. Rudoi collapsed onto the lake as if he'd been shot.

"Get up you babushka, I hardly touched you," Timur taunted, laying a boot into his side.

Curled up like a ball, Rudoi felt for the hunting knife he had commandeered from the picnic table earlier. He braced himself for the next blow. But it didn't come. Instead, pocketing his pistol, Timur grabbed Rudoi by the jacket, and dragged him towards the hole.

It was exactly as Rudoi intended. Lurching forward, he wrapped his huge arm around Timur's neck. As they rolled on the ice, Rudoi plunged the long blade up under Timur's ribcage, piercing his heart. Adrenaline surging, Rudoi gripped the knife firmly in two hands, and lifted Timur's quivering body into the air.

"And the Motherland also thanks you for your service," Rudoi snarled, dropping Timur's limp body to the ground.

With the keys and the pistol, Rudoi glanced about as he ran flat out towards the boat shed, lucky to be alive. But for how long?

8

CIA operative Catherine Doherty left home at sixteen. A dead mother and an abusive father was more than she could take. Cathy headed to Los Angeles and waited tables on Hollywood Boulevard. Out celebrating her seventeenth birthday, she made the acquaintance of a wealthy Russian businessman. Despite being thirty years his junior, she became his paramour. Given a second chance, Cathy went back to school to make something of her life.

Their nine-year relationship ended when he divorced his wife and moved in with a two-bit actress. By that time Cathy was financially independent. Fluent in Russian, and with a Master's degree in International Affairs from Columbia, she was accepted into the CIA's professional training programme.

Three years ago, much to her delight, she was assigned to the Moscow bureau as part of a deep immersion programme. The programme was introduced following a review of the shortcomings in intelligence analysis, which came to light in the wake of several major intelligence failures. The concept was to train young field agents to better comprehend the subtleties and nuances of certain target countries to improve the insightfulness of their analysis.

Cathy's specific role was to collect intelligence on Russia's political elite, in particular President Alexander Volkov and FSB Director, Evgeny Chernik – the two dominant figures in Russian politics.

Now sitting in the CIA Moscow bureau bullpen, Cathy checked her watch, surprised that anyone would call on her office landline so late in the evening. "Hello," she answered, expecting it to be a wrong number. "Okay, put him through."

She listened attentively, trying to make sense of what was being said. "Stop, Mr Rudoi," Cathy demanded. "You've been put through to the wrong department. You need immigration. Write this number down…" Cathy hung up and scribbled a record of the call in her notebook.

Cathy worked for another twenty minutes before she decided to call it a night. She thought she'd head down to the gym for a boxing workout and then grab a bite to eat on the way home.

"Hi, Cathy," came a voice from the dark.

"Charlie, what are you doing here? Shouldn't you be in the bar?

"I've come from there. The boys sent me to fetch you."

"You make me sound like a dog."

"In need of a bone."

"Charlie, I'm perfectly happy here."

"Come on, Cathy. Play the game. You prance around all day in those sexy tight skirts getting the boys all worked up – then you disappear off home every night. That's just not done."

"I've got things to do, Charlie. No offence."

"Bullshit! You think you're better than us."

"Charlie, don't. It's not worth it."

"The boys reckon you're a dyke. But I know better."

"That's rather offensive, Charlie. If you weren't so drunk I'd kick your pretty little arse."

"I'm not drunk. I'll show you," he said undoing his pants and flopping his pride and joy onto her desk.

Cathy instinctively picked up her iPad and swatted at it as if it was a fly.

"Jesus," Charlie cried out in pain. "What'd you do that for?"

"The boys reckon you like it," Cathy said, taking a disinfectant wipe from her desk drawer and cleaning her iPad.

"Fuck you," Charlie said, pulling up his pants.

"See you tomorrow morning, Charlie."

9

The rumble of distant thunder played on Rossi's nerves as he entered the terminal building at Rome-Fiumicino Airport. The departure hall was chaotic. He gazed up at the flight information display. Delayed.

At the airline check-in counter he opened his carry-on bag and removed a small firearm case and checked it in. He had been in two minds whether to pack it, but instinct told him to expect trouble.

He glanced at his watch. Two hours to kill. With the meeting tonight, heading to the bar was not an option. Instead, he took the escalator to the mezzanine floor in search of the pharmacy he had been told was there.

The store was quiet, though not empty. Near the entrance, an elderly couple quarrelled. Further in, an attractive blonde, who Rossi decided was Finnish, studied the label on a bottle of organic shampoo.

"Can I help you, sir?" one of the pharmacists said.

"*Sì.*" Rossi motioned with his eyes to the far end of the counter.

The woman followed without question.

"Thunderstorms," Rossi said, smiling awkwardly. "I need something to calm my nerves."

"Have you tried the bar?"

Rossi pouted. "Teetotaller, I'm afraid."

"Good for you," the pharmacist said, glancing suspiciously down at the large bottle of duty-free hanging from the extended handle of Rossi's carry-on.

Rossi craned his neck as he peered through the doorway to the dispensary. "Surely you've got something out the back?"

"Only with a doctor's prescription."

"Isn't there anything?"

The pharmacist led Rossi to a rotating book stand out front. "This comes highly recommended."

"Overcome your fear of flying." Rossi flicked through the first few chapters, blew out a breath, and then handed the book back to the pharmacist. "I'm dead."

"No you're not," the pharmacist said, touching him reassuringly on the arm. "Fear of flying is nothing more than negative thinking."

"Relax and clear your mind," Rossi nodded politely, having heard it all before.

"Try chatting up the flight attendant."

"Interesting."

"Download some New Age music and breathe deeply anytime you feel tense."

"Deep breathing while harassing the flight attendant?" Rossi smiled. "You'll get me arrested."

"You're funny."

"More anxious than funny."

"Wait here," the pharmacist whispered, before disappearing into the dispensary.

"Good choice," Rossi said as the attentive blonde brushed past him on the way out. A bottle of obscenely expensive shampoo.

For a while Rossi stood in silence, wondering whether he had misunderstood the pharmacist. Then she reappeared, carrying a pill envelope.

"I shouldn't be doing this," she said, handing it to Rossi. "It's for anxiety and panic disorders. I've written the name of the drug on the envelope – in case you experience any side effects."

Rossi shook her hand. "I don't know how to thank you."

"Next time, see your doctor first, please."

"I promise. How much do I owe you?"

"Nothing. It's one of mine," the pharmacist shrugged. "I've got two teenage boys at home."

10

Maximilian Wolf locked his bicycle to the railing next to the circular eastern wall of the Bonner Basilica. Münsterplatz would have been closer, but the Bonn Christmas market was in full swing and access was limited. The light snow that had been falling all day had stopped, and the evening sky cleared. He checked his watch, then lit a cigarette to steady his nerves. It didn't help. Wolf, a thin-framed man with fragile mental health, had never been good at dealing with authority. And tonight, with so much at stake, he was an absolute wreck.

Since finding the Concordat, Wolf had spent many hours surfing the internet. He came up blank. But he wasn't discouraged, as he had found thousands of results for a similar treaty dated six years earlier. Wolf was convinced the Roman Catholic Church, the richest and most powerful organisation in the world, had expunged all traces of his document from history. And if this was true, they would be prepared to pay a tidy sum for its return.

Wolf turned his head as a gust of wind peppered his eyes with ice crystals. He shuddered as he realised he was standing in front of the enormous carved stone heads of Roman legionnaires Saints Cassius and Florentius – the beheaded martyrs over whose graves the basilica was built. "Bad omen."

He took two short, nervous drags and headed towards the basilica's main entrance on the north side. A homeless man opened the towering wooden door. Wolf flicked his cigarette butt into his begging bowl and entered.

Inside the narthex, he removed his beanie and raked his fingers through his wild brown hair.

The church was dimly lit and empty, except for a woman silhouetted against the yellow glow from candles burning in front of the Magdalene altar on the far side.

Despite being a non-believer, Wolf had visited the church on many occasions, mostly with his students. He knew his way around. Looking anxious, he moved slowly towards the bronze portal behind the Magdalene altar.

As he advanced, his small beady eyes were drawn to the church's lone worshipper kneeling at the prie-dieu. Her dark auburn hair was covered with a delicate white laced scarf. The glow from the prayer candles burning in the pricket stand shrouded the lady in a halo of light. Seemingly unaware, Wolf stood trance-like staring at her unnatural beauty.

The lady glanced up, her burning amber eyes meeting his.

"Good evening," Wolf said, looking awkward for having disturbed her.

The angelic lady smiled politely before returning to prayer.

Refocused, Wolf descended the stone steps to the head-high portal. His heart pounded as he pulled open the heavy bronze door and stepped into the cloister.

Built in the mid-twelfth century, the cloister and the accompanying two-storeyed collegiate building had stood largely unchanged for nine hundred years. Wolf walked slowly along the western wing of the arched portico that ran along three sides of the quadrangle.

As he moved deeper, Wolf sensed a blast of warm mouldy air hit him from behind. A strange chill ran through his veins, as though the spirits of those buried in the cloister had awoken. "What the hell was that?" he mumbled to himself, quickening his pace.

Wolf headed intuitively towards a faint blue light that was visible between the eastern portico's thin columns. As he drew closer, he noticed a door set back from the wall with a sign attached that read 'Privat'. He slipped the Concordat into his overcoat pocket and with trembling hands knocked lightly on the door. No response, so he knocked again, harder. Still nothing.

He tried the door. It was unlocked.

"Bishop Muellenbach," he called out, opening the door.

"Herr Wolf, please come in," a disarmingly pleasant voice echoed from deep inside. "I'll be with you in a minute."

Wolf took a few tentative steps, but stopped short in the small entrance hall.

"Come in and make yourself comfortable," the bishop called out, realising Wolf's reluctance.

Wolf pushed gently on the door. The room was cluttered with old furniture and books. On his left, a writing desk. To the right, a faded green Chesterfield sofa and a leather tub chair. Religious icons and symbols occupied every free space. Nothing matched and everything seemed out of place.

Removing his overcoat, Wolf hung it next to the door. Before long, the bishop appeared from down a narrow hallway, moving gracefully for a man of his bulk. He was wearing an apron over his black cassock and carrying a tea service for three on a silver tray.

"I thought you might like a nice hot cup of tea and *Schokoladen Printen*," the bishop said, placing the tray on the coffee table in front of the sofa.

"No thanks."

"Perhaps you'd prefer coffee?"

"Tea's fine."

The bishop motioned towards the Chesterfield. "Please make yourself comfortable."

Wolf sat quietly as the tea was poured.

"I'll let you add your own milk," the bishop said, sliding the white porcelain jug towards Wolf. "I find it's such a personal thing."

"I take mine black."

"Oh dear! I'm not sure we have lemons."

"Black – no lemon, no sugar," Wolf said sharply.

"Then that makes it a lot easier," the bishop said, lowering himself onto the tub chair opposite his visitor.

"Now how do we do this?" Wolf said, sitting forward.

The bishop picked up his cup and took a sip. "Before we start, let me express my gratitude to you for coming out on such a cold night to do God's work."

The suggestion he was here to do God's work seemed to upset Wolf.

"*Schokoladen Printen*," the bishop said, holding up the plate. "Freshly baked by the Ladies' Auxiliary."

"No thanks, Bishop. I'm in a bit of a hurry."

The bishop glanced down at the third teacup. "That reminds me. A gentleman from the Vatican Police will join us tonight."

Wolf sat bolt upright and gazed anxiously at the bishop.

"Nothing to be alarmed about."

"No cops. I've done nothing wrong. I found the document in my father's apartment and now it's mine to sell," Wolf said in a furious tone, standing to leave.

"Inspector General Rossi is the head of the Vatican Gendarmerie, but he's not here in that capacity. He's here to help us agree terms."

"Wouldn't an accountant or a lawyer be more appropriate?"

Bishop Muellenbach stuttered as he searched for the right words, not wanting to inflame the situation further. "Inspector General Rossi and I are jointly accountable for determining what risk your forgery poses to…"

"Forgery!" Wolf snarled. "On the telephone you told me you were interested in acquiring the Concordat. Now you're telling me it's a fake?"

"With due respect, Herr Wolf, you misunderstood me. It's beyond a shadow of a doubt that the Concordat is a counterfeit. No such document ever existed. The question is, how good is the forgery and what risk does it pose to the Church? The answer will determine the price."

"I guess that's what I'd expect you to say. Call it a counterfeit if that makes you feel virtuous. But you're not getting it, unless you pay."

"That goes without saying, Herr Wolf. You must protect what is supposedly yours."

"Where's your Inspector General, anyway? Why isn't he already here?"

"His flight from Rome was delayed," the bishop said, glancing across at the clock on the wall. "He shouldn't be much longer."

Wolf sighed angrily. "Can't we start without him?"

"The examination of the document? That's up to you."

Wolf retrieved a loosely rolled manila envelope from his overcoat pocket and handed it to the bishop.

"I'll need to wash my hands," the bishop said, rising from his seat.

After a few minutes the bishop returned from the kitchen carrying a suede briefcase. He cleared the writing desk and laid down a white cotton cloth. Switching on the lamp, he carefully removed the seven-page document from the envelope. "Now, let's see what we have."

Wolf held his breath. But the bishop's countenance gave nothing away.

The bishop pulled the fluorescent lamp closer. His thinning fuzzy hair was accentuated in the light. "What do you know about the document?"

"My father was a colonel in the Stasi. He was killed last week in a hit-and-run accident in Berlin…"

"Deepest condolences. May God rest his soul," the bishop interrupted.

"My father was not one of God's biggest fans. He despised religion and all it stands for. But, if by chance he was wrong, God would have banished him straight to hell."

"Only God can judge such matters," the bishop said vaguely.

"That's funny. My father used to say something similar. 'Only I can judge such matters.' Then he'd have some poor innocent *Scheißer* shot dead, often for no reason. His death couldn't have come soon enough."

"I'm sorry, I have a call," the bishop said, taking his mobile phone from his pocket. "Good evening, Inspector General… yes he's already here… good… good… God bless you."

"Is he coming?"

"He'll be another ten minutes. So please continue."

"I was saying that my father was killed, and as the only living relative it fell on me to arrange his funeral and deal with his estate. Ha, such a grand word, estate. He died with nothing. I had to fork out eight hundred euros of my own money for his funeral."

"Where did you find it?" the bishop said, continuing to scrutinise the Concordat.

"In my father's study – well at least that's what he called it. It was nothing more than an enclosed balcony. Only big enough for a desk and a filing cabinet."

"In the filing cabinet?"

"No. It was lying open on the desk."

"Amongst the clutter."

Wolf hesitated. "Come to think of it, his desk was clear."

"Do you have any idea how the document came to be in his possession?"

"The time leading up to the collapse of communist East Germany was chaotic. My father started to bring home boxes of secret Stasi files – I assumed at the time for insurance. The Concordat must've been amongst them."

"You said it was open on his desk. Why?"

"It's obvious, isn't it? My father must've been planning to blackmail someone."

"Do you intend to follow in his footsteps?"

"Not at all," Wolf stuttered with indignation. "I'm trying to prevent such a thing from ever happening."

The bishop raised an eyebrow. "By selling the document to the Church?"

"If I was only interested in the money, I would have put it on eBay."

"And what if the Church refuses to buy it?"

"I'll find another buyer. Historical World War II documents are in great demand. Someone will be interested."

There was a long silence while the bishop finalised his initial review. "This is really superb," the bishop said. "If

I had to hazard a guess – it's the work of Soviet master forger David Krotsky."

"How can you possibly tell that?"

"Two things. First, because the document specifically mentions the annexing of the Soviet Union. That suggests to me that the USSR or Russia is behind this. Second, the document is superb. Which leads me to Krotsky. He's the best the Soviets ever had."

"Perhaps it's flawless because it's genuine?"

Wolf's face turned pale with fear.

"What's wrong?" the bishop asked.

"It's possible my father's death was no accident. Perhaps he was murdered to keep someone's dark secret from seeing the light of day."

"Who on earth would do such a thing?" the bishop said in a dismissive tone.

Wolf hesitated. "I can think of only one possibility… the Catholic Church."

"That's ridiculous," the bishop said, his voice losing its softness.

"Am I next?" Wolf cried, pacing in small circles and mumbling to himself. Then with frightening suddenness he leapt forward and grabbed the Concordat, knocking the bishop backwards off his seat as he bolted.

By the time Bishop Muellenbach grasped what had happened, Wolf, and the Concordat were nowhere to be seen.

"That went well," the bishop said, regaining his feet and dusting himself off.

11

Inspector General Rossi's late model Mercedes taxi had not moved for five minutes.

"How much longer?" Rossi asked, picking up his brown felt pork-pie hat that had fallen from his knee.

"It could take some time. Looks like a fire."

As Rossi shifted in his seat trying to get his bearings, his gaze locked on to a partly obscured signpost. "Can you move forward?"

"Where to?" the driver asked, glancing back over his shoulder.

"Half a metre."

"If it will help."

"Münsterplatz one kilometre," Rossi read softly to himself as the taxi inched forward.

"Is that better?"

"I thought the Bonner Basilica was on Münsterplatz?"

"Last time I checked."

"But the sign's pointing to the right," Rossi said, his tone growing more serious.

"That's the pedestrian precinct. The second largest in Germany," the Iranian-born driver said proudly. "No vehicle access. Besides the streets are blocked with the Christmas markets."

"So by foot from here, it's what – one kilometre?"

"If you can believe the sign."

"Then what the hell am I doing sitting here?" Rossi said, buttoning up his beige cashmere duffle coat.

"Because you like chatting with me?"

Rossi paid the driver, grabbed his overnight bag from the boot, and set off at a smart pace in the direction indicated by the signpost. He quickly learned that the narrow, twisting cobblestone lanes, lined with shops and restaurants, were not suited to a mad dash in Italian leather-soled shoes in search of a church unseen.

As he moved deeper into the precinct, the sirens and the traffic noise were replaced by footsteps and voices. Rossi heard his mobile phone. He pulled it from his coat pocket, but it had already stopped ringing. *Bishop Muellenbach*. No point wasting time; almost there.

Sensing he was heading in the wrong direction, Rossi skidded to a halt. The twisting, turning lanes seemed to be leading him in circles. He searched the evening sky between rooftops for one of the basilica's five spires, but saw only Christmas lights hanging overhead.

"*Entschuldigung*, can you help me?" Rossi asked a bearded old man wearing a dark grey homburg. "I'm looking for the Münster Basilica."

The old man took a firm puff on his pipe as he glanced about. "See the tobacco shop at the end of the lane?" Rossi did. "Hundred metres to the right is Münsterplatz. Diagonally opposite you'll find the church. Can't miss it."

With renewed confidence, Rossi hurried off, repeating the old man's instructions in his head as he went.

"*Cavolo,* the Christmas market," Rossi mumbled, standing at the edge of Münsterplatz, gazing over a sea of heads and huts and carousels, towards the basilica.

The Bonner *Weihnachtsmarkt* that runs through Advent each year, occupies every square centimetre of the pedestrian precinct between Friedensplatz and Münsterplatz. The fair's offering of hot *Glühwein*, cold *Kölsch*, grilled sausages, *reibekuchen* and stewed mushrooms, guarantees shoulder to shoulder crowds every night. Unfortunately for Rossi, tonight was no exception.

12

The external door to the cloister opened. Bishop Muellenbach rose quickly from the Chesterfield. "Inspector General Rossi, thank God you've arrived. Oh! Herr Wolf, it's you."

Wolf stood momentarily in the doorway, his eyes bulging with terror. "Not of my own accord."

"Stand over next to the bishop," a husky accented woman's voice ordered.

The colour drained from Bishop Muellenbach's face as Oksana Koroleva emerged from behind Wolf, holding a Glock 23 fitted with an Osprey 40 silencer.

"Never trust a Catholic," Wolf said.

"This has nothing to do with me, I can assure you."

"Then who's she, Mother Teresa?"

"Monsieur Wolf, if you want to live, shut up and listen," Oksana said, scanning the room for security cameras.

There were none.

The bishop held open his hands and took a tentative step forward. "My dear child, I really think…"

"That goes for you too. And don't call me 'my dear child,'" Oksana said, training her gun at the bishop's head.

Bishop Muellenbach raised his eyes to meet hers. "Who are you and what do you want?"

"Who I am is not important. What I want is the Concordat."

"It's a forgery. It has no value."

"That's irrelevant," she said.

"Bullshit it's a forgery," Wolf protested. "You're in this together. You're trying to scam me out of my money."

Oksana swung her pistol back towards Wolf. "I thought I told you to shut up."

Wolf stood, pale and delicate. He opened his mouth to speak, but the words died on his lips.

"That's better," Oksana said, turning to the bishop. "Now where's the Concordat?"

"Not with me." The bishop sneaked a peek at his watch. Fifteen minutes since Rossi had phoned from the taxi.

"So you prefer to play Russian roulette? Are you sure you have the stomach for it?"

"I don't know," the bishop insisted.

Oksana didn't react. Instead she turned to Wolf and repeated the question. "Where's the Concordat? Maybe you know, Monsieur Wolf?"

Wolf appeared confused. "What's a Concordat?"

"Monsieur Wolf, you're playing a dangerous game. I saw you walk in with it."

"Oh, the envelope! I had no idea. I was asked to drop it off by a friend."

"So where is it?"

"I gave it to the bishop. That's why I was leaving."

"You're even more stupid than I imagined. Or maybe you've got big balls."

"Herr Wolf, I strongly recommend you cooperate. The lady is deadly serious."

"That's good advice, Bishop Muellenbach," Oksana said, glancing about. Her eyes paused on an old radio in the corner of the room. "Does that work?"

The bishop shrugged. "I assume so."

"Now Monsieur Wolf, before I remove the first of your big balls, I'll ask you one more time. Where's the Concordat?"

While Wolf considered his answer, Oksana moved over and switched on the radio. "Christian music. Now that's a surprise. And wouldn't you know it, one of my favourites – 'Are You Washed in the Blood?'"

"I assume the music is not for our benefit?" Bishop Muellenbach said.

"We don't want to scare the neighbours, do we? Having a testicle removed in such a crude manner can be painful."

"Killing us would be a terrible mistake," the bishop said.

"Who said anything about killing?"

"You've made no attempt to hide your face."

Oksana looked surprised. "Most people like my face."

The bishop held out his hands, as if beseeching her. "I wonder whether there isn't another way, Madame."

Oksana trained her pistol on Wolf's groin.

"Stop," Wolf cried. "I know where the Concordat is. Make me an offer."

"Herr Wolf, please understand. Once the lady gets her hands on the document, she'll have no further need of you."

Wolf scoffed. "You have a vivid imagination for someone who believes in the goodness of humankind."

Oksana moved back to the radio and turned up the volume. "I offer you your life, Monsieur Wolf, in return for the Concordat. That seems more than fair."

"Wouldn't you know it – my father has even managed to bring me misfortune from the grave."

"Is that your answer?" Oksana said, straightening her aim.

"Go to hell," Wolf blurted out.

"You're an extremely stubborn man. It seems that a little encouragement is needed."

"You're bluffing."

"Is that so?"

Wolf closed his eyes and hummed along with the soul-stirring music. But that didn't stop Oksana from pulling the trigger. His eyes flew open wondering why he felt no pain. "Are you crazy?" Wolf cried out, throwing Bishop Muellenbach a sideways glance. But the bishop wasn't there.

Wolf did a double-take, finding the cleric slumped on the Chesterfield with a neat bullet hole in his forehead. He half turned to run, but his feet seemed to be glued to the floor.

SEAN HEARY

"For the last time Monsieur Wolf, where's the Concordat?" Oksana said calmly.

"Stop, stop – I'll give you what you want. Just let me go," Wolf said blubbering, tears running down his cheeks.

"It's a little late for that isn't it, Monsieur Wolf? You're now a witness to a murder."

"If you kill me, you'll never find the Concordat."

Oksana smiled coldly. "I know exactly where it is. I saw you put it inside your coat when you tried to leave."

"But it's a copy. Do you really think I would bring the original with me?"

"That's what I needed to find out. And you gave me the answer. Nobody risks their life over a worthless facsimile – do they?"

"Okay, you win," he said angrily, unbuttoning his coat and removing the document.

"That's better. Now pass it to me."

Wolf raised his arms, holding the Concordat tightly between his thumbs and forefingers. "Put down your gun or I'll tear it to shreds."

Oksana didn't argue. She simply pulled the trigger, then watched stone-faced as the .40-calibre S&W hollow point bullet ploughed through Wolf's forehead and exited in a spray of grey and red.

Oksana's second victim for the evening dropped to his knees, as though he had finally found God. He then tipped slowly forward and came to rest face down in the plate of *Schokoladen Printen*.

As Wolf dropped, the Concordat floated from his hands and landed at Oksana's feet. Picking it up, she flicked through the pages. "A lot of fuss about nothing," she murmured to herself.

Assignment complete, Oksana turned off the radio and hurried outside. The temperature had continued to drop and a bitter cold wind swirled in the courtyard. Oksana turned up the collar of her mink coat and covered her face. Startled, she looked up. Someone had entered the cloister through the bronze portal. In the distance she saw the silhouette of a tall man moving tenaciously towards her.

"Good evening," Rossi said, throwing her a fleeting glance as he hurried past. Although Rossi had never visited Bonn, let alone the Münster Basilica, the bishop's instructions were straightforward enough. He found the presbytery door without a false step. Keen to get inside he entered without knocking. *Hopefully, this won't take long.*

Oksana glanced over her shoulder as she opened the portal and slipped into the church. Out of the corner of her eye, she saw the eastern portico return to darkness as the presbytery door closed.

A chill ran through Rossi's bones as he stood in the doorway staring down at Bishop Muellenbach and a man he assumed was Maximilian Wolf. He thought it was odd that he didn't feel surprised. Then his mind promptly turned to the Concordat. He glanced over at the desk where they had been working. Nothing. Not a moment to lose, he turned in place and bolted for the exit.

By the time Rossi flung open the basilica's main door and burst onto Münsterplatz, the woman was gone. In front of him was the Christmas market and a wall of lively faces. He glanced right, then left. Which way to go?

The basilica's massive wooden door, caught by a gust of wind as a tourist entered, slammed closed behind him. The vagrant doorman apologised by holding up his hand. Rossi hadn't noticed him in his haste.

"*Entschuldigung*, you didn't happen to catch which way my wife went? You couldn't have missed her. She was wearing a brown mink coat and a white scarf."

"*Tut mir leid*," the vagrant said. "I saw no one."

"You must have," Rossi said, with a worried expression. "She has a medical condition – she suffers from depression."

"She told me not to tell you."

"You have to – it's a matter of life and death," Rossi said, slipping a twenty euro note in the doorman's palm.

The doorman pointed to the balustrade rising from the cobblestones. "Down the stairs to the car park."

"Where's the car park exit?"

"Do I look like I own a car?"

Rossi bolted towards the stairs, descending in leaps and bounds. Thirty metres to his right he spotted a high performance sports car pulling up behind an old Beetle at the boom gate. *Please God, let it be her*, Rossi prayed, ducking and weaving between parked vehicles.

From a distance Rossi watched anxiously as the car window wound down. A broad smile came to his face when a mink-clad arm reached out and inserted a parking ticket into the validation machine. "Got you."

Being careful to stay out of sight, Rossi crept closer with his iPhone ready. Then in an instant the boom gate lifted. In desperation, Rossi snapped rapid-fire pictures of the silver Audi R8 GT as it sped up the ramp. He felt physically sick as he flicked from one blurred image to the next.

Then, "Thank God," he murmured, studying the final shot. The skewed image of the tyre-marked garage floor wasn't his best work, but it did capture the R8's registration plate.

Rossi gazed at the image, not wanting to believe his eyes. 115 CD 238. *The stakes just keep getting higher*. He recognised the orange and jasper green plate from his numerous trips to Paris. "Corps Diplomatique," he mumbled, opening Google and typing in – 'French vehicle registration diplomatic codes'.

He ran his eyes down the tiny screen and opened the most promising result. A simple table popped up. Rossi's expression darkened. 115, the Russian Federation. What the hell are they up to now?

As Rossi headed back to collect his overnight bag from the presbytery, a million half-formed scenarios played in his head. But one thing was as clear as day – he needed to get to Paris before the Russian Embassy opened for business tomorrow morning.

On Münsterplatz the *craic* of the crowd had grown louder and the drinking more ferocious. By happy chance, the vagrant doorman had already called it a night. Inside the church, an old lady arranged flowers on the steps of the high altar in preparation for tomorrow morning's service.

Rossi opened the bronze portal and peered into the cloister. Although it was quiet, he used the dark shadowy portico. Approaching the presbytery entrance, his eyes narrowed. The door was ajar. Rossi was certain he had pulled it closed – but maybe not. He stopped at the door and listened. It was as peaceful as death.

Rossi entered warily. His overnight bag lay where he had dropped it. The two bodies were just as he had left them – the bishop gazing up to Heaven, and Wolf peering down to hell.

Without ceremony, Rossi grabbed his bag and made for the exit. *Bishop Muellenbach's mobile phone*, he thought, stopping dead in his tracks.

A short while later, Rossi sat gazing out of the taxi window on his way to the airport. His last words to Cardinal Capelli kept repeating in his head. I promise you that by tomorrow night the forgery will be secure in my possession, and on its way to the Vatican archives.

13

Sixty-five metres underground, inside atomic Bunker-42, the sirens wailed and the red lights flashed. A ten-megaton nuclear bomb had struck Moscow.

"We have a radiation leak inside the complex," the guard screamed. "You've got ninety seconds to get into your protective clothing."

Cathy grabbed the nearest radiation suit and put it on.

"We've got enough food and air for two weeks. By then we'll be able to return to the surface and assess the damage," the guard said.

"A chilling thought," said newly arrived CIA Agent Paul Lawrence.

"I don't know what would be worse. Radiation poisoning or those blasted sirens," Cathy said, laughing. "Let's go and have a drink."

They rode the lift up from the once top secret military control bunker and headed out onto the street to find their driver.

Fifteen minutes later they pulled up in front of the Lucky Noodle on Ulitsa Petrovka.

"You're a wild one," Lawrence joked. "What've you got in mind? Red plum wine?"

"Trust me."

"Do I have a choice?"

Cathy always enjoyed showing new colleagues around Moscow. She liked to shock and surprise. She couldn't wait to see the expression on Lawrence's face as she led him behind the cashier to the purple curtain concealing the stairs to the basement.

"After you."

Lawrence hesitated. "I trust this isn't an opium den?"

"Mendeleev Bar? Avant-garde maybe, but to the best of my knowledge no opium," Cathy said as they descended.

"Wow! This is nice. And look at those dresses. I think I'm going to enjoy my posting here."

Dresses? The comment seemed odd, but Cathy said nothing.

They took a seat in one of the arched limestone recesses opposite the long bar and ordered a couple of Moscow Mules.

"Welcome to Russia," Cathy said, raising her glass.

"Thank you. It's kind of you to show me round."

"I couldn't let the boys do it. They'd take you straight to Night Flight."

"Night Flight?"

"If anyone suggests it, say no," she said with a wink.

"I'm going there tomorrow night with Charlie."

"Good choice."

For a while they chatted about nothing. But then as always, the conversation turned to Volkov.

"How would you describe him?" Lawrence asked.

"On a domestic level he's xenophobic and nationalistic. But his life mission is to rule the world. Everything he does is to strengthen his own position, and that of the Russian state. Unfortunately he doesn't give a rat's arse how he achieves it. He's a power-crazy despot."

"When the power of love overcomes the love of power, the world will know peace," Lawrence said.

"That's certainly not Kissinger."

"Jimi Hendrix," Lawrence smiled. "Is he smart?"

"Hell yeah, but in a madman sort of way. He's obsessed with his legacy. To him the world is a zero-sum game. Win-win is a Western concept he doesn't buy into."

"So you think he wants to rebuild the USSR?"

"Russian Empire to be more precise. The Soviet communist ideology has gone – if it ever really existed. It was certainly nothing like what Marx or Engels had in mind. After Lenin's death and Trotsky's exile, any real chance of establishing a Russian utopia disappeared."

"That's the problem with social experiments. The moment power is transferred, self-interest and greed kicks in."

"From an admirer," the waitress said, setting two more Moscow Mules on their table.

Lawrence sat up and scanned the room. "I hope there's two of them."

"I don't think he's your type."

"Where?"

"That guy sitting at the bar," Cathy said, motioning with her eyes. "But be warned, he's one of them."

"Gay?"

"FSB. He came down the stairs not long after us."

"How can you be so confident?"

Cathy wasn't sure whether Lawrence was messing with her. "Look around. The bar is crawling with unaccompanied women. Why would he waste his time on me? We could be married for all he knows."

"Ménage à trois – it's very popular in the States right now."

"Trust me on this one."

"Does that mean we should refuse the Mules?"

"Hell no," Cathy said, taking a sip.

"The interactive Cold War museum you took me to earlier – is Volkov capable of pushing the button?"

"If he's painted into a corner – absolutely. That's why I take visitors there. It's a not so subtle way of reminding them that when the shit hits the fan it's best to leave Volkov some face-saving back-down option. Otherwise he'll go out with a bang."

"I'd imagine that would end rather poorly," Lawrence said, raising his glass and saluting the FSB agent.

For a while neither spoke as they looked over the crowd, like judges at a beauty pageant. "By the way," Cathy finally said, "how's your Russian?"

"Pretty good," Lawrence said, switching the conversation to Russian. "My original family name was Larionov. My parents were both Soviet skaters. They defected during the 1980 Lake Placid Winter Games."

"So you're sort of coming home."

"Hardly. I was born and raised in the U.S. and I spent most of my life concealing my Russian heritage."

"So how'd you end up here?"

"I applied."

"You know what I mean."

Lawrence took a long sip on his Mule. "When my father died last year, I realised how little I knew him. I was so hung up on being American I never spoke to him about his formative years inside the Soviet Union. And I regret that because there is so much of him in me."

"Sounds like you're here to discover who you are – more than who your father was."

"I guess there's some truth in that," Lawrence said, knocking down the rest of his drink.

14

Rossi drove his French-blue hire car slowly down Avenue Louis Barthou towards the Russian Embassy. He was still kicking himself over yesterday's delayed flight. *If only I'd left earlier, none of this would've happened.*

He tucked the micro mini Renault in between two parked cars, well short of the Embassy's perimeter fence. Ahead he could see the automatic gates that controlled vehicle access to the compound's underground car park. Although he was some distance from the entrance, the one-way street ensured that he got a good look at any vehicle that passed. *Google Street View – certainly takes the legwork out of spying.*

Rossi checked his watch. 7am. Well before any self-respecting diplomat would think of showing up for work. But Rossi was taking no chances.

He landed at Charles de Gaulle late last night and had taken a room at the nearby Hotel Villa Glamour. His plan was to get some shut-eye before tackling the seemingly impossible task of recovering the Concordat in the morning. But every time he closed his eyes he imagined himself kneeling in front of Cardinal Capelli, begging for forgiveness.

So instead of sleeping, Rossi scoured the internet for information on the Kremlin and its symbiotic relationship with the Russian Orthodox Church. One thing he knew – they were joined at the hip. Despite the Russian constitution guaranteeing the separation of church and state, and equal legal status for all religions, the reality was quite different. The Russian Orthodox Church was, for all intents and purposes, the recognised state religion of the Russian Federation. It operated at the Kremlin's beck and call. This led him to believe that if the Kremlin was behind last night's murders, then the Russian Patriarch was somehow involved. A thought that terrified him. He surmised that no matter what the Russians were playing at, the Catholic Church would inevitably be drawn into a very public spat with the Russian Church. A fight where Christianity would be the loser.

As the morning lightened and the first of the vehicles arrived, Rossi's spirits lifted. At least he now had something to occupy his time. He watched every car as it approached, studying each driver's face in his rear-view mirror. But by ten, no one resembling the assassin had driven past.

15

Five hundred kilometres to the east, Sabine Reich, a highly respected staff writer at the *Frankfurter Allgemeine Zeitung*, was looking forward to her evening. She had invited her boyfriend, a *Luftwaffe* fitness instructor, to her city centre apartment for dinner.

Sabine hurried through the bustling newsroom towards the office of the city editor and barged in without knocking.

"Hey Dirk, don't forget, I'm off early this afternoon."

"The fitness instructor?"

"Classified," she said with a wink.

"Okay, but if I need you, I'll call."

"Don't bother. I'll be tied up all night – with a bit of luck," she said, handing him her copy. It was the third instalment of a four-part feature she was writing on the death of traditional religions in Western society. The first two episodes had caused such a storm amongst the German faithful that Sabine and her blasphemous views had become the story. Which was not only good for circulation, but also served to enhance her hard-earned notoriety.

Before Dirk had time to protest, Sabine was already heading back to her workstation to pack up for the day.

"Sabine, that's your phone," a paunchy middle-aged colleague bellowed from amongst the field of desks.

She quickened her pace, grabbing the phone on the sixth ring. "This had better be important, I'm in a meeting."

"I have information about a Catholic conspiracy," a man said in heavily accented English.

"Go on."

"The Vatican is responsible for the death of three innocent people."

"Only three?" Sabine quipped.

"Murdered to conceal the existence of a newly discovered Concordat with Hitler, dated June 1939."

Sabine took a notepad and pencil from her desk drawer. "Who were the victims?"

"Bernd Wolf. Killed in a hit-and-run accident in Berlin last week…"

"Did the police rule his death a murder?" Sabine asked, her tone sceptical.

"If you're not interested, I'll take the story elsewhere."

"Sorry, it's been a long day," Sabine said, pulling a mocking face at the phone. "And the other two?"

"Maximilian Wolf and Bishop Muellenbach… murdered last night in Bonn."

Sabine keyed the information into Google as the caller spoke. "And the Concordat? I thought you said 1939?"

"I did."

"Not 1933?"

"I'm emailing you a copy now."

"Can we meet?"

The line was already dead.

16

Rossi glanced at his watch as the street lights came on. It was already five. The streets were filled with office workers under umbrellas hurrying home. He felt edgy and anxious – not sure what to do. Without the lady in the mink coat, he had nothing. *A long shot,* Rossi thought, opening the car door and emptying a bottle full of urine onto the tarmac.

Commotion up ahead. The Russian Embassy's gate opened. Heavily armed security guards moved with military precision and blocked off the empty street. Moments later the ambassador's black Mercedes limo, bearing the Russian flag, ascended from the underground car park.

With the boss gone, the rest of the embassy staff soon followed. Within minutes the deluge of vehicles exiting the car park had slowed to a trickle. Rossi's heart filled with anger and disappointment as reality struck. Time to return to Villa Glamour and call Cardinal Capelli. With a shake of his head, he fired up the engine, slammed the Clio into gear and hit the accelerator.

From over his left shoulder came the sound of screeching tyres. He leant to his right and braced for impact. Nothing. Without remonstrance, the driver straightened the fishtailing vehicle and sped off.

Rossi sat motionless behind the wheel, annoyed with himself for having caused such a scene so close to the embassy. *Where the hell did he come from?*

As Rossi regained his composure, he noticed the vehicle slowing in front of the embassy gate. The glare from the brake lights made it impossible to make out the model.

Slowly the gate rolled back, and the car turned sideways as it descended. Rossi slapped the steering wheel with gusto. The unmistakable low profile of an Audi R8. Squinting, he tried to see who was behind the wheel, but from that distance it was impossible.

Fifteen minutes later the car park gate opened once more, and the 610-horsepower Audi rumbled back onto the street and sped off in a shower of surface spray. Rossi planted his foot on the accelerator pedal. Instantly he regretted not having paid the extra €10 for the GT upgrade.

Threading his way through Paris's evening traffic, Rossi stayed within a few car lengths of the R8 as they raced west on Avenue Foch towards the Arc de Triomphe. Although he still hadn't eyeballed the driver, he was sure it was her.

The rain had stopped, and the streets were drying out as the R8 exited onto the Champs-Élysées and headed south-east at a more leisurely pace. Rossi wound down the window to knock off a bit of his tiredness. As he cruised down the most famous avenue in the world, he couldn't help but feel a strange sense of gratitude to the Germans and General von Choltitz for surrendering Paris to the Allied forces, and not destroying it as supposedly ordered by Hitler.

Then, without warning, the R8 turned right and shot down a narrow one-way lane. Rossi was ready. He followed at close range with the sun visor down.

We must be close, Rossi thought, pulling into a loading bay as the R8 slowed. He watched from a safe distance as the driver carefully manoeuvred the Audi down the entrance ramp of a 24-hour garage located under the three-star London Hotel.

Rossi, certain it was not the abode of a well-paid hitman, waited in the car. It wasn't long before the bishop's killer appeared wearing the same mink that she had worn at the basilica. Rossi felt his blood pressure rise.

As she waited on the pavement for a vehicle to pass, he got a good look at her for the first time. She was striking. He couldn't help but wonder what had happened in her life to bring her to this point.

Rossi lifted his phone to his ear as she crossed to the other side. He was sure she hadn't noticed him, but it was dangerous to assume. Professional killers by necessity were observant. And in the last twenty-four hours their paths have crossed on no fewer than four occasions.

Rossi watched in the wing mirror as she stopped in front of a fashionable nineteenth-century apartment building and removed a set of keys from her messenger bag. He was in two minds whether to jump her there and then, or to wait. Suddenly from behind came a loud bang. The La Maison Maubert florist was shutting for the evening. Rossi couldn't help but notice her hand shoot back into her bag. *She's armed.*

With mixed feelings he scrutinised her as she turned the key in the blue double door then disappeared inside. He was pleased to have found her lair, but he knew in all probability the Concordat was at the embassy. There was only one way to find out.

Rossi grabbed his handgun from the glove compartment and went and stood in an unlit doorway opposite the killer's apartment building. Gazing up at the cut-stone façade of the five-storey structure, he quickly confirmed that the only way in was through the front entrance. *I should have jumped her when she opened the door.* The thought was soon forgotten when the third-floor light came on.

Rossi scurried across the street and checked the mailbox. He now had a name to go with the face, 'Koroleva'. A setback. A video intercom system with a wide-angle camera.

Returning to his vehicle, Rossi felt like a hunter whose prey had just vanished into thick woods. His only option was to trick his way inside. But how? The camera, and the killer's acute sense of observation and mistrust, was no small obstacle.

Despair turned to hope. A DHL van pulled up and a middle-aged man jumped out. Rossi had an idea.

He waited until the courier was out of sight, then nonchalantly walked up to the van and tested the rear shutter door. Unlocked. Rossi peered inside. A broad smile came to his face. A yellow DHL spray jacket hung from a hook. No one paid him any attention as he put it on. To complete the disguise, he grabbed a shoebox-size parcel and tucked it under his arm.

Rossi glanced up at the third-floor window. The lights were still on and the curtains drawn open. Positioning himself close to the intercom camera, he took a deep calming breath, and pushed on the button.

"*Allo.*"

"DHL. Delivery for Mademoiselle Koroleva," Rossi said in immigrant French.

Silence.

"DHL – Mademoiselle."

"Who's it from?"

Rossi turned the box slowly while he thought. "Moscow."

"It's late."

"It's Christmas. We're working around the clock. Blame Amazon for that," Rossi said, in a chatty tone.

"Wait." Oksana hurried to her living room window and glanced below at the DHL van parked in front of the florist.

Rossi fought to contain his joy as the magnetic lock released. He flung open the door and entered. The impressive marble-floored foyer, with its curved polished limestone staircase and gilded wrought iron banister reminded him of Rome. He stood momentarily at the bottom of the staircase and listened. Stillness. Rossi checked the foyer for cameras, then pulled his Heckler & Koch pistol from its holster and hid it under the delivery.

His pulse raced as he ascended the stairs in much the same way as a courier might – efficiently and at an even pace. The third-floor landing was no different from the others. Red woollen carpet, patterned beige wall covering, white skirting boards and one oversized glossy black door, framed with white architraves. There was a small discreet security camera mounted high on the wall and a peephole in the door.

Knowing he was being watched, Rossi rounded his shoulders and jutted out his chin as he approached. "Mademoiselle," he called out, pressing the doorbell.

There was a brief delay while Oksana removed her Glock 23 from her bag and placed it on the green marble hall console. Slowly she opened the door to the limit of the security chain.

"Pass it through, please."

"Mademoiselle, it's clearly too big – besides, you'll need to sign for it," Rossi said, avoiding her eyes.

Oksana pulled her gun closer, then unlatched the chain. Standing in the doorway in a white cotton bathrobe, she beckoned Rossi nearer. As Rossi stepped forward his eyes were drawn to hers as if under an enchantress's spell. Instantly she recognised him from the cloister.

Oksana recoiled backwards, her hand frantically feeling for her pistol. But it was too late. Rossi had charged forward, sending her crashing onto the parquet floor.

Before she could recover, Rossi was standing over her, pistol trained at her head. "Don't move," Rossi ordered, flicking the door closed with his foot.

Keeping his distance, Rossi peered down the unlit hallway. He was sure she was alone.

"You're the security guy from the Münster Basilica."

"Something like that."

"Aren't you going to help me up?"

Rossi picked up her gun and removed the magazine. "Place your hands slowly above your head, then roll over onto your stomach."

"Everyone has a preference."

"Hands behind your back."

As she did, Rossi reached down and ripped off her bathrobe. "Nothing personal, Mademoiselle. But my quest comes before your modesty."

"If you say so."

Rossi planted his heavy knee into the small of her back and tied her hands with the cotton belt from the bathrobe.

"I picked you as a deviant," Oksana said, smiling seductively over her shoulder. "What's your fantasy?"

"You're all class."

"I do an excellent schoolgirl."

"Aren't you a little old for that?"

Taking her by the arm, Rossi pulled her to her feet. He gazed at her a long moment as she stood naked under the entrance hall chandelier. She was exquisite. But it wasn't her beauty he saw. He was peering into her soul. The spell had been broken. In place of the alluring temptress he had seen earlier on the street, Rossi now saw only a narcissistic, evil whore who was bound for hell.

With her messenger bag slung over his shoulder, Rossi shoved Oksana down the hallway.

"Christmas pisses me off," Oksana said.

"Perhaps deep down you were yearning for someone to send you a present."

"How did you find me?"

"You were too slow."

"The car park in Bonn?" Oksana said, twisting and stretching the cotton belt with her wrist.

"What idiot would wear a mink to a hit?"

"It was cold."

Rossi glanced about as they entered the living area. He quickly lowered his pistol, realising the curtains were drawn open. "On your knees!"

"Don't tell me we're going to recite the rosary?"

Rossi half-heartedly glanced about the room. "Where is it?"

"The toilet?"

"You know when I saw you on the street, your beauty struck me. I thought this lady could have anything she wanted," Rossi said, moving to the open kitchen. "But then you opened your foul mouth."

"You don't know what you're talking about."

Rossi shrugged his shoulders, then emptied the messenger bag onto the kitchen island. "Oksana Koroleva," he read from her diplomatic passport. "Your mother must be proud of you."

"I have no mother," she said coldly, discreetly slipping her wrists free of the binds.

"So you're one of those. No personal accountability."

"We're all products of our environment."

"Even better. A Darwinian atheist. We exist to evolve to survive – the meaning of life."

"Would you prefer that we exist to serve humanity – or to serve your God?" Oksana scoffed. "I serve myself."

"We could chat all night. But let's not. Hand over the Concordat, and I'll be on my way."

"You're too late."

Rossi made quickly for the window. He had caught something out of the corner of his eye. Movement; a man perhaps? "The Russian Embassy?"

"Shit! That was you who pulled out on me," Oksana said, throwing her head back, laughing. "Rather amateurish – wouldn't you agree?"

"You're the one naked on your knees."

"For now."

"What do the Russians want with the Concordat?"

"I have no idea."

Back at the kitchen island, Rossi picked up a garrotte which had come from Oksana's messenger bag. "You ever used this?"

"Only to neuter pricks like you."

"Why did you kill Bishop Muellenbach and Maximilian Wolf? They were both unarmed."

"Following orders."

"Orders? Soldiers follow orders. You're a contract killer for God's sake. Don't make it sound like it was for a greater cause. You killed two innocent men for money. Nothing more."

"You're wasting your time – I feel no shame. I'm comfortable with who I am. Are you?"

"Who gave you your orders?" Rossi said, standing in front of her.

No answer.

Rossi turned his gaze sharply to the apartment opposite. A window had opened, and a curtain flapped in the breeze. Pistol down by his side, Rossi moved closer. Still no one. *Fresh air.*

"Why didn't you send the Concordat directly to Moscow?"

Oksana rolled back her shoulders and thrust out her teardrop-shaped breasts. "Do I look like a postman?"

"You ran an unnecessary risk turning up at the embassy like that."

"What business is it of yours?"

Rossi gazed vacantly at Oksana. He needed to recover the Concordat – nothing else mattered. But breaking into the Russian Embassy was not remotely realistic. He needed Oksana's help.

"Well, you are human after all," Oksana said, as Rossi's gaze fell lazily to her well-groomed pussy.

"Go to hell."

"But I saw it move. Maybe I can help you. I know a thing or two about fellatio," Oksana said, gliding the tip of her tongue seductively over her upper lip.

Rossi blew out a sigh of disgust. "Classy proposal – but no thanks."

"Perhaps something more Catholic? I've got a nun's outfit in my wardrobe. Untie me, and we can play hypocrite."

"Shut the hell up."

"Silly me. I forgot. You guys from the Vatican prefer altar boys."

Enraged, Rossi raised his hand, and stepped forward. But he stopped short. It wasn't his style.

Oksana was ready. She smashed the heel of her palm into Rossi's groin and grabbed his testicles, twisting him to his knees. "You miserable perverted bastard," she cried, driving the knuckles of her free hand into his wrist. Rossi's pistol dropped to the floor.

Before he had a chance to curse his stupidity, Oksana was standing over him with his gun trained at his heart.

"Now it's your turn to die. You humiliated me, and that is one thing I refuse to accept from anyone."

"Wait," Rossi pleaded, looking up through watery eyes, willing himself not to vomit. "Don't let me die wondering. Who are you working for?"

"Figure it out."

"I would only be guessing."

"Isn't it obvious?" she said, switching on the television. *If only it was.* "Russian Foreign Intelligence…"

"Why are you so interested in such trivial earthly matters, when you are about to discover whether God really exists?"

Rossi rose to his knees. He could almost hear Koroleva

pulling back on the trigger as he closed his eyes to pray. By faith he believed in life after death. And on balance, he considered himself a good man. But Rossi could not find inner peace as he waited to die. All he could think of was the Concordat and having failed his Church in her hour of need.

Finally a shot rang out. Rossi collapsed to the ground. A pool of blood formed on the waxed wooden floor around his head. For a long moment the room was silent.

Dazed and hurting, Rossi wondered how she had missed from such close range. He opened his eyes slowly and gazed up at the moulded ceilings. The stench of flesh and gunpowder hung in the air. Putting his hand to his ear, he felt the warm blood streaming through his fingers. He wanted to stay down, but there was too much at stake. Drawing a deep breath, he propped himself up on his elbows.

Rossi's head jerked back. A pair of amber eyes stared at him. He sat up further and wiped the blood from his face. Slumped against the sofa, with a gaping hole in the side of her head, sat the bishop's killer.

Instinctively he turned his gaze to the large panelled window and the apartment building beyond. There was a bullet hole through the middle pane, about head height. Someone had fired from the building opposite. But he had heard only one shot – or maybe two shots fired precisely at the same time. His head throbbed too much to think.

He scrambled across the room and killed the lights, then crawled to the window. In the apartment opposite, he saw a man disassembling a sniper's rifle. Rossi rose to his feet, expecting him to take flight. Instead, the shooter stepped calmly out of the shadows and smiled at Rossi as if to say, 'I'm not afraid of you.'

Rossi glanced about the room and then down at Oksana's lifeless body. The more he learned about the Concordat the less he understood. And that terrified him. *What now?* Rossi was certain the Concordat was on its way to Moscow. But instinct told him to head to Berlin where the Concordat had first surfaced.

Recovering his pistol from the naked corpse, he headed to the bathroom. He flung open the cupboards and quickly found what he knew would be there – a gunshot wound kit and a bottle of painkillers. Hands trembling, he tore open a packet of clotting sponge, and pressed it against his mangled ear. Within a few minutes the bleeding had slowed to a trickle, and the painkillers had kicked in. He washed his face in the sink and taped a fresh gauze dressing over his ear. Then in the mirror he wiped the blood off his spray jacket before heading out to the car to change his clothes for the drive to Charles de Gaulle.

17

Sleep was not something Rossi needed a lot of. But the relentless pace of the investigation, exacerbated by an all-night stopover at the Berlin Memorial Hospital to patch up his ear, had taken its toll.

Rossi glanced up at the clock on the meeting room wall as he popped a couple more painkillers. It was 8.45am – he was fifteen minutes early. He rested his heavy eyelids, just for a moment, and sank into a deep sleep.

Detective Lieutenant Axel Huff of the Berlin *Kriminalpolizei*, colloquially known as the Kripo, was taken by surprise as he entered. "Heavy night," he mumbled to himself, clearing his throat. As an added measure he slapped his black leather organiser down onto the conference table.

Rossi woke with a start and sprang to his feet. He was not sure how long he had been napping or whether he had been caught. He glanced up at the clock. It was 9.05.

"Detective Lieutenant Huff?" Rossi said, thrusting out his hand.

"Welcome to Berlin, Inspector General. It's a great honour to meet you."

"Thank you," Rossi said, turning his good ear in the direction of the voice. "What a pleasure to be in Berlin – one of the world's great cities."

"I'm from Munich," Huff said dryly.

Rossi took it as a joke and smiled politely.

"I understand from your colleague, Commandant Waldmann, that you are interested in Bernd Wolf."

"Correct. I would like to establish if there's a connection between his death and the double murder in the Bonner Münster Basilica the night before last."

"If you don't mind me asking," Huff said hesitantly, "why has the Vatican sent someone of your standing to investigate what appears to be a rather routine matter – notwithstanding a Catholic bishop was one of the victims?"

"I asked myself the same question," Rossi said. "It goes without saying that the Vatican has complete confidence in the German police force. But the truth be known, Bishop Muellenbach is – was an old friend of the Dean of the College of Cardinals. He asked me to personally take charge of the matter as a sign of respect for the deceased and his family."

"Do you know the purpose of the basilica meeting?"

"Unfortunately no," Rossi shrugged.

"My understanding is that the younger Wolf was not a churchgoer, and that Bishop Muellenbach was based in Cologne. So it doesn't appear to be a chance meeting."

"Difficult to say."

"Blackmail?" Huff said, stretching his shirt collar with his finger. "Maybe some personal indiscretion from the past."

"Why would you think that?"

"The Church is not without her faults."

"None of us are," Rossi said, wondering what Huff was playing at.

Huff motioned to Rossi's bloodstained bandaged ear. "You look as though you've been in the wars – what happened? The wound looks fresh."

"Hunting accident. Wild boar."

A sharp rap on the door. A man in his early forties, with the face of a journeyman, poked his head into the room.

"Inspector General, this is Senior Detective Schmidt," Huff said, motioning to the detective to enter. "I've assigned Schmidt to assist you. He's at your beck and call."

"So to speak," Schmidt added.

Huff smiled. "I understand you have a late afternoon flight back to Rome?"

"That's right," Rossi said, glancing unnecessarily at his watch.

"So we don't have much time. I assume you'd like to start with the files?"

"I'd also like to visit Wolf's apartment."

"Schmidt will organise that. Now, if you don't mind, I must excuse myself. I have a meeting with the

Bürgermeister. He's not happy about something – again," Huff said, rolling his eyes as he left the room.

"Inspector General, I'm sure it hasn't escaped your notice, but the office coffee is *Scheiße*," Schmidt said, pushing aside his mug. "May I suggest we continue our conversation in the café across the street?"

"*Un'idea eccellente!*" Rossi said, standing and following Schmidt out of the door.

A few minutes later they were sitting in Café Roma.

"So what's your reading of all this?" Rossi asked, cradling a double espresso in his hands.

"*Leberkäse* and fried eggs?" the waitress interrupted.

"That's mine," Schmidt said, tucking a large paper napkin into his unironed shirt.

"Enjoy your breakfast," the waitress said, turning and walking away.

"We had it down as joyriders. The burnt-out vehicle was found the next day on a forest service road. It had been stolen. The owner was overseas at the time," Schmidt said, shovelling a forkful of *Leberkäse* into his strangely narrow mouth. "So there was no reason to suspect foul play."

"Really?"

"Well that was until Commandant Waldmann called last night."

Rossi handed Schmidt a fresh napkin.

"Incidentally, you wouldn't happen to know how Commandant Waldmann knew about the Wolf family connection?" Schmidt asked, glancing up from his plate.

Rossi shrugged his shoulders. "TV, I guess."

"Those guys move fast."

"What was found in Wolf's apartment?" Rossi asked, changing the subject.

"Not sure. Kripo's only there now."

"What?"

"Prior to the Bonn murders, it didn't seem necessary."

18

"*Scheiße.*" Schmidt hit the brakes hard and threw the unmarked police car into reverse. "All buildings around here look the same," he said, accelerating backwards.

Rossi's head exploded in pain as he was tossed about. Memories of yesterday's near-death experience came flooding back as he lobbed a couple of painkillers into his mouth.

Even though the day was bright and sunny, it was bitterly cold. The cul-de-sac was deserted except for three young truants drawing stick figures on the pavement with broken pieces of chalk. Fifty metres back from where they had just come, a neighbourhood dog sniffed at the wheels of a kebab van parked on the grass verge. The Kripo vehicles that had been standing in front of Wolf's apartment earlier in the day were long gone.

Rossi felt distracted as he climbed from the vehicle. The Concordat was on its way to Moscow, but here he was in Berlin.

They walked behind the vehicle and stood in the middle of the road. The crayon outline of Wolf's contorted body was still visible, albeit sporting genitalia that had recently been added in blue chalk.

"The vehicle came from that direction," Schmidt said, pointing west towards the closed end of the long curving cul-de-sac. "The attending officer took statements from three witnesses. All of little use. The only real lead was the mirror knocked off on impact. But you already know all that."

Schmidt led Rossi to Wolf's apartment building. The entrance was damp and uninviting. There was a panel of cast-iron radiators fixed to the wall on the right, but judging by the room temperature they hadn't worked for some time. To the left was the emergency stairwell, and in front of them was a lift with *'KAPUT'* taped to the door.

"Trust me. We're lucky," Schmidt said, winking.

Keen to get inside, Rossi bolted up the stairwell, two steps at a time.

"Fifth floor," Schmidt called out, struggling to keep up.

"Which apartment?"

Schmidt, breathless when he arrived, could only manage to point and hold out the key.

Rossi stepped inside. The gloomy sixty-square-metre flat was soulless, sparsely furnished and devoid of all personal objects that make a house a home. A Soviet-era chandelier hung from the living room ceiling.

"A sad and lonely man, by all accounts," Schmidt said, lighting a cigarette to catch his breath.

"Is this him?" Rossi asked, picking up a framed photograph that was standing on the sideboard. "He's in uniform?"

"Wolf was a Stasi colonel in his day."

Rossi wondered whether that was significant. It could help explain the origins of the document. An Iron Curtain relic, perhaps? "That wasn't in the file."

"It was nearly thirty years ago. It didn't seem relevant. As far as the traffic guys were concerned he was a pensioner."

Not wanting to show his hand, Rossi started in the bedroom. It was musty and dark, like a cheap motel room in a run-down part of town. He drew the curtains and opened the windows. Rifling through the cupboards and drawers, he had only one thing on his mind – the colonel's study.

"Nothing in the bedroom," Rossi said, already standing in the study doorway.

The room was minuscule with windows covering the far wall. There was a desk, a chair and a filing cabinet with a printer on top.

"Are you looking for anything in particular?" Schmidt asked, joining Rossi from the kitchen.

"Something worth killing for."

"So you think the colonel was murdered?"

"What was there?" Rossi said, pointing to a dark rectangular patch on the faded blue carpet.

"Boxes of old Stasi surveillance files. An employee from the Federal Commissioner for Stasi Records picked them up an hour ago."

"What the hell were they doing here?"

"At a guess – Wolf stole them. Probably just before the wall came down."

"Blackmail?"

"If that was his intention, he seemed to have had a change of heart."

Rossi squeezed behind the desk and opened the filing cabinet. Empty. "Why do you say that?"

"The boxes were sealed and covered in dust. According to the forensic team, they hadn't been opened in years – if at all."

"And the desk?"

"Just what you see. Nothing."

There was a long silence. Rossi gazed at the dark patch on the carpet; Schmidt puffed on his cigarette. Something was odd.

"Shall we try the neighbour?" Schmidt eventually said, motioning to leave.

Arno Reinder, like Wolf, had lived in the apartment block since its construction in the early eighties.

Schmidt knocked loudly on the door. "Round here people don't take kindly to foreigners. Best I do the talking."

Footsteps could be heard from within, then a brief silence.

"What do you want?" came a grumpy voice from behind the peephole.

"Police, Herr Reinder," Schmidt said. "I'd like to speak to you about Bernd Wolf."

The door opened a few centimetres at first, and then all the way. Reinder, unshaven and dressed in a tattered woollen dressing gown, stood in the doorway squinting at Schmidt's identification.

"I've spoken to the police already," he complained, eyeing Rossi suspiciously.

"A few follow-up questions," Schmidt said, his tone firm.

Reinder mumbled something inaudible and shrugged his shoulders.

"When did you last see Bernd Wolf?"

"Alive?"

A roll of his eyes. "Of course alive."

"The evening of the accident," Reinder said, slowly scratching his arse. "He dropped in on his way to the shop."

Rossi, not happy with the pace, barged in. "How'd he look – nervous, agitated?"

"Bernd always looked like death."

"Did he have any unusual visitors prior to the accident?" Rossi asked.

"Not that I know of."

"What about his son?"

"Max was here after the accident – not before. I had to let the ratbag in. He knew I kept a spare key in case of emergencies."

"Didn't he have his own?" Rossi asked.

"No. They were estranged. More through apathy than any great falling out."

SEAN HEARY

Rossi turned to Schmidt. "The keys! Were they amongst Wolf's personal effects at the morgue?"

"I'd need to check."

Instantly Rossi thought about the man in the green flat cap mentioned in the police files. "It's time to visit Frau Becker."

19

Cardinal Capelli's office had a distinct rotten egg smell about it when Waldmann entered. He sniffed at the air. Mistake. The cardinal glanced up from the police report he was reading and indicated a seat. Waldmann sat down, his hand cupped over his nose and mouth, pretending to clear his throat.

"Any news from Rossi?" the cardinal asked. His voice was weak and thin. "He seems to be avoiding me."

"I'm afraid that's my fault, Your Eminence," Waldmann lied. "I convinced him it would be better to channel all communications through me. He's already got too much on his plate."

The cardinal leant forward, his elbows on the table, his hands under his chin. "I've read the preliminary police report. Distressing to say the least... it doesn't mention Rossi or the Concordat."

SEAN HEARY

"No. Rossi arrived after the murders and left before the police turned up. He thought it best not to get involved."

"And the Concordat?"

"Somehow the Russians have ended up with it."

The cardinal blew out a sigh. "Old enemy; new game – so what does the Inspector General intend to do about it?"

"Rossi's heading to Moscow tonight."

"Alone?" The cardinal's eyes narrowed behind his round steel-rimmed glasses. "Is that advisable?"

"By the time he arrives in Moscow, I'm hoping to have the Americans on…" Waldmann stopped breathing for a short moment. His body's defence system had automatically kicked in. Schoolday memories of St. Michael's Catholic Boys' School were suddenly revived; sitting at the back of the classroom with his hooligan mates releasing ammonia and match head stink bombs whenever the teacher approached. Only this was worse.

"I didn't understand," the cardinal said, seemingly without a speck of shame. "What's that about the Americans?"

Waldmann recalled reading in some lightweight publication how people like to smell their own flatulence. But surely not in the company of others. *Was this the first sign of dementia in one of the Church's most powerful leaders?*

A slight gag and cough. "Your Eminence, do you mind if I open one of the windows? I'm feeling a little warm."

"Maybe you're coming down with something," the cardinal said. "A cold draught running through the room is the last thing you need."

"I'm perfectly fine, Your Eminence. I just need some fresh air."

"Nonsense," the cardinal said, with a dismissive wave of the hand. "I'll ask Monsignor Polak to prepare some tea with lemon."

Waldmann sat sniffing his fingers while the cardinal dialled.

"Now what were you saying?" Cardinal Capelli asked, replacing the receiver.

"I'm hoping to have the Americans on board by the time Rossi arrives in Moscow."

"Excellent idea. Involve them if you can. They like this sort of thing. And I'll contact Massachusetts Senator Carrick Maloney – to give it a bit of a nudge. He's Opus Dei, you know."

"That would be greatly appreciated, Your Eminence."

"No need to mention the Concordat, of course," the cardinal said softly, as if talking to himself.

"The Senator's not to be trusted?" Waldmann asked, clumsily.

"He's a politician, Christian."

A hint of a smile came to Waldmann's face, unsure whether the cardinal was joking.

By the time Monsignor Polak rapped on the door with the tea, Waldmann had finished his account of the Münster Basilica bloodshed and was starting on Paris.

Monsignor Polak entered. "Good Lord," he proclaimed, abandoning the tea tray on a side table and hurrying across and opening several of the windows.

Waldmann immediately felt vindicated.

"My apologies, Commandant Waldmann," the Monsignor said, taking an ironed white hankie from his pocket and covering his nose and mouth. "Cardinal Capelli was born with anosmia."

A smile of incomprehension on Waldmann's face prompted further explanation from the Monsignor. "No sense of smell."

The cardinal shrugged. "A minor affliction. Except in the case of house fires and dogs with flatulence." Laughter.

Monsignor Polak lowered himself on all fours and crawled under the cardinal's oversized desk. "You're coming with me, mister," he said, gently persuading the cardinal's geriatric pug towards the door.

20

Rossi stood in front of Frau Becker's door, waiting for Schmidt to catch his breath.

"*Polizei*," Schmidt said, holding his ID in front of the peephole.

The door opened wide. Oozing enthusiasm, Frau Becker stepped into the corridor. "At your service, officers," she said in a loud *Thälmann Pioneer's* voice, standing to attention, if possible to tell for a woman that size.

It was plain Schmidt disliked Becker straight away. The traits and peculiarities of an 'unofficial collaborator' were evident – even to the man from the Vatican.

"I understand you witnessed Herr Wolf's accident," Rossi said.

"Yes, I did."

"Can you tell me what happened?"

"There was a thump and a yelp. I thought a dog had

been hit. By the time I got to the window the vehicle had gone. Then I noticed the colonel lying there. At once I phoned the police."

"Did you see anyone near him?"

Frau Becker hesitated. "Yes. A man trying to help him. Why, I don't know. It was clear, even from where I stood, the colonel was gone. Such a lovely man too."

"Did you recognise him?"

"Not at first. It wasn't until I went downstairs I realised it was the colonel."

"Not Herr Wolf. The other man."

"You mean the man wearing the flat hat?"

"The man you saw from the window next to the body," Rossi said, wanting to slap her.

"Yes. That's the man with the flat hat," Frau Becker said.

"Yes, you recognised him?"

Frau Becker gave Rossi an odd look. "No – I'd never seen him before in my life."

Rossi turned to Schmidt. "We're done here."

"Now what?" Schmidt asked, following Rossi back down onto the street.

"Turkish kebab."

"Good idea. I'm starving."

Rossi threw Schmidt a sideways glance. "To interview the owner."

"Closed," Schmidt said, lighting another cigarette. "It was in the file."

Rossi shrugged. "I know. But let's hear it from Muhammed."

"That's a bit racist isn't it?" Schmidt chuckled.

"That's his name. Also in the file."

Schmidt held up his ID as they approached. "*Polizei…*"

"Like to ask you a few questions about the hit-and-run," Rossi jumped in.

Muhammed, a thin man with a bushy black moustache and a matching monobrow, pursed his lips in disappointment. "I closed early that night. My cousin arrived from Istanbul."

As if he hadn't heard, Rossi asked, "You didn't happen to see a Mercedes van?"

"Mercedes van?" Schmidt mumbled to himself.

"Interesting you would ask. There was one parked opposite for a couple of days." Muhammed hesitated, then nodded. "Immediately after the accident – not before."

Rossi felt his heart skip a beat. "Did you see the owner?"

"Someone – two men. They took turns buying the coffee."

"What were they up to?"

"I did ask one of them. He said something about witness protection. Sounded like bullshit to me."

"What did they look like?" Rossi asked.

"Like a pair of nightclub bouncers. Both tall. One was beefy and bald, the other lean with curly fair hair. They dressed more or less the same – dark suits, roll-neck sweaters, shiny black shoes. Except the fair-haired guy always wore a dark green flat cap."

Schmidt wrote frantically in his notebook. All news.

"Accents?"

"They were Russian, if that's what you mean."

Rossi's face lit up. "That's a guess?"

"The guy with the cap took a call in Russian while ordering."

"How can you be so sure?"

"I was married to one for seven miserable years. Great sex but high maintenance."

"So what do you make of that?" Schmidt called out, scurrying after Rossi, who was already on his way back to Wolf's apartment.

"The two Russians killed Wolf, stole his keys and then staked out his apartment," Rossi said over his shoulder.

"What the fuck for?"

"Good question."

"The Stasi files?" Schmidt suggested.

"Then why didn't they take them when they had the chance? Besides, they didn't have to kill Wolf if that's all they were after."

"How did you know about the Mercedes van?"

"It was in the background of one of the police photographs. It stuck out like a Ferrari in a Trabant factory."

Schmidt shot Rossi a confused glance.

"Take a look around. There isn't a vehicle on the estate worth pinching."

Schmidt nodded, though whether he understood it was difficult to tell.

"The Mercedes simply didn't belong."

"So what are we looking for?" Schmidt asked, re-entering the colonel's apartment.

"Audio surveillance bugs. You can be sure they weren't sitting in the van all that time playing Scopa."

Schmidt got the picture and joined Rossi in the hunt.

It didn't take long. "I've found something," Rossi called out from the study.

Schmidt, standing precariously on the back of the sofa checking the chandelier, glanced down at Rossi. "What is it?"

"*La prova*," Rossi said, holding up a short piece of black electrical duct tape. "It was stuck to the bottom of the desk."

"And?"

"The tape's clean. It's only been put there recently."

"Sorry," Schmidt said, climbing down. "I'm not sure I follow."

"It was used to hold a microphone in place," Rossi said emphatically.

"That's a stretch."

"Then keep looking."

After a minute or two, Schmidt felt something behind the heavy sideboard, but he couldn't quite get his fingers to it. "Give me a hand," he called out.

Rossi rushed in from the kitchen and together they dragged the sideboard away from the wall. On the back was another piece of the same black tape – only this time there was a short length of electrical wire stuck to it. They examined it closely and then unanimously agreed. It was the aerial from an audio bug's transmitter. The Russians had been careless.

"What on earth were they listening to?" Schmidt said.

"Poltergeists."

Schmidt was in no hurry as he drove Rossi to Berlin-Schönefeld Airport for what he believed was a late afternoon flight to Rome. Keen to hear Rossi's view on the ever-expanding mystery, he caught every red light he could.

"It's clear the three deaths are related," Rossi said. "In what way, I'm not sure. One possible scenario is that Colonel Wolf had compromising information on someone the Russians were interested in."

"Bishop Muellenbach?"

"The bishop certainly seems to be the odd man out."

"It's not without precedent," Schmidt said. "There were a number of clergy, from all denominations, that were identified as collaborators through the examination of the surviving Stasi records."

Rossi felt bad about wrongly implicating the bishop, but he needed to set a false trail to keep Schmidt away from the truth. At all costs, the existence of the Concordat needed to remain secret.

"And the stakeout?"

"That I'm struggling with. But it certainly had something to do with Maximilian Wolf, given he was the only one in the apartment at the time."

"It's as though the Russians murdered the colonel simply to lure the son to Berlin."

Rossi instantly realised he had grossly underestimated Schmidt.

21

"Have a good flight," the border protection officer said, handing Rossi back his passport.

Head pounding and in desperate need of sleep, Rossi strode through the concourse area in search of a café sheltered from the omnipresent public address blare. He spotted a booth behind a 1963 Chevrolet Corvette in the retro Kennedy Café. "Double espresso," he said as he passed a waitress in a red polka-dot rockabilly dress.

Rossi flopped onto the seat and downed a couple of painkillers. Sweeping aside the clutter, he laid his iPad on the table to check the news. Memories from his childhood flashed through his mind. His extended family crowded in the living room watching the six o'clock news on a television the size of a washing machine. Now it's all real-time, on a device lighter and thinner than a newspaper. It brought a faint smile to his weary face.

Reading, he felt physically ill. 'Murders Conceal Secret Vatican Nazi Concordat' – posted by *Frankfurter Allgemeine Zeitung*, just eighteen minutes ago.

"Evil is upon us," he murmured, shaking his head in sheer disbelief.

"Sorry sir, did you say something?" the waitress said as she placed the double espresso on the table in front of him.

Rossi sat forward, his elbows planted on the table grasping his head between his hands. "Yes. Bring me a large Laphroaig."

When the Scotch arrived, Rossi took a deep gulp, braced himself, and read.

Murders Conceal Secret Vatican Nazi Concordat
by Sabine Reich

All eyes will be on the Vatican today as it tries once again to explain its relationship with Hitler during World War II. The discovery of an unknown Concordat between the Holy See and the German Reich, dated 1 June 1939, just three months before the start of World War II, is damning.

In the agreement, signed by Pope Pius XII, the Vatican undertook to cease all resistance against the Nazi government including a renouncement of the Papal Encyclical 'With Burning Concern dated 14 March 1937'.

In return the Nazis agreed to recognise the Catholic Church as the state religion of the German Reich. Terms and conditions of the Concordat apply to all countries of the Third Reich, including countries annexed as a result of war. Specific mention is made to the annexing of the Soviet Union.

Nazi Germany invaded the USSR on 22 June 1941. It has been a long-held view by many experts that the Vatican had secretly supported Nazi Germany's invasion of communist Russia due to the Soviet's treatment of the Church post-revolution.

Yesterday when contacted, the Vatican declined to comment on the grounds that it had not seen the alleged document. However, a Vatican spokesman said later that the only Concordat executed between the Holy See and the German Reich was the well-documented agreement of 1933. 'Any new document now circulating is a counterfeit aimed at undermining the good and necessary work of the Church in Europe,' the spokesman said.

Experts contacted for comment suggest that if the Concordat is genuine, it is possible that after the Nazis invaded Catholic Poland in

September 1939, the Church got cold feet and unilaterally withdrew from the agreement.

According to one source, the Concordat was amongst several boxes of secret files stolen by a former Stasi colonel, Bernd Wolf, in the days leading up to the collapse of communist East Germany.

German police have refused to comment on whether the recent death of Bernd Wolf, and the subsequent murders of his son Maximilian Wolf and Bishop Muellenbach from Cologne, are related to the newly discovered treaty.

Speculation is that the Church was in negotiations with Maximilian Wolf to acquire the document at the time of his death.

Rossi sat in disbelief, trying to make sense of it all. The story could have only been leaked by the Russians, and to him the implication was clear. *The Concordat is not the endgame. It's a means to an end. But what end?*

"Flight SU112 to Sheremetyevo, Moscow now boarding at gate sixteen," echoed through the cavernous hall.

Rossi glanced up at the monitor. *Time to take the fight to the enemy,* he thought, calling for the bill.

On his way to the gate, a shiver ran down his spine. Cardinal Capelli had called for discretion. For now, containment was the best Rossi could hope for.

22

Classified by the State Properties Agency as a dacha, Gorki-9 on the upper reaches of the Moscow River was anything but a country house. Hidden away in a pine and birch forest, the palatial presidential residence was surrounded by well-manicured gardens, maintained by a small army of carefully vetted workers.

Tonight, alone in his walnut panelled office, President Alexander Volkov sat at his desk reading a leather-bound copy of Dostoyevsky's *Demons*.

Volkov's interest in literature arose suddenly when a visiting head of state asked him who his favourite Russian author was. With his usual bravado, Volkov declared Anton Chekhov, although he'd never read a page of his work. When his guest enthused about *The Lady with the Dog*, Volkov's ever-alert Foreign Minister quickly stepped in and changed the subject.

'If there is no God, then I am God', the forty-eight-year-old Volkov read, closing the book. "I must remember that. I could work it into one of my speeches."

A rap at the door. Anastasia Lebedova, Volkov's executive secretary, poked her head in.

"The Cubans have arrived, Mr President."

"What took them so long?"

"It's the Americans, sir," Anastasia said, entering the room carrying a Spanish cedar cigar humidor.

Volkov opened his desk drawer. "Put them in here. I don't want Chernik filling his pockets again."

Anastasia hid the humidor, then silently withdrew.

Volkov, a short man with thinning grey hair and a watermelon belly, glanced at his watch. "They're late," he murmured, standing in front of the antique drinks cabinet tucked away in the back corner of his office like a shrine.

On top of the cabinet stood a nineteenth-century globe showing the Russian Empire stretching from Warsaw to Vladivostok. Next to it, a solid gold three-barred cross of the Russian Church, and a bust of Felix Dzerzhinsky.

For Volkov, these were not just symbols of Russia's past glory, but poignant reminders of the task that lay ahead – to rebuild the Russian Empire. Volkov was a Slavophile. He rejected the Western notion of globalisation and the loss of cultural identity. Volkov was not interested in European integration or a minor role for Russia on the world stage. The 'new world order', touted by Western leaders, was not how he foresaw the future.

Hanging on the wall above the drinks cabinet was a framed black-and-white photograph of Joseph Stalin, superimposed over a red Soviet flag. Volkov lifted it off its hook and laid it face down on the floor.

Attached to the back was his handwritten mission statement. Volkov had penned it three years ago when elected President. He wrote it in response to the West's encroachment into what he considered being Russia's traditional sphere of influence. It was not eloquently written, as he had no flare or patience for such an artistic undertaking. But it didn't need to be, as it was for his eyes only.

'Always and Forever Great' was written across the top. He skimmed down the page.

- Absolute power in the hands of the President...
- Take back the Empire...
- Racism and religious intolerance helps protect cultural identity...
- Opposition is treason...
- Revolutions require terror, therefore terror is good...
- War is inevitable so prepare well...
- Propaganda is truth...
- The West will always be our enemy...
- Establish Godhead...

Volkov felt energised as he hung Stalin back on the wall. He was in no doubt that global domination was his destiny and that fate was on his side.

He had had nothing but good fortune since his rise to power. Crude oil prices, on which the Russian economy depended, tripled during his first two years in office. Awash in hard currency, he increased pensions, boosted military spending and annexed several neighbouring countries – unchallenged by the West.

Moreover, the constant state of war provided Volkov with the justification for amending the Russian constitution; amendments that gave him power to enact laws without parliament's involvement.

In three short years, in spite of Russia's increased isolation, the Russian people had willingly entrusted Volkov with dictatorial powers, to rule Russia as he saw fit. In return he promised a new era of Russian greatness and prosperity. Volkov had managed to wind back the clock of history while its citizens slept.

Turning his attention again to the drinks cabinet, he reached in and grabbed an unopened bottle of Rémy Martin XO Cognac and three tulip glasses. He held the bottle up to the light, admiring its amber glow. "Such a small bottle." He grabbed a second.

The phone rang.

Volkov placed the cognac and glasses on the large circular table which stood in the recess of a soaring five-panel bay window, then picked up the phone.

"The Prime Minister has entered the compound," Anastasia said.

"Where's Chernik?"

"I'm not sure, sir. His phone's off."

When Volkov drafted his mission statement, he knew he needed help with one task more than any other – controlling the Russian Orthodox Church.

Despite having only recently approved the appointment of the Russian Patriarch, Volkov sensed that he was not to be trusted; a situation not without precedent. Ever since the creation of the Russian Church in 988, a game of cat-and-mouse has been played between the Church and the state for control over the hearts and minds of the common people. Notwithstanding Volkov's political savvy, he was never sure whether he was the cat or the mouse.

To help manage this dilemma, Volkov established the Godhead Society. Godhead has only ever had three members: Volkov himself, Prime Minister Sergei Kalinin and the Director of the Federal Security Service, Evgeny Chernik. The number and its members coincide precisely with Volkov's circle of trust.

Volkov was acutely aware that neither Imperial Russia nor the communists had ever fully controlled the Russian Church, despite the state's immense resources.

'If you can't beat them join them', was how Volkov explained the concept to Kalinin and Chernik.

Anastasia rapped on the door for a second time. "The Prime Minister has arrived."

"Show him in," Volkov said, looking up to find the Prime Minister already in the room.

Kalinin, a short fit man in his fifties, appeared in an ebullient mood.

"How nice of you to come," Volkov said, tapping the tip of his index finger on the face of his diamond-encrusted watch.

Anastasia, a girlish thirty-five, chin-length black hair and emerald eyes, took Kalinin's overcoat. "Can I bring you something, Prime Minister?"

"I'll look after him, Nastya. You go home."

Kalinin's lecherous eyes followed Anastasia as she left the room. "Well aren't you going to offer me a celebratory drink, Mr President?"

"Why should I?"

"Judging by your mood, you haven't heard."

Volkov looked up curiously as Kalinin lay his briefcase on the table. "Heard what?"

"About the Concordat."

Another rap on the door and Chernik entered.

"What an opportune time to call a Godhead meeting," he said, greeting his colleagues as if he hadn't seen them for years.

"He doesn't know," Kalinin scoffed.

Chernik, a large well-groomed man with dyed jet black hair, took a step back. "Have you been in a cave all day?"

"Very clever," Volkov said, his tone rough.

Kalinin pulled a translated copy of the German newspaper article from his briefcase. "The Catholics have shot themselves in the foot again. Three months prior to the Nazis invading Poland, the Vatican signed a concordat with Hitler."

"What the *fuck's* a concordat?"

"A fancy name for a treaty between the Vatican and a sovereign state on religious matters," Kalinin said, putting on his glasses. "Let me read you some of the article."

Volkov reached over and flipped on a switch. The crystal chandelier, hanging from the centre of the decagon-shaped ornate ceiling, lit up.

"That's better." Kalinin took a seat and read out loud. 'All eyes are on the Vatican as it tries to explain its relationship with Hitler following the discovery of a secret Concordat dated 1 June 1939. In the agreement the Vatican undertook to cease all opposition to the Nazi government, in return for being recognised as the state religion of the Third Reich, including the Soviet Union when annexed'.

Volkov turned to Chernik. "This is your doing?"

"I'm not that smart."

"Is it authentic?"

Kalinin waved the article in the air, like a barrister waving evidence in front of a jury. "It says the Catholics were negotiating to acquire it. What more proof do you need?"

"Where's the document now?" Volkov asked.

Chernik cleared his throat. "It's in a diplomatic bag on its way to Moscow."

"How's that possible?" Volkov said, gazing suspiciously at his security chief.

"It was offered to our Berlin bureau some time back. But we declined – it smelt wrong. Then last week, we received intelligence that the Catholics were about to acquire it. So we stepped back in."

"Why wasn't I informed?"

"I wanted to run some tests on it first," Chernik explained. "Didn't want you going off half-cocked, Mr President."

Volkov rubbed his hands together, the quintessential cartoon villain. "If we play this well, we'll control the Eastern Orthodox Church by summer."

"Pope Pyotr I," Kalinin said. "It has a certain *je ne sais quoi* that commands respect."

Volkov had long recognised the inseparable relationship between church and culture. For him, there was no better example throughout history than the role the Roman Catholic Church had played in shaping Western civilisation. It was part of Volkov's strategy to emulate the Catholics' success. He planned to unite the fourteen autocephalous Eastern Orthodox churches into one, with the Russian Patriarch as its undisputed head. The glue to hold his empire together for a thousand years.

Now looking more relaxed, Volkov poured the cognac. "To the success of the Holy Russian Empire," he said, holding up his glass.

Before the crystal had time to resonate, the *eau de vie* vanished in one crude gulp and the glasses slapped back onto the table for a refill.

"We must brief Patriarch Pyotr as soon as possible. Stop him heading off in the wrong direction," Kalinin said.

"That will not be easy," Volkov said. "Although he's venomously opposed to the presence of the Catholic Church on Russian territory, he won't want to go down in history as the cleric responsible for starting another holy war."

Kalinin scoffed. "History is written by the victors, and this is a battle we will not lose."

"It's best you speak to him," Chernik said, slapping the President on the back. "He trusts you – well at least more than he trusts me."

Volkov nodded in agreement. "So what do I say?"

"He's greedy like the rest of us," Chernik said. "Emphasise what's in it for him."

"Tell him we intend to expel the Catholics from the Russian Federation," Kalinin added, patting down the back of his hairpiece.

Chernik held up a cautionary finger. "Stalin tried that, but the bloodsuckers are still here."

Volkov gave a sneering laugh. "Stalin was a softie."

"He was a psychopath."

Volkov wandered over to his desk and removed the cigar humidor and a large butane lighter from one of the drawers. "How much do we tell the Patriarch?"

"Keep it vague," Chernik said. "Tell him that Constantinople plans to re-establish communion with the Vatican and to concede to Papal Supremacy over all Christianity."

"He won't believe it," Volkov said.

"It depends on how convincing you are," Chernik said, lighting a Montecristo.

Kalinin shook his head. "It's too easy to disprove. The Patriarch of Constantinople will simply deny it."

Chernik blew a cloud of cigar smoke towards the ceiling. "Of course he will. Conspirators always do."

23

alf a dozen pairs of eyes followed Agent Doherty as she sashayed through the CIA bullpen.

Dressed in a tight stretchy black mini dress and knee-high stilettos, she knocked sharply on the station chief's open door. "You're after me?"

"Come on in," Chief James said, gawking unashamedly as she moved across the room.

Cathy sat down and crossed her long legs, and with an exaggerated wiggling of her backside, tugged her dress back down over her thighs. "I'm all ears," she said, folding her arms and deliberately pushing up her cleavage.

"Heck, Cathy, stop doing that. You know I have little self-control."

"I'm sure I don't know what you're talking about, Chief," she said, flicking her long wavy chestnut hair back off her face.

"Dressed to kill. Who's the lucky man?"

"I've got a blind date with a tall, dark handsome Italian," Cathy said, her smile teasing. "But you would know – you set it up. Are you still trying to marry me off?"

"God knows you need help finding a decent man. And this one's from the Vatican, no less."

"What's he doing in Moscow?" Cathy asked, in a more serious tone.

"Good question. No one seems quite sure. Yesterday evening I received an official, unofficial request from Langley to assist him on a matter – wait for it – of the utmost delicacy."

"Official, unofficial, utmost delicacy. Sounds like a train crash waiting to happen."

"It has something to do with this German newspaper article," the chief said, turning his computer screen towards Cathy.

The English version of the *Frankfurter Allgemeine Zeitung* article. "I've read it. The notion that such a document exists is intriguing. And the timing ironic. It was supposedly executed just before the German-Soviet Non-Aggression Pact came into force."

"Which cleared the way for the Nazis to invade Poland," the chief added.

"And in return for staying on the sidelines, Stalin was promised the Baltic States and parts of Poland – which he ended up getting."

"So at the time this Concordat was supposedly being signed, the Soviets, and the Nazis were already bedfellows."

Cathy shifted in her seat and adjusted her dress. "A classic Hitler double-cross or a forgery?"

"Only time will tell."

"And the Vatican suspects the Russians are behind it?" Cathy enquired.

"As if Volkov needs more enemies," the chief said, shaking his head. "I spoke briefly with Commandant Waldmann of the Vatican's Swiss Guard this morning. He requested that we provide Inspector General Rossi security protection while he's here. Fortunately, I was able to convince Waldmann that he needed you instead – someone to put things into context, while causing the least amount of damage. Besides, you're rather handy with a gun, if it comes to that."

"Thanks, Chief – I think."

"If the Kremlin's involved, what do you think they're up to?"

"Simplest scenario – they plan to use the document to kick the Catholics out of Russia. The Orthodox Church has long accused them of proselytism."

"Sounds like a foot fungus."

"Poaching from their flock."

"And the more complicated scenario?"

"At a pinch, Volkov plans to use the Concordat as a rallying cry for his expansionary policies. Expelling the Catholics could be just the first step – aimed at destabilising the region. The fact that the Concordat mentions annexing the USSR, and not just Russia, in effect invites all fifteen former Soviet states into the controversy – many of which are Muslim."

"God, I miss the Cold War. Those were the days," the chief said.

"As you know, Volkov has been pushing hard to re-establish Russia's sphere of interest. His main tools to date have been regional military superiority, energy and economics. Religion would be a logical extension," Cathy said.

"It wouldn't be the first time religion was used to achieve a political end."

"You never know with the Russians. Most of what they do defies Western logic."

"A riddle wrapped in a mystery inside an enigma – Churchill got it spot on," the chief said, now standing at the sideboard, pouring himself a cup of freshly brewed coffee.

"Every Western leader makes the same mistake. Russians look European, so we expect them to behave like Europeans – not Neanderthals."

Cathy glanced up at the wall clock. Almost noon. "I'd better skedaddle if I'm going to catch me a husband," she said, with a hillbilly twang.

"Well I wish you luck."

Cathy stopped in the doorway and half turned. "Incidentally, do you know what Signor Rossi looks like?"

"The Commandant said he's a tall Italian with effortless grace – but straight men don't say things like that about their colleagues unless they're joking. So look for a short, round bald man wearing a sheriff's badge."

"Life can be so cruel," Cathy said, playfully flicking back her hair as she exited.

24

After breakfast, with the help of the concierge, Rossi ventured into the city and acquired a stylish new wardrobe. Now sitting in the crowded foyer of the Marriott Royal dressed in a dark grey casual suit, a navy roll-neck sweater, and oxblood cordovan brogues, he oozed Italian *sprezzatura*.

Rossi eyed every young lady that entered the lobby from outside, most of whom reciprocated with an appreciative smile.

"Inspector General Rossi," came a voice from behind.

Rossi swung round in surprise. "Yes," he answered, not sure what to make of the sexy brunette wearing a sable coat.

"I'm Agent Catherine Doherty," she said, offering her hand. "Welcome to Moscow."

"Agent Doherty," Rossi said, springing to his feet. "I wasn't expecting, um... how did you pick me out? Am I that obvious?"

"You're the only foreigner in the lobby that doesn't look like he's selling something. Besides," she said, taking half a step back and cocking her head to one side, "I was told to look out for a stylish Italian with sea-green eyes."

She's dangerous, Rossi thought, shaking her hand warmly.

"How are you finding the infamous Russian winter?"

"Cold."

"Not the best time to be visiting Moscow."

"Trust me, there's no other place I'd prefer to be right now."

"I know you're itching to see Red Square, but we really should go somewhere quiet to talk. There's an Uzbek restaurant near the US Embassy on Novy Arbat."

Rossi grabbed his green double-breasted wool coat from the sofa. "Lead the way, Agent Doherty."

"Call me Cathy."

"If you call me Enzo."

Outside on the bleak treeless street, the CIA driver was waiting with the engine running. Leaning back, he pushed open the rear door as they approached. Cathy gave him instructions. A stiff nod, then he sped off in the direction of the Boulevard Ring.

"How was the flight?"

"Coffee was good."

Cathy turned in her seat, her knees touching his. "Enzo, if you don't mind me asking. What's it like working inside the Vatican? It must be so fascinating."

"It's a piece of cake, as long as you appreciate and respect the traditions and history of the Church. Like Washington, I imagine."

"How'd you end up there?"

"My mother wanted grandchildren."

"Have you made your mother happy?"

"Not yet."

"Oh!" Cathy said. "No time?"

"No wife."

Cathy smiled and fell silent as the Escalade sped west along the busy Boulevard Ring towards Arbat.

"I assume the double-headed eagle is the Russian coat of arms?" Rossi said, pointing to a string of tricolour flags hanging from a souvenir kiosk.

"That flag is the Presidential Standard. But you're right, the double-headed eagle is the coat of arms," Cathy nodded. "It dates back to the fifteenth century and Ivan the Great. To me it represents the Russian Imperial Court. The communists replaced it with the hammer and sickle in 1917. After the collapse of the Soviet Union it was reinstated by the ruling elite. They're doing everything possible to wind back history. The ruling class would prefer to pretend that the communist nightmare never happened."

"Interesting. I've always associated it with the Holy Roman Empire. The two heads representing Church and State."

"In Russia the historical meaning is unclear. Stolen no doubt, like the tricolour from the Dutch."

"During the Byzantine Empire, the two heads represented the emperor's authority over religious and civil matters," Rossi said, grinning. "A bit like Russia today."

"Really," Cathy said. "I like to think the two heads represent the Russian character of schizophrenia and self-destruction."

Rossi laughed. "Or Squealer and Moses the Raven."

The driver swung hard right and hammered the Escalade down a narrow side street. A series of hard turns and they arrived back on the Boulevard Ring.

"That's the monument to Russia's Shakespeare," Cathy said, pointing to a bronze statue of Alexander Pushkin.

"Are there two of them?"

The driver looked up, catching Rossi's eyes in the rear-view mirror. "We doubled back. We've got a G-Wagon on our tail. It's a game we play with the Russians now and then."

Cathy rubbed Rossi's knee. "They're on to you."

"Me?" Rossi asked in a concerned tone.

"I'm nowhere near important enough for the honour, so it must be you."

"Should I be worried?"

"Not yet. Besides, they rarely harm foreigners unless they have a very good reason."

"I might be about to give them one."

"Volkov is a short-arsed paranoid expansionist, but he's not stupid. Harming the Inspector General of the Vatican Police would be against all international diplomatic norms. So you shouldn't worry. Deportation is the worst you can expect."

"Until I'm finished here, deportation is a fate worse than death."

Cathy cast Rossi an inquisitive glance but said nothing.

The Escalade pulled up in front of the restaurant and Cathy and Rossi piled out.

"Short-arsed paranoid expansionist," Rossi repeated as they entered. "I'll have to Google that."

"Good evening. A table for two at the back," Cathy said, pointing to a windowless area in the far corner.

The maître d' clapped his hands sharply, and a waitress dressed in a brightly coloured Uzbek tunic stepped forward from behind a curtain. They followed her in silence to an elevated area of mostly empty tables.

"From here we can see who comes and goes," Cathy said, allowing her sable to drop from her shoulders into Rossi's waiting arms.

"*Che bello!*" Rossi said, his eyes fixed on Cathy's shapely backside.

"Do you like it?"

"Very much so."

Cathy sat with her back to the wall, facing the entrance. "Sorry about the view, but under the circumstances…"

Nearby, within earshot, the waitress hovered. Cathy passed Rossi a menu.

"This is all Greek. Best you order."

"I hope you're up to it," Cathy said, as the waitress left. "I've ordered a mixture of traditional Uzbek dishes."

"Funny isn't it? My first meal in Russia, and I'm eating Uzbek cuisine."

"No need to be disappointed. Uzbekistan was part of the Russian Empire from the second half of the nineteenth century. And then part of the Soviet Union until the collapse. So you're in fact eating former Russian Empire food. Besides, the way things are going, Uzbekistan will be back in the Russian fold very soon."

"That makes me feel a lot better."

"Here comes something much more Russian."

The waitress brought over a half-litre bottle of ice-cold vodka and filled their ryumkas.

"For lunch?"

Cathy raised her glass. "For new friendships."

With the empty ryumkas back on the table, Rossi was keen to get down to business. But before they could start, the waitress had returned with lunch.

25

Father Arkady entered the subterranean chamber beneath the Cathedral of the Holy Apostle John and stepped up onto the solid wooden chair that had been brought down for the occasion. Without ceremony he began simply. "The trap is set."

The white stone chamber reverberated with murmurs of excitement from the forty-odd prelates and priests standing shoulder to shoulder within.

"Saturday evening, God willing, you will receive an encrypted message from Metropolitan Anatoly confirming the untimely death of our beloved leader Patriarch Pyotr."

Utterings of solemn prayer resounded through the chamber.

Father Arkady held up his hands. "This will be your call to action."

"It's time," the gathering called out with one accord.

"The plan remains unchanged," Father Arkady said, barely audible over the din. "Metropolitans Anatoly, Viktor and Nikodim, as permanent members of the Holy Synod, will ensure Metropolitan Paul is elected Patriarchal Locum Tenens immediately on Patriarch Pyotr's passing. We have four of the eight permanent seats so we can assume that's a given."

The three Metropolitans nodded their understanding.

"It is for the rest of you," Father Arkady said, pausing to make sure he had their full attention, "to ensure that by the time the Local Council convene to elect the new Patriarch of the Russian Church, Metropolitan Paul has overwhelming support from the 700 voting delegates. We must send a strong message to the Kremlin – the puppet theatre has finally closed."

A hand rose slowly amongst the sea of black. Father Arkady's jaw clenched when he realised who it was. "Bishop Protev, you have a question?"

"Father Arkady, your plan is based on a number of assumptions that carry substantial risk, not least being an over-reliance on the Metropolitan of St Petersburg."

"Bishop Protev, we discussed this at length last meeting. What purpose does it serve to go over it again?"

"Indulge me please," the bishop said.

Father Arkady shrugged his shoulders and nodded, knowing regardless of his answer, the bishop would speak.

"How can we be certain that Metropolitan Paul will stand up to the Kremlin after he is elevated to the Patriarchal throne?"

"Metropolitan Paul is dedicated to our cause."

"But if he betrays us? Revealing Light will cease to exist. Power does strange things to people. No one escapes her attention. We are taking a great risk," Bishop Protev said.

"For three hundred years Revealing Light has maintained its peaceful struggle – and achieved nothing. So what are we risking?"

"Our lives," the bishop called out.

"But our lives have no value if we're not serving God."

The gathering erupted in a chorus of support and Bishop Protev fell silent.

Father Arkady motioned for the room to come to order. "Any other issues?"

"Yes," a young priest said, holding up his hand. "Will the newly discovered Concordat between the Vatican and Hitler impact our mission?"

Father Arkady drew a deep troubled breath before he spoke. "That very much depends on President Volkov. If he does not involve himself in the scandal, then the document will generally be viewed as a forgery. It will be left for the crackpots and fanatics to milk it for what it's worth."

"And if he does?"

"I can only speculate. But one possible, unthinkable scenario is that a war of the creeds breaks out, in which Patriarch Pyotr becomes so embroiled that he is unable to attend the judo opening ceremony."

The chamber erupted into a cacophony of discussion.

"As I've already pointed out, the plan carries risk," Bishop Protev shouted over the racket.

"My dear brothers," Father Arkady said, again motioning for silence. "This too can be managed. There is nothing to fear. Let's put our faith in God."

26

The table was cleared, and the coffee arrived. Rossi had already divulged freely everything he knew. With Cathy he held nothing back. There was no point. The *Frankfurter Allgemeine Zeitung* had ensured that the worst of it was already in the public domain.

"You must bear in mind that no such document ever existed – not even in draft."

"How can you be so sure?"

"The Church knows her own history."

Cathy blew out a short dismissive breath. "Precisely."

Silence.

"And the lady in Paris. Does she have a name?"

Rossi opened a photo of the assassin's passport on his phone and held it up. "You know her?"

A short sharp breath. "Oksana Koroleva. You have been busy. This lady's a legend. A Kremlin hired gun.

Drop-dead gorgeous. This photo doesn't do her justice."

"Passport photos rarely do."

"Chief James has a mad crush on her. Maybe you can introduce her."

"She's dead."

"Is there anyone you've met recently that isn't dead?"

Rossi considered the question, then shrugged.

"One thing that makes little sense. If the Vatican knew the Concordat was fake, why negotiate?"

"The Church trades on her reputation. The facsimile we received was so convincing, Cardinal Capelli decided to remove the threat rather than try to prove the negative later. People have become far too cynical. They are only too willing to believe in such lies."

Cathy slowly stirred sugar into her coffee. "Especially if Volkov is controlling the narrative."

"And of course at the time we had no idea who was behind it. That was the main reason I travelled to Bonn – to interrogate Wolf. Tragically it all went pear-shaped, and I blame myself."

"That's nonsense. A delayed flight doesn't make you responsible," Cathy said, staring at a monstrous man who had just entered the restaurant.

Rossi glanced back over his shoulder. "Signor G-Wagon?"

"Dark suit, square jaw, small eyes. Certainly FSB."

"Do we need to go?"

"No. He'll keep his distance for now," Cathy said, removing a pepper spray canister from her handbag. "And from Paris you headed to Berlin where you established the colonel was indeed murdered."

Rossi nodded. "To lure the colonel's son to Berlin."

"But why?"

"Because he knew where the Concordat was hidden?"

"Unlikely," Cathy said bluntly. "At that point the Concordat was only of secondary interest."

There was a long silence. Rossi figured she had misspoken. "Why would you think that? This whole despicable affair has only ever been about the Concordat."

"Because, if your Berlin spooks were really interested in the Concordat, they would never have allowed Wolf to escape back to Bonn with the document. Not even the FSB are that incompetent."

"So what then?" Rossi said, his tone more reticent.

"The Concordat wasn't there in the first place."

"How does that make sense?"

"Wolf was telling you the truth. He did stumble on the Concordat in his father's study – but only after the Russians had planted it there for him to find."

Rossi pushed back in his seat, speechless.

Cathy rested a consoling hand on his arm. "They were surfacing the Concordat. Historical document found amongst a stash of old Stasi files in Berlin, etcetera. You know the drill."

"But all this only makes sense if the Russians knew about Bernd Wolf's Stasi past and the stolen files – doesn't it?"

"You're right, and they did," Cathy said, glancing over at Signor G-Wagon. "Strategies for surfacing forged paintings or documents are usually built around opportunity. My guess is that Colonel Wolf pitched the

143

Stasi files to the Russian Embassy in Berlin some time back. There's a limited clientele for such files, but the Russians definitely would be on the shortlist."

"*Sì*. So they built a story around an ex-Stasi colonel with boxes of stolen top-secret documents."

"To give the Concordat life. It needed a history, which thanks to the Bonn murders and Lois Lane, it now has. The biggest risk to the Russians' plan was if Maximilian Wolf failed to take advantage of his good fortune."

"Not much chance of that happening," Rossi said, touching his ear, surprised that it no longer hurt. "Greed has infected an entire generation. Capitalism is the new religion."

Pleased with herself, Cathy rubbed her palms together. "Now that's the how. As for the why – we'll need to work on that."

"That's brilliant. How the hell did you work that out so quickly?"

"It's what I do for a living."

"But it's what I also do."

"Then I must be smarter than you."

Rossi smiled. *Brains masked behind a bimbo's façade – there's got to be a fascinating story that goes with that.*

Suddenly Cathy sat bolt upright. "Damn, I might have something for you. A man claiming to be an FSB operative based in Berlin phoned the other day. I told him to call back on a secure line. To the best of my knowledge he didn't. But I'll check."

"Do you have a name? I'll pass it onto the German police."

Cathy took a small notebook from her handbag and thumbed to the second-last entry. "Mikhail Rudoi. Give me a minute, I'll call the office."

While Cathy phoned, Rossi sent a message to Senior Detective Schmidt.

"Good news," Cathy said, ending the call. "We're meeting Rudoi later today."

"Let's pray he knows where the Concordat is kept. I must recover it before any further damage is done."

"Pray you must, because recovering the Concordat is not possible. It's insane to think otherwise."

"How can we find out who forged it? That'd be a good place to start."

"Slow down, Enzo. Excluding the possibility that the Concordat is genuine, there's another complication. We have no idea when the document was forged. It could have been sitting dormant since the War. The Soviets had a huge 'active measures programme' that, amongst other sins, created and counterfeited documents."

"So discounting that possibility – where do we start?"

Cathy leant closer and whispered, "I'll tell you this because I trust you. But don't go screwing me."

Rossi nodded his assurance.

"We have a high-level mole inside the FSB."

"Doesn't everyone?"

"I like you already, Inspector General."

"That's great. But what do we do next?"

Rossi listened intently as Cathy explained the procedure. First she would post a coded message on one of the online chat rooms, spelling out her interest. Then the mole would collect the requested intelligence and drop it off at a prearranged location for her to collect.

"That doesn't sound quick."

"There'll be a dead drop in two days."

"Can't it be sped up?"

"Not without risking lives. The dead drops are agreed way in advance. Besides, our man will need time to gather the information."

Rossi sat biting his lip, knowing Cathy was right.

"So what's on your agenda?"

"I've got a meeting with Archbishop Joseph Esposito, the head of the Archdiocese of Moscow, in a couple of hours."

"And?"

"That's it," Rossi said with a shrug of the shoulders.

A broad grin. "Not much of a plan."

"I thought I'd let trouble come to me."

"And it will," Cathy said, looking into his eyes. "The FSB have let you in for a reason."

"I'm not sure I follow."

"Do you really think you sneaked in under the radar?"

"Well…"

"You're a pawn in one of Volkov's political games. Together with Bishop Muellenbach and the Wolfs. You're being used to give credibility to the forgery. Imagine the reaction from the world press when the Inspector General of the Vatican Police is arrested in Moscow, trying to recover the Concordat. A document the Vatican insists is a vicious fabrication."

"I guess the moral of the story is don't get caught."

Cathy rubbed Rossi's hand. "Be careful, that's all I'm saying."

"So are you in?"

"I wouldn't miss it for the world," Cathy said, pausing as a question popped into her mind. "The scanned copy of the Concordat, you said it was convincing. Why?"

"The historical context is beyond reproach. And the language and the layout is perfect. It is totally consistent in format and style to the 1933 Reichskonkordat; which unquestionably is the real deal."

"That's because the forger used it as a template," Cathy said.

"That's what I concluded too."

"And the Papal Encyclical mentioned in the text. What is that?"

"*Mit Brennender Sorge*," Rossi said. "A papal letter dated 14 March 1937. It denounced breaches by the Nazis of the 1933 Reichskonkordat, and many of the Nazi ideologies, including the idolatrous cults of state and race."

"Is there any significance to it being included?"

"Most probably not. Just another historical touchpoint for those who wish to believe the document is real."

"Well let's hope it's a recent forgery and that the artist is still alive. He's our best chance."

Cathy glanced at her watch and motioned to the waitress for the bill.

"What's the Vatican's view of the Russian Patriarch?" Cathy asked.

"The previous incumbent, Patriarch Alexander, was extremely sympathetic towards the Kremlin. He fought fiercely to expel the Catholic Church from Russia. More Russian than divine, you might say. He would have considered the use of such skulduggery reasonable and necessary."

"In much the same way Stalin considered the gulags reasonable and necessary."

Rossi laughed at the comparison. "The Vatican is praying that the newly elected Patriarch is different."

"He's different all right. *Ta Eschata.* His regressive statements on the Apocalypse and the Second Coming are straight off the ark. A CIA psychological assessment concluded that he is a delusional, hallucinatory psychotic."

"Granted, his colourful language is old-school, and his claim God speaks to him is just a little off-putting, but…"

"Why? Does God only speak to the Pope?"

"Very good."

A cheeky smile. "Sorry. Continue."

"In some ways Patriarch Pyotr is right. If the world doesn't get its house in order, the final battle between the forces of good and the forces of evil is closer than we think."

"That's too depressing."

"Look about us. Wars raging on all continents. Confrontation between the rising power of China and the United States seems inevitable…"

"The 'Thucydides Trap,'" Cathy said.

"Nuclear weapons in the hands of madmen. Who's going to stop it? The United Nations Security Council?"

"Off your soapbox, Enzo."

"Sorry," Rossi said, cringing a little.

Cathy smiled for a moment, then her expression grew serious again. "So you were saying…"

"The Vatican would like to think Patriarch Pyotr intends to put Christianity ahead of his personal ambition. But the reality is he's most likely to be another Kremlin puppet."

"The CIA has truckloads of contradictory evidence. But on balance we also have him down as a Volkov stooge. Think about it. With 2,000 nukes ready to be launched at a moment's notice, no country is willing to challenge Russia – not even the good old USA."

"It would result in global annihilation," Rossi added.

"Therefore the only real threat to Volkov is internal. And given Volkov's suppression of all forms of political opposition, it is left to Patriarch Pyotr and the Russian Church to be the voice of dissent and defiance in Russia."

"But he remains silent." Rossi paused. "I guess that's the answer."

It was already 2.30. Rossi needed to get back to the hotel where Archbishop Esposito's driver was waiting to take him to the Cathedral of the Immaculate Conception.

Cathy took a business card from her handbag and wrote her personal mobile phone number on the back. "In case of an emergency, or if you just need to talk," she said, handing Rossi the card. "Moscow can be a lonely city at night."

She's something else, Rossi thought, helping her on with her coat.

Outside on the pavement the Escalade was waiting, engine running. "Quick! Jump in," the driver yelled, pushing open the door.

"I trust that wasn't you," Cathy said, scrambling into the back next to Rossi.

"You mean the G-Wagon? No way. The tyres deflated on their own," the driver laughed, gunning the Escalade west on Novy Arbat.

27

The archbishop's driver slowed the Toyota to a halt in front of the Cathedral of the Immaculate Conception's main gate. He reminded Rossi, in broken English, that His Eminence would be waiting for him in the sacristy, which was located to the right of the high altar. They had planned to meet at the archbishop's residence nearby, but as Rossi had been stuck in traffic for over an hour, the location was changed to accommodate the prelate's busy schedule.

Built in the early part of the twentieth century, the cathedral provided sanctuary to Moscow's Catholic community, which at the time had swollen to more than thirty thousand. The neo-Gothic red brick building with lancet windows operated as a place of worship until it was commandeered by the communists in 1938. The interior was then converted into four floors of communal apartments and office space for government use.

Rossi stood momentarily glancing up at the façade, imagining what the cathedral looked like with the hammer and sickle flying from its bell tower.

Returned to the Church in the 1990s, the cathedral was now home to the Metropolitan Archbishop of the Archdiocese of Mother of God, Joseph Esposito. *But for how long?*

Rossi ascended the snow-covered stone steps to the main entrance. He pulled hard on the heavy wooden doors and entered the narthex. He removed his hat and gloves and dipped his fingers into the holy water stoup and blessed himself. Through a second set of doors he entered the nave which was white and simple in design.

He glanced about to get his bearings. Two old ladies shuffled between benches tidying up after a wedding; a handful of worshippers prayed in the front pews. He bowed his body towards the altar and then moved to the right.

In the distance, at the end of the side aisle, he spotted a single door. *That must be the sacristy*, he thought, checking his watch as he hastened towards it, upset with himself for being so late.

Rossi listened at the door. He could hear voices speaking softly on the other side. He knocked and waited.

"Come," a voice called from within.

Rossi opened the door. In front of him stood three novices in deep conversation. Archbishop Esposito appeared from behind them and approached with open arms. The two men, who had met at the Vatican on numerous occasions, embraced each other warmly.

"*Mi dispiace per il ritardo,*" Rossi said humbly. "The traffic in Moscow is diabolical."

"It's always like that. Even worse than Rome."

"Have I come at a bad time?" Rossi asked, motioning towards the novices.

"For you – there's never a bad time. They're local candidates who are being ordained tomorrow. Our Russian flock is growing fast and we need more priests. I thank God for sending strong young men to help with our mission," the archbishop said, leading Rossi back towards the apse.

The tall, withered archbishop took Rossi's arm as they climbed the steps to the high altar chatting about news from home.

Archbishop Esposito lowered himself into the cathedra, positioned directly under the nine-metre-high crucifix attached to the wall, in the centre of the windowless apse. "Now tell me everything you know."

Rossi pulled over one of the adjoining chairs, placed it in front of the archbishop and sat down. He leant forward, and in a soft, weighty voice explained the events of the last few days.

Archbishop Esposito listened without interrupting. Occasionally he pursed his lips or raised an eyebrow, to express surprise or concern.

"That's as much as we know," Rossi said after twenty minutes.

The archbishop sighed deeply. "The inventiveness of evil. It never ceases to amaze me."

The peaceful reverie inside the cathedral was shattered

by the sound of raised voices, speaking in broken English, emanating from the narthex.

Father Francis, one of the resident priests, was in an animated discussion with two men in hats. From where Rossi was sitting it was difficult to make out what was going on.

"They would like to speak with the candidates," Archbishop Esposito explained. "Father Francis is trying to convince them they're not here."

I guess he's got his fingers crossed, Rossi thought. "Is this common?"

"Regrettably after Volkov became President, intimidation and harassment has become a daily affair. And with the rite of ordination tomorrow it's only to be expected." Archbishop Esposito slowly rose to his feet. "Stay here, Lorenzo. It's better if I handle this alone. Discretion is the better part of valour."

Rossi remained seated, obscured from the narthex by the high altar, as the archbishop moved with an air of authority to the point of commotion. Although it wasn't his style to hide from controversy, Rossi knew his involvement would only further complicate matters. He quietened his breath and turned his good ear towards the open door.

"Gentlemen, I'm Archbishop Esposito. How can I help you?"

"Good evening, Archbishop. My name Prickov," a stout man said, holding out his identification card. "I from FSB. I want speak with young Russian boys you have here."

"What would you like to speak to them about?" Archbishop Esposito asked politely.

"I need confirm they are not forced in joining church," Prickov said, with an unpleasant tone and a steely gaze. "Why ruin young Russian boys' lives? We have own church. Don't need another," he said, in rapid order.

"I'm afraid they're not in the nave at this moment," Archbishop Esposito said calmly.

"I return tomorrow morning, sharp ten. All three hostages here – or I burn down church," Prickov barked.

Rossi, who had caught most of the conversation, met the archbishop and Father Francis in front of the high altar as they returned.

There was no utterance of indignation or outrage. After a brief discussion, in which the archbishop did most of the talking, it was agreed that the candidates would be ordained tonight in a secret ceremony under candlelight, reminiscent of the Cold War.

Father Francis was sent off to muster all involved while Archbishop Esposito and Rossi returned to the apse to finish their conversation.

"I couldn't have imagined the rate of deterioration," Rossi said, shaking his head. "How could the Russian people allow this to happen all over again? And so soon after the horrors of the Soviet Union. Don't they remember what it was like?"

"The answers are long and complicated, and we have no time today," Archbishop Esposito said with urgency. "Regarding the Concordat; what is it you'd like me to do?"

"It would be greatly appreciated if you could raise the matter with Patriarch Pyotr."

Rossi waited while the archbishop thought.

"I will do my best with God's help. But you do understand that if the Kremlin's involved, as you have suggested, President Volkov will forbid such a meeting."

"Will the Patriarch obey Volkov?"

"He shouldn't, but he most likely will. There has been an unwritten rule of mutual benefit down the ages. But if the truth be spoken, it is one-sided. The Kremlin has always called the shots."

"So, can I conclude, that if the Concordat is a Kremlin offspring, the Patriarch is unlikely to interfere?"

The archbishop nodded. "Sadly, that is correct."

"Then there's no point in meeting with him?"

"Most probably not – but I will try. Miracles often happen when you least expect them," Archbishop Esposito said, standing.

Rossi gave the archbishop his arm and they descended from the high altar together.

28

Dirty and unshaven, Rudoi gazed up at the rows of dark windows as he approached the Khrushchev-era apartment building. He punched the four-digit code into the electronic keypad mounted on the metal door frame. The buzzing of the electric strike confirmed he was at the right address.

The foyer was stark and dimly lit. He entered and summoned the lift. The lopsided doors sprung open with a bang and the stench of stale urine wafted out. He pushed the button for the sixth floor.

As the lift climbed, Rudoi grew increasingly distraught. Impulsively he slammed his fist against the chunky control panel. Fifth. The instant the door opened he bolted to the adjoining stairwell and ascended three steps at a time. On the sixth-floor landing he heard the lift door open. He listened for a moment. Stillness. Warily he opened the door and poked his head out.

To his left a shaft of white light emanating from a doorway down the long unlit corridor. Beads of sweat gathered across his brow as he stepped anxiously into the open. Taking up a position hard against the wall, he shuffled towards the light.

"Come in, Mr Rudoi," a man's voice commanded from deep inside.

Rudoi froze in place.

"Mr Rudoi."

Several slow deep breaths. "I'm unarmed," Rudoi called out, raising his hands in the air. He pushed open the door with the toe of his dirty shoe and stepped into the light. The windows of the apartment were blacked out; the room uncomfortably hot. In front of him a wooden chair, illuminated by two strategically placed spotlights. He held up his right hand to shield his eyes, but it was impossible to see what lay beyond.

"Close the door."

Rudoi appeared relieved to be inside.

"Turn around and place your hands against the wall."

In silence Rudoi followed instructions. He knew the drill.

Agent Lawrence stepped out from behind the light, his gun trained on Rudoi's back. "Are you armed?"

"No."

Holstering his pistol, Lawrence frisked the Russian from head to toe. Other than an unpleasant stench, Rudoi was clean.

Rudoi took his seat. Gaze fixed on the floor, he seemed disorientated and confused as he described events leading up to his escape from the dacha.

"You mentioned Red Dove. What was the brief?" Lawrence growled, maintaining the pressure.

"To terminate Colonel Wolf, and to plant a document in his apartment for his son to find."

"What document?"

"An agreement between the Vatican and Hitler."

"Where did the document come from?"

"Moscow."

From the corridor came the sound of children running, accompanied by the scream of their mother. Rudoi looked nervously over his shoulder at the door.

"Who forged it?"

"Who said it was forged?"

"Why Bernd Wolf?"

Shielding his eyes again, Rudoi tried to see beyond the blazing lamps. Still nothing. "Bad timing."

Lawrence hammered his fist on something; probably a table. "Am I meant to guess what that means?"

"Wolf came to the Russian Embassy in Berlin last summer. He wanted to sell three or four boxes of old Stasi surveillance files he had taken home before the fall of the wall. Lubyanka was informed, and we received orders to buy them."

"Last summer?" Lawrence repeated.

Something dropped on the floor in the adjoining room. Rudoi shot a nervous glance to his left. Nothing. "July."

"Then why were they still in Wolf's apartment, even after you murdered him?"

"We were told by Moscow not to collect them. Wolf had already been paid, so what did he care?"

"Do you know why?"

"At the time, no. But it's obvious now," Rudoi said, his brow covered in sweat.

"Amuse me."

"Make it appear as though the Concordat was part of the cache stolen by Wolf."

"So you placed it open on the colonel's desk. But you left the boxes sealed and covered in dust. Didn't you think it would look odd?"

"We were instructed to place the Concordat in a prominent place. Nothing was mentioned about opening boxes."

"Poor 'tradecraft,'" Lawrence said, pausing. "And what if someone else had come along before Maximilian Wolf?"

"The probability of that happening was assessed to be low. We made the death look like an accident; there was no need for the police to visit the apartment. Besides, we bugged the joint to monitor all outcomes."

"Then you murdered Wolf's son and Bishop Muellenbach in Bonn and stole back the Concordat. And the pièce de résistance – you leaked the whole story to the *Frankfurter Allgemeine Zeitung*. The article is then referenced all over the world and fiction became the fact. A tried and trusted Soviet modus operandi?"

"My role began and ended in Berlin. The deaths in Bonn, and the leaking of the story, had nothing to do with me. In fact it's the first I've heard of it. I've been on the run – no newspaper with my breakfast."

"Then who do you think was behind Bonn?"

The sweat on Rudoi's face was unbearable. He removed a stained handkerchief from his pocket and mopped his brow.

"I have no idea. The mission was classified need-to-know. Moscow was pulling the strings." Rudoi paused, closing his eyes out of tiredness. "Can we stop? I'm exhausted. I haven't slept in two days."

"That's enough for now."

"Will you help me?"

"Yes. We'll get you out. It'll be tricky. But there are ways."

"Spasiba."

"In three days a CIA agent, resembling you, will enter Russia by car from Finland at the Karelia border crossing. His cover will be as a German automation engineer. You will go out the next day as him."

"How's that going to work?"

"You either trust us or you don't."

"It's more a question of competence than trust," Rudoi said, pausing. "But what choice do I have?"

"Precisely! Now, you'll need to stay here while we arrange things. Don't leave the apartment. Don't even look out of the window. There's food in the kitchen. Someone will come tomorrow and put you in make-up for the passport photo. He'll identify himself as Woodpecker."

Rudoi grunted his understanding.

"There's a bathroom on your left. Go in and close the door. And don't come out for ten minutes."

As soon as the door clicked shut, Lawrence locked it. "Here's the key," he said, flicking it under the door. "And take a bath. You stink."

On tiptoes, Agent Doherty stepped quietly out of an adjoining room carrying her stilettoes. She winked at Lawrence as if to say well done. They then exited the apartment without a word.

29

Martin Burke, the general manager of the Marriott Royal, lived in a small studio apartment near the hotel. Several times a month when guests of high standing arrive Burke feels obliged to stay overnight to help manage their over-inflated egos.

Although Inspector General Rossi didn't quite fall into that category, Burke had agreed to take extra care of him as a favour to Archbishop Esposito.

"Yes," Burke said, grabbing the phone.

"This is Gisela, Mr Burke. Inspector General Rossi has returned. I did what you told me to do," the duty manager said.

"Keep him there," Burke said, jumping up from behind his desk. He hurried down the stairs from his office on the mezzanine floor to the lobby. At a more dignified pace he moved attentively towards Gisela, who was standing near the front desk.

"Did anyone notice him come in?" Burke whispered.

"I don't think so, but I can't be sure," she said apologetically. "The FSB agent that was here earlier vanished when I was attending to a guest."

Burke, a conservatively dressed man with curly salt and pepper hair, scrutinised every face in the lobby. Satisfied there was no immediate threat, he moved discreetly across the palatial void towards the storeroom.

Burke glanced one final time over his shoulder before unlocking the door. He drew back in dismay. A well-fed man with a flat-top haircut was making a beeline for the front desk.

"Has Inspector General Rossi returned yet?" he growled in his habitual tone of intimidation.

"Let me check, sir," Gisela said, picking up the telephone.

"He's not in his room," he snapped. "Is he in any of the restaurants?"

"I wouldn't know, sir. I have no way of telling," she said, with a well-practised smile. "One minute. I will ask my colleagues whether they've seen him."

Gisela moved to the other end of the long, narrow reception counter where three desk clerks were busily attending to guests. She questioned each of them in turn in a soft, clear voice. "Did anyone hand in a Nigerian passport this morning; a gentleman has misplaced it?"

Each answered, "no," with an emphatic shake of the head.

Gisela strode confidently back towards the impatient FSB agent. "I'm sorry, sir. No one seems to have seen him since he left the hotel after lunch."

"Useless lot…" he scoffed, mumbling an inaudible

obscenity. He then deposited himself on a sofa facing the hotel entrance.

Gisela looked over and caught Burke's eye. With a discreet gesture, he signalled for her to stay put. At that moment, a tall, scraggly-haired woman approached from reception pulling a suitcase with UN stickers displayed prominently on both sides.

"Can I help you, madam?" a porter said.

"Yes. Store this, please."

Frantically, Burke rushed forward and snatched the bag from the porter's hand. "I've got it."

Confused, the porter stood upright and placed his hands on his hips.

"Anton, go and help the arriving guests," Gisela called out.

"Yes, ma'am," he said, turning and heading towards the revolving doors.

Burke, now in undisputed possession, unlocked the storeroom and wheeled the suitcase inside. Against the back wall, sitting on a stack of boxes filled with printer paper, was Rossi.

"Hello, Inspector General," Burke said sheepishly, wiping perspiration from his upper lip.

"Is this how you treat all your guests?"

"We try very hard not to."

"What's happened?"

"The FSB are here. Two in your room and at least one in the lobby."

Rossi blew out a deep breath as he jumped off the boxes. "Do you know what they want?"

"Apparently they have a court order to arrest and deport you for visa violations."

"Cathy was right," Rossi murmured. "How do I get out, without being seen?"

"With great difficulty."

"Don't you have secret passageways for celebrity guests?"

"You mean like the Vatican?"

Rossi managed a smile.

"The best I can offer is the service entrance. Give me a minute." Burke picked up a ream of copy paper, opened the door and stepped cautiously into the lobby.

Gisela hurried over. "Thank you, sir," she said, taking the paper.

"Listen carefully," Burke whispered. "Here's the plan. You distract the buffoon while I smuggle the Inspector General out the back way."

"Bad news I'm afraid. There's an FSB agent posted there too."

"I can't keep the staff out of the storeroom for ever. We need to come up with something quick."

Gisela glanced outside. An airport shuttle bus carrying an Etihad flight crew had just pulled up. "Get the Inspector General to phone the hotel and ask for me. I'll inform the agent he's on the line. While they're talking, the Inspector General can sneak out the front, using the flight crew as a screen. Tell him to keep the agent on the phone as long as possible."

"That could just work. He doesn't seem to scrutinise the departing guests," Burke said.

SEAN HEARY

No alternative proposal presented, Rossi agreed.

Gisela stood behind the front desk waiting. "Marriott Royal... Good evening, Inspector General Rossi," she said, in a loud voice.

The FSB agent's ears pricked up.

"Excuse me, sir. It's Inspector General Rossi. He would like to speak to you," she said, holding up the phone.

"Stupid girl," the agent boomed, already standing at the desk. "How dare you warn him I'm here?"

"I don't understand, sir. I thought you wanted to speak to him," Gisela said, looking suitably surprised.

Foam forming in the corners of his mouth, the agent snatched the phone out of Gisela's hand and grunted down the line.

"This is the Inspector General of the Vatican Corpo della Gendarmeria. I understand you're looking for me," Rossi said, peering out from behind the storeroom door at Burke.

"Where are you?" the agent said, his lustful gaze locking onto the bobbing backside of one of the air hostesses.

"Go," Burke said, in a frantic whisper.

"I'm in traffic. I'll be another ten minutes. Can you wait?" Rossi said, weaving his way between two porters pushing trolleys stacked high with the flight crew's luggage.

"I'll be in the lobby," the agent said, swinging his gaze towards the front entrance as if he had sensed something.

Rossi had gone.

167

30

An unexpected knock on the door sent Rudoi's heart racing. He grabbed the screwdriver he had found earlier and tucked it into his sock.

Rudoi peered anxiously through the spy hole. The corridor was poorly lit; the visitor's round face heavily shadowed. "Who's there?"

"Woodpecker," came a deep voice.

"You're a day early."

"We're ahead of plan," the visitor said in American English.

There was a long silence. "Show me some ID."

Woodpecker pulled an American passport from his pocket and held it up to the spy hole.

"Where's the agent who was here earlier?"

"Do I sound like his fucking mother?"

Rudoi opened the door.

Carrying a large black makeup case, Woodpecker glanced about as he stepped inside. "No more games."

The room was large and cheaply furnished. On the right a threadbare sofa and two armchairs. Between them a laminated wooden coffee table. To the left a tired-looking open kitchen with a small dining table and three mismatched chairs. Against the front wall next to the entrance, the two spotlights that Lawrence had used earlier that day.

Woodpecker removed his coat and flung it on to the sofa. "Why all the hysteria?"

"Trying to stay alive," Rudoi said, studying his visitor. "Not sure who to trust these days."

"That's because you're in with the wrong crowd."

Rudoi didn't react. He just continued to eye his visitor as he spoke.

In an exaggerated arch through the air, Woodpecker swung the make-up case onto the kitchen table. "This shouldn't take long."

"What do you have in mind?"

"A few props."

"How's that going to work? By now my mugshot is hanging on the wall of every checkpoint and border crossing in the Russian Federation."

"You'd think so. You're a dangerous felon."

Woodpecker pulled one of the wooden chairs away from the table and positioned it under the shadeless ceiling light. As he did, Rudoi glimpsed his holstered handgun beneath his jacket.

"When you're standing in front of a case-hardened

border guard, you don't want anything catching his eye."

"That's reassuring. But what does it mean?"

"Wigs and FX prosthetics to be avoided at all costs."

"That doesn't leave much."

Woodpecker took a step back and cast a critical eye over Rudoi. "I'll hazard a guess that the description accompanying your mugshot reads – tall male, thick sandy-coloured hair, grey eyes, clean shaven."

Rudoi shrugged his shoulders. "Me and a million others."

"That's the point."

"You make it sound so simple."

"I might even give you a little birthmark," Woodpecker said, examining Rudoi's forehead.

"Like Gorbachev," Rudoi scoffed. "That would be ironic. Russians hate him too. We blame him for the collapse of the Soviet Union."

"Nothing so grand as to be obvious. Large enough to show up in a passport photo, but small enough to go unnoticed in everyday life."

Woodpecker removed a pair of hairdressing shears from the makeup case and worked on Rudoi's hair as they spoke. "Do the Russians know about the documents you passed on to Lawrence this morning?"

"What are you talking about?" Rudoi said, knitting his brow. "I was lucky to escape with my life."

"Someone's got their wires crossed."

"Clearly."

There was a long, thoughtful silence before Woodpecker spoke. "What's it like being a defector?"

Rudoi's face grew grim. "What was I meant to do? Stand there and take it like Kutin. No thanks."

"I couldn't do it myself," Woodpecker continued. "Reaching for your gun every time the dog barks. Never knowing when that bullet will come."

"What's your point?"

"No point. Just curious."

Rudoi reached over and picked up the pack of cigarettes on the table. "Mind if I smoke?"

"Go ahead, kill yourself," Woodpecker scoffed. "Might as well, you're dead anyway. Betraying your deep-cover colleagues; it's a death sentence. They'll find you. They always do."

Rudoi took his time lighting his cigarette. "You trying to cheer me up?"

Woodpecker stood behind Rudoi resting his heavy hands firmly on Rudoi's shoulder; the sharp tips of the shears brushing against his earlobe. "How many names did you give them?"

"Enough to blow the cover on several key operations." Rudoi winced and arched his back as if he was expecting the shears to be plunged into his neck.

"Is something wrong?" Woodpecker asked, circling Rudoi as he checked the evenness of the cut.

"I couldn't help but notice your weapon."

"Are you afraid of guns?"

"That one I am. It's a Russian PSS silent pistol. An unusual choice of a weapon for an American agent."

"A souvenir."

"If you're CIA, I'm Chairman Mao."

Woodpecker sprung backwards and drew the pistol. Rudoi stayed seated.

"Good. This way we can have a grown-up conversation without all the pretence," Woodpecker said.

Rudoi looked up without emotion. "You must be Timur's friend?"

"Who did you betray, Agent Rudoi? The names."

"Why should I cooperate?"

"Because my bag contains instruments of torture that I'm more than willing to use."

"Crap! This is not my week. Instead of Woodpecker, I get Klaus Barbie."

"Mikhail, my friend," Woodpecker said, switching to Russian. "You know our methods better than most. We do what it takes, without mercy."

"*Idik chertu*," Rudoi said, spitting in Woodpecker's face.

Woodpecker pulled the trigger. A round lodged in the wooden chair between Rudoi's open legs. "Don't fuck with me, you traitorous piece of shit. I was up all night and I'm in a terrible mood."

"You kill me and you don't get the names, Einstein. Then the European deep-cover programme will be set back twenty years."

Woodpecker straightened his aim. "That's why I'll start by shooting out your kneecaps."

"That sounds painful," Rudoi said, popping a yellow capsule into his mouth. Almost instantly, Rudoi collapsed to the floor in convulsions.

"You coward," Woodpecker cried, dropping to his

knees, and shaking Rudoi violently. "Who did you betray?"

"No one," Rudoi said, plunging the long shaft of the screwdriver deep into Woodpecker's neck. "That's the irony of it all."

Gasping for air, Woodpecker fell to the floor.

No time to hang around. Rudoi flung open the apartment door and bolted down the corridor. He put his weight to the emergency exit. Locked. Not daring to look back, he scrambled across to the lift and pounded on the call button. The sound from the shaft told him that the lift was near. "Open," Rudoi pleaded, as the lift clunked to a stop in front of him.

"Don't move," Woodpecker said in a low, gurgling tone. Bloody shoulder resting on the wall, he lifted his pistol with both hands.

Rudoi swung around in disbelief. Woodpecker looked sunken and weak. But his eyes were sharp and his gun hand steady.

"Where are you hurrying to? We haven't finished."

A smile came slowly to Rudoi's tired face as he raised his hands. "There's a screwdriver sticking out of your neck. You should get that seen to."

The lift door, at last, sprung open. Rudoi fought off the urge to dive forward. He could see the colour fading from Woodpecker's face. He knew it was only a matter of time before his visitor lost consciousness. Patience.

"Step away from the lift," Woodpecker said, his voice powerless and lacking authority.

Rudoi coiled his body; eyes flashing between the gun

and the open lift. Woodpecker was having none of it. A single noiseless round hit Rudoi above the ear. He fell with a thud. Then, as if death wasn't enough, the lift doors closed and opened on his head.

31

Rossi climbed out of the taxi near the Uzbek restaurant where he had taken lunch. Cathy had mentioned the US Embassy was nearby. He figured it was as good a place as any. Turning his back to the icy wind, Rossi waited for the taxi to disappear.

Disorientated and alone, he descended into a subterranean walkway and crossed to the south side of the busy six-lane avenue. Russian pop music blared out of speakers mounted on the roofs of the shops and restaurants that lined the strip.

He hurried east in the direction of the Kremlin. Best to put some distance between himself and the US Embassy.

Looks promising, Rossi thought, peering through the window of the 'Petit Café'. It was all but empty, which didn't say much for the coffee. But it was quiet and commanded an uninterrupted view of the street.

Inside it was warm, with Provençal charm. *Petit all right.* Rossi counted no more than a dozen tables. He glanced over at the leggy waitress as he hung his coat near the door; too busy flirting with the barista to even turn her head. He sat down by the window facing west and scanned the area where he was dropped off.

In front of him was the café's only other guest – a stylish woman with long swept-back brunette hair, not yet forty. She looked up and smiled softly, as if to say hello, then continued reading one of the fashion magazines that were scattered about the café.

"A double espresso please," Rossi called to the waitress.

She turned her head back over her shoulder and nodded; then said something to the barista that made them both snigger.

I need to call Cathy, Rossi thought, patting his pockets. A wry smile. He had dropped his phone into the shopping bag of a passer-by as he fled the hotel. It seemed to be a smart thing to do at the time. Now he wasn't so sure.

"Do you speak English?" Rossi asked the waitress when she brought over his coffee.

"*Nyet,*" she said, shaking her head unapologetically.

"Is there a payphone nearby?"

"*Ne-panimiyou.*"

"Te-le-phone," Rossi repeated, gesturing with his hand.

The waitress shrugged her shoulders and moved back to the bar.

"The arrogance of youth and the naivety of beauty," the brunette said, standing unnoticed at Rossi's shoulder.

He looked up with a start. "Sorry, I was somewhere else."

"I couldn't help but overhear your conversation," she said, holding out a Swarovski-encrusted smartphone.

No thought of refusing, Rossi snatched at the phone. "You're so kind. I wouldn't normally impose, but…"

"Not at all," she said, returning to her table.

The sound of sirens filled the street as Rossi fished about in his pockets for Cathy's business card. He gazed nervously at the stream of police vehicles racing past towards the Moscow River. *Seems I'm not the only one causing trouble tonight.*

Rossi dialled. No answer. His heart sank as Cathy's voicemail activated. He rang off and dialled again. Voicemail. He left a short message.

"Is everything all right?" the brunette asked, as Rossi handed back the phone.

"She didn't answer."

"Maybe your wife didn't recognise the number?" she said, putting on her fur coat to leave.

Rossi knew a proposition when he heard one. "Regrettably, I'm not married."

"How fascinating," she said, tilting her head to one side.

Rossi's strong primal instinct burst forth. He thought to ask for her number. Then his brain kicked in. This was not the time or the place.

As the door closed behind the brunette, Rossi heard sirens approaching from the east. He hurried to the window. In the distance, three police vehicles escorting a VIP through traffic. Come on Cathy – where the hell are you? Then the café door swung open again. *She's keen*, Rossi thought.

"Signor Rossi, I assume?" the brunette said, holding out her phone. "It's for you."

"I'm so sorry," he said, taking the phone.

"Don't mention it."

"Cathy?"

"I got your message. I'll be there in two minutes. And keep away from strange Russian ladies."

Rossi felt an overwhelming sense of relief. "Please hurry," he said, ending the call.

"You found her?" the brunette said, scribbling her telephone number on a napkin.

"Yes. She's on her way."

"Pity," the brunette said, tucking the napkin into Rossi's breast pocket.

"Thank you again," Rossi said with a schoolboy grin as the brunette turned for the exit.

As the door opened, Rossi again heard sirens. But this time the sound was static. "Christ," he said, staring at a dozen police vehicles, pulling up in front of the Uzbek restaurant.

Out of the corner of his eye he noticed the waitress looking his way. "Bill please," he called out, motioning with his hands.

At the exact spot he had exited the taxi, thirty armed policemen had gathered under a street lamp. Dressed in grey trench coats and trooper hats, they were receiving instructions from the officer in charge.

Rossi felt his stomach tighten as half their number

vanished down the same subterranean crossing he had used twenty minutes earlier. Within seconds they were on his side of the street. Four, maybe five turned towards the river; the majority headed east in his direction.

Rossi watched in horror as they paired off, then with weapons raised stormed into the first half-dozen establishments. Terrified patrons flooded onto Novy Arbat. The commotion brought the waitress and the barista to the window.

"They're looking for someone," the barista said, in accented English, turning to Rossi.

"Really?" Rossi said, smiling, more surprised by the fact the young man spoke English than by his ridiculously obvious observation.

"Look," the barista cried, "they're coming our way."

Time to go. Rossi rose abruptly and grabbed his coat.

"Be careful out there. The Moscow police like to use their guns."

"That's reassuring." Rossi reached for the door then stopped. "I'm parked out the back. Do you have a service entrance?"

"I wish," the barista said, too wide-eyed to suspect that the well-dressed man in his café was the fugitive at the centre of the manhunt.

"Pity. It's a bit of a hike."

Rossi scurried east without looking back. In front of him a glass door swung open and a small group of diners came onto the street. Rossi caught the reflection of a tall man in a fur hat approaching quickly from behind.

"Inspector General Rossi," came a faint voice.

Friend or foe? Rossi ran.

"Stop! Where are you going?"

Between buildings, Rossi spotted the halo of a street lamp at the end of a roofed passageway. He pivoted towards the opening. But his leather-soled shoes refused to follow. "Christ," Rossi cried out as his feet flew out from under him. Landing with a thump, he came to rest against a giant fibreglass Mexican promoting the 'Hat Dance Cantina'. Dazed and winded, Rossi lay motionless, unable to move.

"Are you Rossi?" the man enquired, grabbing him by the arm.

Rossi tried to break free, but he wasn't up to it.

"Come with me," the man insisted, pulling Rossi to his feet.

"Release me," Rossi said, his speech slurred. "I have full diplomatic status."

"CIA, Special Agent Lawrence. Can you walk?"

"I'm fine," Rossi said relieved, his legs collapsing under him.

Lawrence took Rossi's weight. "Let's get out of here before you're spotted."

Blurry-eyed, Rossi glanced back at the 'Petit Café'. On the pavement the waitress and the barista were talking to three portly policemen. "It's too late."

"I doubt it," Lawrence said. "Look at the size of those guys. They're more likely to go inside for a piece of cake than chase after you."

Rossi's head throbbed and his ears rang as he followed Lawrence through the passageway and out onto the back lanes of Arbat. The sight of Cathy sitting behind the wheel of the Escalade lifted his spirits.

"Who phoned for a cab?" Cathy called out as they approached.

"I told you trouble would come to me," Rossi said, climbing delicately into the back.

"Were you spotted?" Cathy asked, hitting the accelerator pedal hard.

Torment. Rossi felt an invisible hand reach inside his skull and squeeze his brain. Frantically his fingers danced about in his pockets searching for his painkillers.

"Possibly," Lawrence answered.

Cathy glanced at Rossi in the rear-view mirror. "What happened to you this time?"

With one hand, Rossi threw a couple of painkillers into his mouth. With the other he held a bloody handkerchief to the back of his head. "I ran into a big Mexican."

Cathy laughed. "A little accident-prone, aren't you?"

The vehicle fell white-knuckled silent as Cathy raced the heavy SUV down a narrow icy road and through an intersection without even a tap on the brake.

"You've done this before," Rossi said.

"Holidays on my uncle's farm in Wisconsin. We used to go ice racing on the nearby lakes during winter."

"Summer wouldn't work."

"It was before my mother died. I must have been twelve or thirteen. Jeez, it was fun."

"What was she like?"

Cathy looked straight ahead. "She was an angel. I miss her so much."

"What happened, if you don't mind me asking?"

"I came home from school one day and found her hanging from the ceiling," Cathy said, her voice brittle.

An uncomfortable silence.

Rossi kept glancing back over his shoulder expecting to see a response. After a while he stopped looking. "What happened to the police?"

"I told you. They're eating cake," Lawrence said.

Suddenly Cathy hit the brakes and skidded the Escalade to a halt. "The road's closed." She leant forward and scanned the area.

The traffic on the Boulevard Ring was building in both directions. To the right a lone policeman stood in the middle of the Prechistenka Ulitsa intersection waving a black-and-white baton. Quickly the streets grew eerily silent. Rossi looked about anxiously. He couldn't quite understand why only he looked nervous. Then the faint sound of sirens drifted in from the direction of the Kremlin.

"Is this *all* for me?"

Cathy smiled at Rossi in the rear-view mirror. "I hate to disappoint you. It's the President's motorcade."

Rossi blew out a short tense breath. "Trust me, I'm not disappointed."

The shrill of the sirens from the accompanying armoured vehicles grew louder as the convoy climbed towards Kropotkinskaya.

"This area will be at a standstill for hours," Cathy said.

Through the bare poplar trees running down the centre of Gogolevsky Boulevard, Rossi watched as the motorcade sped through the intersection. Blue flashing lights appeared and disappeared between the stationary traffic as they went.

Cathy glimpsed a black Pullman Guard limousine in the middle of the heavily armed pack. "It's the President all right. An unusual route for him. He must be going to dedicate a new tank factory."

The sirens faded, and the streets grew noisy, but the traffic barely moved – gridlock.

"Where are we heading?" Rossi asked. "Back to the Marriott?"

"A safe house. We need to come up with a new plan. Your 'trouble will come to me' strategy, seems to have run its course."

"Yeah. It wasn't very good, was it?"

"Incidentally, what happened back at the hotel?"

Rossi told his story with all the colour and enthusiasm of a teenager returning to school after summer break. "It's an experience I'll remember for the rest of my life."

"Let's hope Volkov doesn't cut it short."

"My experience?"

"Your life."

"You're joking," Rossi said, as if the truth was the last thing he wanted to hear.

"Taking a taxi from outside the hotel wasn't your smartest move," Cathy said. "With the driveway CCTV, it was only a matter of time before they tracked down the cab. I'm surprised you had time to drink your cappuccino."

"Double espresso – only an Australian would order a cappuccino after lunch."

"Of course."

32

It was already past eight. The wintry night sky hung low and heavy as the President's limousine rolled up the driveway of Patriarch Pyotr's working residence on Chisty Pereulok.

Dressed in a black cassock and wearing a white koukoulion embroidered with the image of Seraphim, the Patriarch ambled onto the porch. Stroking his long grey beard, he watched dispassionately as Volkov climbed out of the limousine. Volkov, uncomfortable with the symbolism, hurried up the stairs to be on an equal footing to his host.

Anastasia Lebedova bustled up the driveway waving her index finger in warning. "Delete them now," she said, chastising a state photographer who had snapped several shots of Volkov inadvertently looking up at the Patriarch as he ascended.

Anastasia raised her hand, quietening the large gathering of propagandists, whom she had corralled into a small roped-off section of the front garden. "There will be no interviews given tonight. A statement will be provided later for voiceovers. We expect blanket coverage," she said, in no mood to say it twice.

Volkov shook the Patriarch's hand with insincere, humble reverence; a gesture he had practised to perfection. Anastasia, satisfied the press had sufficient material, nodded to the President and the two leaders moved inside.

"Your Holiness, the matter I wish to speak to you about is confidential. May I suggest we discuss it in private first," Volkov said softly, as they walked from the entrance hall towards the formal meeting room.

"As you wish," the Patriarch said, without a hint of curiosity.

Volkov turned to his following entourage and instructed them to wait.

"This way," the Patriarch said, guiding Volkov along the southern hallway towards the door leading to his sitting room.

The room was symmetrical, but cosy. On the right, two rich red and brown fabric armchairs faced a lit open fireplace that crackled invitingly. A coffee table with an inlaid top and carved legs stood between them. "Please take a seat. I'll organise tea," the Patriarch said, ringing a small brass bell resting on the commode next to the door.

Above the mantelpiece hung an oil painting that Volkov knew well. It was *The Last Judgement*, painted in 1904 by Viktor Vasnetsov. He had recently signed a presidential decree transferring the masterpiece to the Patriarch's residence from a small museum in the Vladimir Region.

"I see you received your painting," Volkov said, flopping into the armchair in an overly familiar manner, having already dropped all pretence of devoutness.

"Yes. Thank you. It depicts Matthew 25:31-33," the Patriarch said in a passionate tone of voice. "And when the Son of Man shall come in his majesty, and all the angels with him, then shall he sit upon the seat of his majesty. And all nations shall be gathered together before him. And he shall separate them one from another, as the shepherd separateth the sheep from the goats. And he shall set the sheep on his right hand, but the goats on his left."

"We are the sheep and the Americans the goats?" Volkov said, jutting his chin forward.

"I can think of a better metaphor."

The housekeeper, who must have been in her eighties, entered pushing a trolley of Darjeeling tea and homemade cake. She arranged the service on the coffee table then, without pouring, left the room.

The Patriarch lowered his corpulent person onto the armchair he preferred, on the right of God. He then cleared his throat as though he intended to speak, but remained silent.

The only son of an Orthodox priest, Patriarch Pyotr grew up in a small Siberian town far from big city temptations. From early childhood he had been obsessed with Armageddon and the fate of humankind. As one of the world's foremost experts on eschatology, he was known as 'Ta Eschata' by fellow theologians. Considered mad by many mainstream Christians, his election to head the Russian Church was naturally viewed with great suspicion.

"You take your tea with honey," the Patriarch said, picking up the large Gzhel porcelain teapot and pouring.

"You're well informed, Your Holiness."

"At least my housekeeper is. Now, what's this delicate matter that has prompted your most unexpected visit, Mr President?"

"The newly discovered Concordat," Volkov said, succinctly.

"I recall reading something about it this morning."

Volkov's gaze expressed his annoyance. "Let me check if I understand you correctly. You read the article, but found it so inconsequential that you can vaguely recall reading it?"

"More unbelievable than inconsequential."

"How is that?" Volkov enquired.

"Well it all seems a little too convenient, does it not? How could such a divisive document exist for all these years and nobody knows about it – not even a whisper?"

Volkov handed the Patriarch a plastic sleeve containing the Concordat. "Maybe this will help to convince you."

The Patriarch studied the document. He flicked back and forth and read some sections twice. "It's conceivable, but is it believable?"

"Of course it's believable," Volkov snapped, unable to hide his frustration. "It's the smoking gun. It shows the Catholics for what they are. If Hitler had succeeded, the state religion of Russia today would be Roman Catholicism, and you would be painting church steeples."

"Don't you consider it strange that after eighty years this document would miraculously appear out of nowhere?"

"Put it down to serendipity. The circumstances surrounding its discovery are easily understood. Lost during the heroic Soviet Army's liberation of Berlin. And now, thanks be to God, found amongst a pile of old Stasi files. I don't see anything sinister in that."

A heavy sigh. "Serendipity! That's one word for it, Mr President. So how did it end up with you?"

Volkov coughed and looked towards the fire. "One of our agents acquired it from an East European criminal gang."

"With Russian accents?"

"They were only hours away from selling it to a powerful group of German anti-clerics."

"So what do you intend to do now you've rescued the Concordat from the forces of evil?"

Volkov fought back a smirk. "Establish the truth."

"Truth has never been one of the Kremlin's strong points," the Patriarch said.

"And humour has never been one of yours."

There was a long silence as the Patriarch sipped his tea. "I trust the Kremlin had nothing to do with the murder of the Catholic bishop?"

"For a man of faith, you show little faith in your country or your President."

"I'm sorry – I'm not sure I understood your answer, Mr President?"

Volkov huffed. "And I'm not sure I understand your lack of enthusiasm, Your Holiness. I thought we were both on the same side."

"Are we?" the Patriarch asked.

"Yes."

They glanced at one another for a long moment. Then the Patriarch said, "War with the Vatican is ill-advised, Mr President."

"That's not a bad idea – a holy war just might play in Russia's favour."

"Religion is not a tool of the state," the Patriarch said firmly, now standing in front of the fireplace.

"Your Holiness, I shouldn't have to remind you I played no small part in your election. In return I expect your trust and loyalty," Volkov said, with a threatening glare. "As we speak, the Catholics are again expanding in Russia – undermining your authority and that of the Kremlin. The Concordat gives us the opportunity to rid ourselves of this pestilence for ever. On this we must stand united."

The Patriarch turned towards the open fireplace and gazed pensively up at *The Last Judgement.* "It's been three months since my enthronement at the Cathedral of Christ the Saviour," he said, almost as if he was talking to himself. "As the bells rang out on that glorious day I promised God that I would turn the tide of moral decline throughout the world, before the Son of Man returns to judge mankind for a final time."

"And God heard you," Volkov said, leaning over and topping up his tea. "The Concordat is God's helping hand? God has chosen you to lead Christianity back to the right path? The Catholic Church has lost its moral authority – the Concordat only serves to remind us of that. A return to Orthodoxy is needed."

"I see your point," the Patriarch said, his tone more collaborative.

Volkov's brow knitted with confusion; perhaps suspicion. "Good."

"You are right, of course, Mr President. I was testing your resolve. We would be totally within our rights to expel the Catholics from Russia. Russians are Orthodox – it is part of our culture. We don't need a second religion confusing the faithful."

"Perhaps Your Holiness should consider engaging other Orthodox Churches. After all, the Concordat has broader implications. Greece, Cyprus, Serbia and Bulgaria – they all should feel equally aggrieved."

The Patriarch nodded, as if in tacit agreement.

With the Patriarch's capitulation, Volkov's style became less constrained. He gaudily unveiled Godhead's ambitious plan that was concocted the night before. "Summon the Holy and Great Council of the Orthodox Church. Tell them that the Orthodox Church must strengthen its structure and fortify its base before it is devoured by Rome. That can only be achieved by uniting under one strong leader – the Patriarch of Moscow and All Russia. Why should the Ecumenical Patriarch of Constantinople be the 'first among equals'? What does that mean anyway? Russia is one thousand times more powerful than any of the other autocephalous churches. For God's sake, Istanbul is not even Christian. Your

Holiness, this will be your legacy. Act now to correct this historical injustice."

"You could well be right, Mr President, but your plan is more complicated than you realise. It will take time. May I suggest that we start with something a little more modest?"

"Like?"

The Patriarch hesitated. "Verifying the authenticity of the Concordat."

"Of course! This is a task I would like you to lead. Politicians rarely bring credibility to such matters."

"Yes. But the process will need to be seen as open, independent and transparent."

"I agree," Volkov said, pulling a folded sheet of paper from his pocket. "Here's a list of those I would like on the review board. You will note it includes clerics, historians, theologians, scientists and even a military representative."

"As you wish, Mr President," the Patriarch said, his expression stolid.

33

It was well past dinner time. They had been driving for two hours and still no sign of the traffic letting up.

Cathy glanced back at Rossi who had been napping. "How's the head?"

"Needs feeding," Rossi said, stroking his blood-matted hair. "Much further?"

"We're almost there."

Abruptly Rossi sat up, wishing at once he hadn't. A savage pain shot through his head. "I almost forgot. Berlin Kripo identified the two Russians. One was the name you gave me – Rudoi. The other Yuri Kutin. Both commercial attachés assigned to the Russian Embassy."

"Yeah, I know. We have Rudoi under protective custody."

Rossi's face lit up. "Finally, some good news. And Kutin?"

"Dead at the bottom of a frozen lake."

Rossi listened full of expectation as Cathy briefed him on the meeting with Rudoi.

"Rudoi said he knew nothing about the Concordat – other than it arrived from Moscow. I'm inclined to believe him."

"Not exactly what I was hoping to hear."

The SUV slowed and turned left. They drove under an archway through a crumbling pre-Revolutionary building into a tarmac courtyard.

"This will be your home for the next couple of days," Cathy said, searching inside her handbag for her mobile phone that was ringing.

Rossi gasped. "Good Lord – is it habitable?"

"Hello." Cathy's expression turned grave as she listened. "Thanks for letting me know."

Rossi held his breath, waiting for Cathy to speak. *The CIA mole inside the FSB has been compromised.* He could think of nothing worse.

"Rudoi's dead."

"That's not possible," Lawrence protested.

"A single shot to the head as he tried to escape," Cathy said, her tone disbelieving. "He let someone in. There was no sign of forced entry."

"Maybe he was followed?"

Cathy shook her head. "No way, Paul. The Russians would've stopped him before he got anywhere near us. The intelligence we gathered is invaluable."

"Misinformation?"

"No, I don't think so. My guess is Rudoi's location was leaked."

Lawrence scoffed. "It's for the best. It was going to be a bitch getting him out."

Rossi grimaced at Lawrence's pragmatism. *Hopefully Cathy's more compassionate.*

"Enzo, Agent Lawrence will introduce you to your new abode. I'm needed back at the office."

"I trust my safe house is safer than Rudoi's."

"As long as you don't phone your mum," Cathy said, handing Rossi a small black leather pouch containing a mobile phone.

"Chic."

"What we save on accommodation we spend on phones," Cathy said. "The pouch has a silver-infused lining. It blocks the signal being transmitted by your phone – stops bad guys tracking you."

"Inspector General, are you armed?" Lawrence asked.

"No. My pistol's in a locker at Berlin-Schönefeld Airport. Wanted to avoid complications on arrival."

"I'll arrange something for you," Lawrence said. "It's about to get a whole lot rougher."

"Can you make it a big one?"

Rossi and Lawrence jumped out of the SUV and went to the door. Cathy swung the Escalade around and shot off back under the archway. As she drove east towards the centre, she couldn't help but wonder who had leaked Rudoi's location, and more importantly was Rossi safe.

34

When Vladimir Ilyich Lenin moved the Soviet government to Moscow from St Petersburg in 1918, he established his private residence and office in the Senate Building within the Kremlin walls. During this time the word Kremlin became a metonym for the Soviet government.

The Kremlin, located on a small hill in the centre of the city, overlooked the Moscow River. The entire perimeter of the sixty-eight-acre triangular site was fortified by an imposing 2.2 kilometre red brick wall. Strategically placed along the wall were twenty defence towers of various designs, the tallest being the Spasskaya Tower on the eastern side overlooking Red Square, under which Muscovites gather every New Year's Eve to watch the tower's large clock strike midnight.

North of the Spasskaya Tower was the mustard-coloured Senate Building, the working residence of the current Russian President.

It was mid-morning. Volkov was sitting at his desk in his oak-panelled office. He gazed blankly at the door through which he had just entered. Kalinin and Chernik were on their way, hungry for news.

While at first Volkov was delighted with last night's outcome, now he was not so sure. *Did Rasputin outsmart me? Why did I ever approve his appointment?*

Anastasia knocked on the door and entered. "It's ten o'clock, sir. The Prime Minister and Director Chernik have arrived. They're on their way up."

"Good. Let them straight in and then make sure we're not disturbed."

Shortly thereafter the door flung open, and Volkov's two most trusted cohorts entered.

"How did it go?" Kalinin asked, greeting Volkov without the usual theatrics.

"The old prick was sceptical at first. But when I reminded him of his duty to the Motherland and his responsibility to the Russian Church, I had him eating out of my hand."

"Well done," Kalinin and Chernik said in unison, as they sat down on the two armchairs in front of Volkov's desk.

"Mind you, I had to constantly feed him. He's far too scholastic to come up with practical steps by himself."

Chernik scoffed. "Scholastic – is that the same as derailed?"

Volkov stood up from behind his desk and straightened the recently hung painting of St Petersburg on the far wall.

"Had he ever heard of the Concordat?" Kalinin enquired.

"Not a whisper. In fact, he lectured me about how improbable the notion was. But I stole his thunder. I advocated that he should lead an independent team of experts to authenticate the document."

Kalinin sat forward. "How independent?"

"I gave him a list of highly credible sycophantic cheerleaders who owe their very existence to me."

"That's reassuring. We shouldn't take unnecessary risks," Kalinin said. "And how far did you get with the rest of the Godhead plan?"

"He agreed to everything. I was extremely persuasive."

Chernik, who had already been briefed by his audio surveillance team, coughed into his fist, masking a snigger.

"Then we need to get on with it or risk losing control of the narrative," Kalinin said. "The social networks are already all over this."

Chernik knitted his brow. "*Bozhe moy*, Sergei, don't worry about the social media. I have my web brigade of sock puppets trolling the online community as we speak. The Kremlin sets public opinion. Remember, we are the conscience of the people."

Arms folded, chin raised, Volkov paced behind his desk. "If there is no God, then I am God."

Chernik glanced up, puzzled. "Sorry?"

"A little imagery I'm experimenting with," Volkov said, sitting down again. "Incidentally, whatever happened to Inspector General Rossi? I thought he would be part of your dog and pony show. Rumour has it you've lost him."

"He had a bit of beginner's luck," Chernik said defensively.

"Or maybe he had help. I wouldn't put it past the Americans to be sticking their noses in where they don't belong."

"You mean into our perfectly legitimate plan to disrupt the world order."

Laughter.

"But it plays to my point," Kalinin said, maintaining his serious tone. "We need to get on with it."

35

ossi stared, mouth agape, at his reflection in the last fragment of mirror still hanging above the water-stained basin in the bathroom.

"Hold still," Cathy said, hacking at his hair as if it was an overgrown hedge.

"Couldn't we have just gone with glasses and a silly hat?"

"That's where you're wrong, Inspector General," Cathy said smugly. "Silly hats come later. First, we must erase all those distinguishing features that make it easy to identify you from a photograph or a description. Like your once-gorgeous long, thick black hair."

"And which other distinguishing features are you planning to erase?" Rossi asked, his gaze catching hers in the remnants of the mirror.

Taking a step back, Cathy pursed her lips and stroked her chin. "Now let me see. Italian confidence –

that'll have to go. Stylish wardrobe – easily fixed. Perfect teeth…"

"That could prove more difficult."

"Not at all. I saw pliers in the kitchen."

Rossi bared his teeth in the mirror. "Couldn't I keep my mouth shut?"

"You?" Cathy scoffed. "Not likely."

"Brother, what happened?" Lawrence said, in the bathroom doorway.

Cathy tenderly ran her soft hands over Rossi's strong naked shoulders, brushing away the hair. "Short and functional. Sit down, Lawrence. I have time for one more customer before I close up."

"In your dreams, Doherty," Lawrence said, moving back into the living room.

Cathy brushed the last few strands of hair off Rossi's back. "You're done. Clothes are on the bed. Put them on."

After a few minutes, Rossi wandered into the lounge transformed. He was wearing dark blue trousers of dubious origin, scuffed black boots, a grey woollen jumper and a rabbit skin ushanka hat.

"Don't you look the part," Cathy said, cupping her hand over her nose. "Almost invisible? I for one wouldn't give you a second look."

"I don't want to appear ungrateful but these clothes have been lived in." Rossi sniffed under the armpit. "More than once."

"But the underpants are new. I picked them out myself."

"Ferrari red is à propos, but they're a trifle small," Rossi said, tugging at the seat of his pants.

Cathy's head shot forward a tad; she appeared to be eyeing his crotch. "Really? You don't look that big."

As Rossi's jaw dropped, she stepped forward and placed a pair of black-rimmed glasses on his nose. "Perfect."

36

Perched precariously on the edge of a bar stool, David Krotsky threw back another shot. "Forbes calls them 'self-made billionaires.'"

"If you regard stealing state assets through rigged privatisation auctions to be self-made, then I guess they are," his pallid-faced companion said with a roll of the eyes.

"Why did we let them get away with it?"

"We were all asleep."

"The young were too naive. They believed fame and fortune didn't discriminate."

"And the old folk had forgotten how to think."

"So it was up to us to prevent the pilfering," Krotsky said. "But we did nothing. Intoxicated by our new-found freedom."

"And a belief in the magical elixirs of capitalism and democracy. We're a country of fools."

The barmaid refilled their ryumkas with cheap chilled vodka. Krotsky, a small man with a pinched face, was out celebrating his fifty-ninth birthday with his only friend, Leonid Kats. They had been at it since early afternoon and intended to go home in wheelbarrows.

Although they caught up regularly, it was usually at one of their apartments, with a light meal of borsch, blinchiki and black tea. Their finances didn't allow for much more. However, each year on three occasions, namely their respective birthdays and Victory Day, they headed to one of the city's fast-disappearing Soviet bars for the purpose of reminiscing their glory days.

As idealistic young members of the Komsomol, they were recruited within a week of each other, thirty-six years ago, by the KGB's Office for Active Measures. Their primary responsibility had been to produce high-quality forgeries and propaganda material to promote the communist ideology. Leonid Brezhnev was still General Secretary and Yuri Andropov was Chairman of the KGB.

"Remember what Solzhenitsyn said – 'Don't lie! Don't participate in lies, don't support lies,'" Kats said, laughing.

"We used to always think he was talking directly to us."

"When I think about the lies we churned out, it makes me cringe – and you're still doing it, David."

Krotsky drummed his finger on the bar. "Despite all its faults, communism gave us certainty."

"Yeah, the State looked after us. Not well, mind you. But there was always food on the table and a roof over our heads."

"We did it for the ideology; a classless society, common ownership…"

"From each according to his ability, to each according to his needs," Kats interrupted, quoting Marx.

Krotsky scoffed. "Instead we got Stalin's state capitalism; Marxism-Leninism."

"And a succession of incompetent peasant leaders."

"And then Mikhail Sergeyevich gave us glasnost and perestroika and destroyed the Soviet Union in the process."

"The Soviet Union collapsed because the system didn't work," Kats said, spilling his vodka as he shook his finger at his friend, "not because of Gorbachev's policies. Sure, he could have violently suppressed the protests in Eastern Europe, but what for? The break-up was inevitable."

Krotsky nodded. Kats was right. "Then the cruel hand of fate saw fit to inflict Tsar Boris upon us. The drunken dancing bear."

"From superpower to flea circus," Kats said, lighting a cigarette. "We never saw that coming."

"And now we're faced with Volkov's totalitarian democracy.

"Stuck in the middle of another social experiment."

Krotsky shook his head. "We're a hopeless lot."

Toast. A splash of glasses. "To old times and innocents."

Krotsky glanced suspiciously at the faces in the room. Close to Kats, he said in a toneless whisper. "I'm worried about Volkov."

"You and the rest of the world."

Krotsky turned to the barmaid and held up his empty ryumka.

"Another one?" she asked, with an old-fashioned smile, emptying the last few drops of the second bottle into his glass.

Krotsky missed the smile. His eyes had drifted to her breasts; cradled in a black low-cut bra, lightly veiled behind a transparent white blouse.

"What's happened? The Concordat?" Kats asked. "You've never let it bother you before."

There was a long silence before Krotsky answered. "In the old days, we were fighting for an ideology. Now there's nothing. No moral high ground. Just power and greed, concentrated in the hands of so few. What is Volkov planning?"

"Revenge. The dwarf feels aggrieved. Never got over losing the Cold War. He'd prefer to live in chaos rather than see Russia disrespected on the world stage. Volkov's the de facto Russian ego."

"And that's at the heart of my concern. Why should I help him?" Krotsky said, his tone solemn.

Kats funnelled a handful of peanuts into his mouth then spoke. "David, you are something rare, a KGB forger with a moral conscience. The two are incompatible. Live with it or retire. Now shut up and relax – it's your birthday."

"I can't relax. This thing could go pear-shaped very quickly. Remember the Protocols of the Learned Elders of Zion?" Krotsky said, referring to the anti-Semitic forgery created by Tsar Nicholas II's security apparatus.

Kats nodded.

"Subsequently used by the Nazis to justify genocide against the Jews – and it is still being circulated by extremist groups today."

As Krotsky's mood darkened, Kats knew it was better to let him talk. Get it off his chest.

It was ten o'clock before Krotsky ran out of steam. He had said all he needed to, and drunk as much as he could. Krotsky, being the only one with an income, paid the bill. Then arm in arm they staggered out of the bar and headed towards the Metro.

37

Heavy snow fell as Cathy bounced the Escalade up onto the pavement next to the western entrance of Kolomenskoye Park. Through the iron railings she saw the apple orchard was deserted. A blue disc nailed to the base of a lamp post signalled the exchange was on.

Thirty minutes earlier, Cathy and Rossi had been on the opposite side of the four-hundred-hectare park. Together they had buried a stash of US dollars in the snow amongst a thicket of pea trees. Before leaving, Cathy had attached a blue disc to a nearby tree.

"Let's see what we've got," Cathy said, putting on her hat and gloves.

Rossi glanced about. "Aren't we going to look a little conspicuous?"

"Not really. Russians do strange things. Besides conspicuous can be interpreted as having nothing to hide."

Like lovers on a romantic early morning stroll, Cathy and Rossi walked arm in arm through the unmanned gate into the park. In front of them lay a field of white. So much snow had fallen that the path running east past the apple orchard to the Church of the Ascension was not visible. If it wasn't for fresh tracks laid down by two horses, finding the path would've been problematic.

"The fifteenth row," Cathy said, looking back and counting from the road. "Now all we need to do is find the marker."

"A blue disc?"

Cathy nodded.

"Don't you have any other colours at the agency?"

"If it was up to me, they'd all be pink."

"Really! I'd never pick you as a pink sort of person."

"It's my lucky colour. I always wear something pink."

Rossi threw her a questioning glance. He could not once recall seeing her in anything pink. Blacks and reds; always short. Never pink. "If you say so."

Their feet sank deeper into the snow as they left the firmer ground of the pathway and headed into the orchard. Bent over like chickens eating corn, they high-stepped their way under the low-hanging branches searching for the disc.

"It's got to be here somewhere."

Rossi made a snowball and tossed it at Cathy. "The best-laid plans of mice and men," he laughed.

"That's why they're called plans," Cathy said, scooping up a handful of snow herself. As she let fly she spotted two mounted policemen on the service track, which ran down the centre of the orchard, riding towards them.

Rossi glanced back over his shoulder at what had caught Cathy's eye. Fumbling, he pulled the earflaps of his ushanka down and fastened it under his chin.

"Best if you keep your mouth shut." Cathy then wrapped her arms around Rossi and gave him a long, wet kiss on the lips.

Rossi wanted to say something clever, but nothing came out.

For the policemen who patrolled the former royal estate several times a day, it was not uncommon to see people playing in the park during the height of winter, especially after a heavy snowfall. It was something Muscovites did. However, given they were on patrol and had not seen a single soul all morning, they decided to make a nuisance of themselves. And maybe earn a few roubles for their trouble.

"Good morning," the older of the two officers said, looking down from his mount.

"Good morning, officers," Cathy said in Russian, with a relaxed pleasant demeanour. "I'm surprised to see you out on patrol in such conditions. Particularly given the park is empty."

"We need to exercise the horses."

"But *you* don't?" the younger policeman said, in a more challenging tone.

"We're in Moscow for a couple of days on business," Cathy said. "We were here eight years ago on our honeymoon – mind you, it was summer then. Some Russian friends brought us here for a picnic. We shouldn't have done it. But we carved our initials into one of these apple trees. We're trying to find it."

Whatever she's saying he seems to be buying it, Rossi thought, impressed with how calm Cathy appeared.

"Your documents," the policeman said, without commenting on Cathy's imaginative story.

"Oh, I'm sorry. They're in the SUV. Should I fetch them?" Cathy said, pointing west.

The policeman traced their footprints back to the path, but could not see further because of the trees. "Under Russian law, you are required to carry your passport at all times," he said, like a reluctant headmaster about to dispense punishment.

"I'm sorry, officer. It's my fault. An oversight, no more – I assure you. There will be a fine?" she said, sliding her hand into her coat pocket, signalling she was ready to negotiate.

The policeman pulled out a well-thumbed copy of the civil and criminal penalties handbook and pretended to study it. "Six thousand roubles."

"Unfortunately we're leaving Moscow tomorrow. Perhaps we can pay in cash? I know it's unusual, but I would feel terrible if we left Russia without paying."

The policeman nodded.

Cathy stuck her hand back into her pocket, took out a small bundle of one-thousand rouble notes and counted off six.

"Each," the younger policeman said sharply.

Cathy smiled and continued to count.

"Next time follow the rules," the older policeman said, turning his gelding about.

Rossi gave Cathy a sideways glance in disbelief as the

police rode away. "That was impressive. Why didn't they recognise me?"

"During Soviet times, the workers had a saying. 'You pretend to pay us and we pretend to work.' Cops like that have one thing on their mind. Money. They're not searching for criminals. They're looking for opportunities."

"Found it," Rossi called out, digging up the package.

Ten minutes later, Cathy swung the Escalade into a quiet residential street and pulled over. "Let's see what we've got," she said, cutting open the package with a Swiss Army knife. Inside was a typed note, a thin document stapled at the corner, a small bottle containing a liquid substance, some strands of hair in a zip-lock bag, and a black-and-white photograph of three men. The head of the man in the middle had been circled with a red marker.

"This document is of no interest to us," Cathy said, laying it aside. "But the note is, together with the photograph."

Rossi shifted in his seat impatiently. "What does it say?"

"Interesting," Cathy said as she read. "The Concordat is part of a highly classified FSB operation called Red Dove. Naturally he couldn't access the files. But he suggests that if the document is an FSB fake, then the forger is probably David Krotsky – the Rembrandt of counterfeited historical documents. That's him circled."

Rossi picked up the photograph and studied it. "Finally we have a name."

"And an address and mobile phone number."

"*Fantastico*. Your man's done well. How soon can we jump him?"

"Enzo, let's not get ahead of ourselves. The message says *if* the document is an FSB fake. For now Krotsky is simply a person of interest."

38

Krotsky took the escalator from the depths of the Park Pobedy station looking tired and worried. Blindly he followed the evening pilgrims through the swinging glass doors onto Kutuzovsky Prospect.

He turned down the dark, empty side street towards his modest apartment. Deep in thought, he didn't hear his phone ring. The caller persisted. Krotsky's gaze rose sharply when the melody finally penetrated his consciousness.

'No Caller ID'. That worried Krotsky. Only a handful of people knew his number. Curiosity then piqued. He answered, but said nothing. A long silence.

"Mr Krotsky, we need to talk," Cathy said in Russian.

Again silence.

"Mr Krotsky," Cathy repeated. "We need to talk."

Krotsky stopped and rechecked his screen. He paid no attention to the windowless van approaching from behind.

Well, at least not until it screeched to a halt beside him. Krotsky froze in place as the side door shot open. Sitting inside was a large man with a pistol trained at his head.

"Get in," Rossi barked.

"What do you want?" Krotsky asked in Russian, climbing in.

"I want to talk to you about the Concordat," Rossi said, guessing what he had asked. Rossi knew from the intelligence that Krotsky spoke five languages. English was one of them.

"I wrong man," the bewildered polyglot protested. "I pensioner. No money."

Rossi slammed the door and switched on the interior dome light. "Stop the pretence, Mr Krotsky. I wish you no harm. Just answer a few questions, and then you can go."

Krotsky nodded, but said nothing.

Rossi held up three photographs in the diffused light. "Do you know these people?"

Krotsky gave a cursory glance, then shook his head. "No."

"It's the team responsible for surfacing the Nazi Concordat in Germany," Rossi said, tossing the photos, one at a time, at Krotsky. "Your team."

"I'm not an operational guy," Krotsky said, dropping the pretence. "But what's the point?"

"They're all dead. Murdered by the FSB to cover the tracks leading back to you – and your evil creation."

"Is that what you've come all the way from Rome to tell me? I assume you're from the Vatican – despite your dishevelled appearance."

"Your life is in danger. They know I'm here. And it's easy to work out who's on my dance card."

214

"By the size of you I'm guessing you're not clergy?"

"My name is Inspector General Rossi of the Vatican Corpo della Gendarmeria."

"The Vatican police," Krotsky said smirking. "Aren't you a little out of your jurisdiction? Russia can be quite a hostile place for enemies of the state."

"I have God and the Church on my side."

"Let's not play games," Krotsky grumbled. "What do you want from me?"

"I need unequivocal proof that the Concordat is forged."

"You want me to betray my country? You overestimate your power of persuasion," Krotsky scoffed at the notion. "If I betray my country, I'm as good as dead anyway. What's the difference – dying a hero or being remembered as a traitor?"

"Why should the dead worry about how they're remembered? Isn't it better to go with a clear conscience and at peace with God?"

"That's all too highbrow for me, Inspector General. Let me concentrate on staying alive."

"Then come with me. The Americans can offer you protection."

"Where? In a foreign land. Always looking over my shoulder, eventually dying of shame. No thanks," Krotsky rebutted angrily. "With all her faults, Russia is my Motherland. She will always be my home."

"Russia is a great country, held back by flawed ideologies and inept leadership," Rossi said, changing tack.

"Maybe so, but that's no reason to turn traitor – what's the euphemism you Westerners use? Whistle-blower, that's right. Under any name and for whatever reason, it's the lowest form of life."

"I'm not asking you to be a traitor. I'm giving you an opportunity to be a revolutionist. A national hero that changes the course of history," Rossi said, assuming a passionate tone. "Volkov is moving the world towards the burning abyss. You can help stop him."

Krotsky sat stone-faced mulling over what Rossi had said. He didn't know how to respond. He wished he had never been asked to create the Concordat. Dark cloudy thoughts raced through his confused mind.

"Mr Krotsky."

"I need time to think."

"There is no time. You're a dead man walking – they know where to find you," Rossi said.

"Yet I'm still alive."

"You're alive because it suits their purpose. Don't be mistaken, they plan to kill you. They have too much invested in your Concordat. They know you don't have the conviction to see it through. You're a walking time bomb."

"They've always trusted me. What makes it so different this time?"

"The stakes… the Concordat is a key plank in Volkov's strategy to rebuild the Russian Empire. And right now you are its weakest link."

Krotsky stared over Rossi's shoulder, avoiding his unyielding gaze. "I'm a simple forger, a foot soldier in Volkov's army. If it wasn't me it would be someone else."

"In Italy we have a saying, *a chi fa male, mai mancano scuse*, which means 'he who does evil is never short of excuses'. Stop making excuses, Mr Krotsky. Don't deceive yourself. You have a choice. You can live and help expose Volkov for what he is – the reincarnation of Stalin. Or die knowing you directly contributed to a nuclear apocalypse."

"Haven't you heard, Volkov is rehabilitating Stalin?" Krotsky smirked. "That makes him someone to be admired."

"That's the equivalent of the Germans rehabilitating Hitler. It's unimaginable. But why am I not surprised?"

Krotsky fell silent again.

"You don't even have the self-belief to speak poorly of Volkov, let alone take him on. Do you, Mr Krotsky?"

"I'm no revolutionist. I'm a simple artisan who provides others with the means to change history."

"David. That's Jewish isn't it?" Rossi said. "Are you Jewish by faith or only by blood?"

Krotsky groaned as he massaged his temples with the tips of his fingers. "They're inseparable and the same. Born a Jew, always a Jew. It's a culture, a race and an ethnicity before it's a religion – there's no escaping it even if you wanted to. The world has always seen us as different."

"How strong is your faith?" Rossi asked.

"My faith is strong, but so is my love for Russia," he said, "if that's where you're heading."

"What does your faith tell you about the Concordat? You must feel its destructive power. The unspeakable harm it will do rests on your shoulders."

"In my job I see evil every day. I'm numb to it."

"This is not everyday evil. This is your very own 'Elders of Zion' moment," Rossi said, pointing his finger accusingly at Krotsky. "Remind me how many Jews have died as a result of that little Russian masterpiece. And you want to hide behind the veil of duty. You're a disgrace."

Another long silence before Krotsky spoke. "As I said, I need time. Now let me go."

"I can't hold you. But be aware, this could be your last chance to confess your secret. An assassin's bullet awaits you."

"What secret? What are you talking about?"

"The glitch in the Concordat."

"You surprise me, Inspector General. Are you suggesting that I would deliberately sabotage my own work?"

"Not sabotage. Just the tiniest of flaws."

Krotsky scoffed. "What on earth for?"

"Revenge, insurance, to be able to undo the wrong. There are many motives. I've read that some great forgers even do it out of vanity. Artists like to leave their mark. Or am I mistaken?"

"Spoken like a true Catholic. Full of hope and prayer. But little fact," Krotsky said, sitting forward to leave. "Now can I go?"

Resigned that he had taken it as far as he could for now, Rossi leant forward and pulled hard on the door. Krotsky sprung out like a caged animal and scurried off down the street.

As the van took off, Rossi pulled the curtain across and slid open the glass window separating the driver's compartment from the rear. "Well?"

"Professional job, Inspector General," Cathy said, sounding a little surprised. "When we get back, I'm going to recommend you for our extraordinary rendition programme. Fun job, provided you have a high tolerance for sand, heat, and waterboarding."

"It did go well, didn't it? He didn't even try to deny forging the Concordat."

"Funny that," Cathy said, tossing the prepaid mobile phone she had used to call Krotsky out onto the snow. "Just in case he panics."

Rossi laughed. "That's five."

39

T he study in the Patriarch's Chisty Pereulok residence. Almost nine thirty. His Holiness lowered himself onto the cabriole sofa and fastidiously arranged the scatter cushions around his massive frame. Nervous excitement. 'Breaking News' flashed across the bottom of the muted television screen as the anchor crossed to the Kremlin. The Patriarch turned up the volume and flicked between channels. They were all broadcasting the same live feed of a stern-faced Russian President arriving at the podium.

Volkov glanced up at the hand-picked propagandists, and then without introduction read in a monotone from a prepared text.

The Patriarch beamed as Volkov announced the expulsion of the Catholic Church from the territory of the Russian Federation.

Listening closely, he checked for any discrepancies between what Volkov said and the text he had negotiated with Prime Minister Kalinin a few hours earlier. "It all seems to be there," he murmured to himself.

He couldn't help but wonder what the Pope was thinking when Volkov explained that the legal basis for his action was the newly enacted anti-terrorism law; a controversial piece of legislation that Volkov insisted was necessary for controlling hostile groups masquerading as NGOs that threaten Russia's security. To the free world, the law was viewed as nothing more than a piece of catch-all legislation, aimed at silencing the Kremlin's critics.

He switched off the television and stretched back on the sofa, satisfied that his current support for Volkov's plan was what God wanted. Yesterday's doubts were a distant memory. He had convinced himself that the end justifies the means.

For now, the Patriarch was prepared to allow Volkov to use him, and the good name of his Church. *Let him do the dirty work and I will pick up the pieces afterwards.*

Weary from the long day, the Patriarch lay down on the sofa and gazed up at the hand-painted images of angels and saints on the study ceiling. Slowly he drifted into a dream-like trance. The angelic panorama churned and surged about him. "Speak to me, God," he cried out, raising his arthritic hands towards the swirling dark sky like a madman.

"Unite Christianity in readiness for Judgement Day, when the Son of Man shall come in his majesty, and all the angels with him. Only then will order be made from the chaos and you will be judged," a deep fatherly voice beseeched him from above.

The apparition was so powerful and the voice so familiar that the Patriarch knew God had spoken to him again – there could be no other explanation.

God has been patient. Almost one thousand years has passed since the Great Schism, and Christianity is still divided, the Patriarch thought, as the vision faded into a raging sea of colour. The Patriarch squinted as the colours settled and a different image took shape. It was medieval Europe – 1054, when Christianity was torn in two by the manoeuvrings of the ambitious Patriarch of Constantinople, Michael Cerularius. A sneering smile lit up the Patriarch's face as the irony became apparent. He recalled how leading up to the Great Schism, Patriarch Michael had provoked Pope Leo IX by criticising various traditions of the Roman Church. In a clumsy attempt to stop Patriarch Michael, the Pope had written a letter to the Patriarch based on a section of the Donation of Constantine – a forged decree of Constantine the Great that conferred privileges and property on the Pope. *Through Volkov's scheming, another forged document will be the catalyst that reunites Christianity – with me as its head.*

Not for one second did the Patriarch consider his vision to be a false hallucination.

The telephone on the small gilded table next to the display cabinets that divided the long room rang. The Patriarch woke from his reverie. His body felt like lead as he picked up the receiver. "Hello," he said, his voice soft and weak.

"Sorry to disturb you, Your Holiness, but the Vatican is on the line," the Patriarch's personal assistant said sobbing, having also just watched Volkov's announcement.

"Tell the Vatican – and Archbishop Esposito for that matter when he rings – that I'm unavailable. Tell them I'm speaking with God."

40

The safe house was always too hot. The Soviet-era radiators had no taps or thermostats. Temperature was regulated by opening and closing the old wooden windows. Or by wearing as little as modesty allowed.

"Short-arsed shit," Cathy said, turning off the TV.

"I'm sure he's a nice guy, once you get to know him," Rossi said, settling in the three-seater sofa, a Laphroaig in each hand.

Cathy went over and opened a window. "Still snowing," she said, leaning out and breaking off an icicle that had formed beneath the sill.

"At least we now know what he's up to."

"I doubt we do."

Rossi shot Cathy a puzzled look. "But he just announced it to the world."

Working her short tight dress down over her thighs, Cathy rested her backside on the armrest of the studded back wing chair opposite Rossi's inquisitive eyes.

"Volkov didn't need a forged document to expel your Church from Russia," Cathy said, sure of herself. "Clearly there's more to come."

Rossi sat forward and handed Cathy her Scotch. "For instance?"

"I'm not sure. And nor is he." Cathy stirred her Scotch with the icicle. "You've heard it said, Volkov is a great strategist."

"Isn't he?"

"Not by a long shot. He can't see beyond tomorrow."

"I'm not sure I follow."

"Volkov's a suck-it-and-see sort of guy. If he gets away with something, he goes for more. So far we've turned a blind eye to his indiscretions because no one wants war." Cathy took a long sip on her Scotch, then continued. "But one day soon he'll reach a tipping point that demands a strong and decisive response. And like a stockbroker experiencing a market crash for the first time, he'll panic and overreact. Everything will go to hell in a handcart."

"For him or for us?"

"For the entire world."

"Is the Concordat the tipping point?"

"Potentially – but not on its own. It depends on what comes with it. For now it's just another disruptive step."

"So if the West understands this, why aren't they doing more to stop him?"

"Domestic politics, war fatigue, economics, self-interest, it's a combination of things," Cathy said, tugging off her boots. "I think we need to speak to Krotsky again."

"Volkov said he had consulted with the Patriarch. Is that true?" Rossi asked, his eyes instinctively drawn to Cathy's soft inner thighs.

"They met for sure. According to the newspaper that's where Volkov was heading when we ran into him the other night. But I doubt there was much consulting going on."

"Only instructions on ways to keep your job."

Cathy rose from the armrest and stood close to Rossi, not bothering to adjust her dress. Rossi tried not to look, but he was Italian. He blew out a slow soft breath and allowed his gaze to sweep over her.

"You know this is the first time we've been alone since we met," she said, taking her Scotch and knocking it back in one long gulp.

"Another?"

Cathy gazed seductively into his eyes. "No. I think it's time we went to bed."

"But I'm not tired," Rossi said, instantly dismayed by his own naivety.

"I would hope not."

Rossi emptied his glass. "We need to talk."

Cathy was taken aback. "Not quite the response I was expecting."

"It's just that I don't want to disappoint you."

"Oh you won't."

"Don't misunderstand me," Rossi said, wishing his glass was full. "I'm not without experience. After all,

SEAN HEARY

I'm a policeman not a priest. It's just that— I'm not as experienced as you."

"How quaint," Cathy said, colouring.

"This is awkward. I didn't mean it that way."

"Then what did you mean?"

"I'm not quite sure how to say this without offending you," Rossi said, dropping his gaze to her feet. "It's just that you're…"

Cathy stood over Rossi, hands on hips. "What?"

"Too experienced," Rossi said, almost to himself.

Fuming, Cathy waited for the next blow.

Smiling awkwardly, Rossi continued. "I'm sorry. I like you a lot. It's just that I need a better reason for making love to you than the physical pleasure."

"What else is there?"

"Love," Rossi said, gazing into her eyes.

"Love?"

"The meeting of souls. Without love it's almost self-gratification. Promiscuity."

"You're judging me, aren't you?"

"Not at all. I'm telling you how I feel."

"I'm a promiscuous slut for suggesting that we go to bed. Is that what you're saying?" Cathy said, tears welling up in her eyes.

Rossi said nothing.

Cathy ran into the bedroom and slammed the door behind her. Rossi stood there, then poured himself another Scotch.

41

lone in the darkness of his kitchen, Krotsky sat staring at his empty glass. Midnight, but there was no chance of sleep. *What is truth?* He poured himself another drink to further lubricate his metaphysical thoughts. He was cognisant that we see the world as we want to see it. And that we create stories that support and reinforce our reality. Everyone must believe in the truth. *But what truth?* It cannot be absolute – for it is only an individual's perception, coloured by their experiences and the environment that surrounds them.

Krotsky was rattled. Rossi had got under his skin. He couldn't think straight. It was as though the man from the Vatican had taken a sledgehammer and smashed his reality into tiny pieces.

The ideology he'd believed in when he first joined the KGB's Office for Active Measures had long gone. Russia was no longer communist. So why was he still caught in the lie? At first he had convinced himself that the collapse of the Soviet Union was temporary. It had failed, not because of the ideology, but because of the frailty of humankind and the incompetence of the Soviet leadership. To have Stalin in charge of such an intellectual undertaking was like putting Genghis Khan in charge of Silicon Valley. The social experiment was doomed to fail from the beginning. There is still time. A new leader could come along with the good of the people in mind. But the people were half the problem. It's through their apathy that communism failed. And then democracy. The small minority that took part in public life were, on the whole, motivated by greed and seduced by power. They never represented the people, nor did the people represent themselves. Someone else will do it. We were wrong. They screwed us.

Where is the enemy now? He knew they were long gone – if they ever existed – but he always suppressed the thought. *So why am I still participating in the lie?* he asked himself again. Was it love of the Motherland? He thought it peculiar he didn't have a better answer.

Slapping both hands on the table, Krotsky stood. He headed to the living room and flopped on the sofa. "I'm no traitor," he growled to himself. Equally he knew he was not what he'd become. Convinced he could not run even if he wanted to, he thought about early retirement. No one could begrudge him that. He had done his bit. For an instant he felt calmer. Then President Volkov's news conference flashed through his mind. Maybe he had done his bit too well. The Concordat had brought the world one step closer to nuclear Armageddon. And for what? Not for the good of all, but for the benefit of the few. He had become the antithesis of what he believed in.

Mumbling to himself, Krotsky grabbed his laptop and typed. Within an hour he was asleep. Tomorrow was a working day. And given all that was going on he didn't want to give anyone a reason to question his commitment to the cause – whatever that might be.

42

Lawrence's dozing eyes lit up when the grey metal door to Krotsky's apartment building swung open. A man in an ushanka hat, his face hidden behind a scarf, glanced about as he stepped onto the pavement.

Is that him? Lawrence wasn't sure. The appearance of a bearded man, from an adjoining alleyway, removed any doubt. Lawrence sunk low behind the wheel as the two men hurried past in turn.

Krotsky removed a glove and dropped it on the snow. He glanced back suddenly as he bent down to pick it up. The FSB tail stood in plain sight. For now, it was only intimidation.

On the opposite side of the road, following at a safe distance, Lawrence pulled his mobile phone from his pocket and dialled. "The target will be with you in four minutes."

"We're in position," Cathy's voice came down the line.

"By the way, you were right. He's got a tail. Dark hair, full goatee, and a black leather coat – like a throwback to the Cold War."

"Can you manage him?"

"Does a bear shit in the woods?" Lawrence said, without hesitation.

"I'll take that as a maybe."

Krotsky glanced back over his shoulder as he turned left onto Kutuzovsky Prospect, fifty metres from the Metro entrance. The tail made no attempt to hide. Lawrence quickened his pace. As he drew within a few metres of the FSB ruffian, he sunk his hand into his pocket, and removed a high voltage stun gun, ready to strike.

"Watch where you're going," a delivery man shouted, striking Lawrence on the shin with the toe plate of a hand trolley.

Lawrence swore out loud and danced around in pain.

The FSB agent shot him a glance, but quickly returned his gaze to the sea of bobbing heads in front of the Metro entrance. "Out of my way," he growled, realising he had fallen too far behind. Panic. He charged the crowd, knocking over a scrawny Tajik carrying a canvas bag full of dried fruits and nuts.

"Careful," the man's larger companion remonstrated, grabbing the agent by the arm.

"FSB," the tail snapped, brushing the Tajik aside.

By the time Lawrence made it inside, the tail was already on the escalator heading down to the platform. Lawrence remained calm. He knew the Park Pobedy escalator, at 126 metres long, was not the quickest ride in town. He barged past the queues and jumped the ticket barrier. "Police business," he called out, holding up his golf club membership.

As Lawrence stepped onto the escalator, he heard two trains departing in quick succession. One city-bound, the other heading out to Mitino. With trains arriving and departing every two minutes, it would be tight.

Elbowing his way past sleepy commuters, the tail made good progress. "Make way, FSB," he continued to call out.

Lawrence stopped. He was out of position. Below he glimpsed Cathy stepping onto the platform behind Krotsky. She glanced up and mouthed something he didn't understand. "Push," she repeated, motioning with both hands. Lawrence nodded, then launched himself into the back of the obese woman dozing on the step below him. The woman let out a yelp as she catapulted into the man in front of her. That was all it took to set off a chain reaction that continued all the way to the bottom.

Screams of terror and pain rang through the station. Inside the glass observation booth, the platform supervisor slammed her fat fist on the red button. The escalator jolted to a halt. Those still standing were thrown forward onto the writhing heap.

Throughout the chaos, Lawrence kept his feet. He stood watching Cathy until she disappeared behind a column. Then movement on the escalator below. Lawrence stood aghast as the leather-clad agent emerged from under two hysterical schoolgirls, who rolled off his back as he rose.

Dazed, the FSB agent looked up at Lawrence blinking, as if taking mental pictures of his face. He then vaulted over the balustrade and slid on his back down the stainless steel divide to the bottom.

"Get out of my way," the tail thundered, as an impenetrable wall of arriving commuters rushed towards him. He never stood a chance.

Lawrence smiled in relief as Krotsky's train roared off, presumably with Rossi and Cathy on board. Down below amongst the congestion, his opposite number was already on the phone.

On board the city-bound train, Rossi and Cathy positioned themselves in the front half of the third wagon, close to the master forger.

Krotsky glanced anxiously about the crammed carriage, expecting to see his tail. Instead, he spotted Rossi threading his way towards him.

"There's a vehicle waiting at the next station," Rossi said, motioning him to follow.

Krotsky turned his back to move away. There was no room.

Rossi leant in and whispered, "You're Volkov's loose end."

Again silence.

Grabbing Krotsky by the wrist, Rossi pulled him closer. "Good or evil. Choose."

Rossi's heart sank as the train slowed, approaching Kievskaya station. In the briefest five minutes of his life, he had failed to convince Krotsky to help. Now it was time to get out before the police sealed off the station. Perhaps after Lawrence's monumental cock-up, it was already too late?

"Russia's future is in your hands," Rossi said, trying one final time.

"Leave me alone," Krotsky blurted out, drawing sideways glances from passengers.

The doors hissed open and half the carriage piled out. Rossi hesitated. Krotsky was his only lead.

"Out," Cathy demanded, shoving Rossi onto the platform, just before the waiting horde surged forward to fill the void.

Rossi's eyes darted about, expecting to see an escalator that would take them to safety. Nothing. "I hope you know the way out."

"We need to change lines," Cathy said, pulling Rossi along by the hand. "The street exit is via the adjoining Koltsevaya station."

As they rushed through the station hall towards the connecting passageway, Rossi couldn't help but glance about. The architecture was impressive. For a split second he forgot where he was. "Is this a Metro or a museum?"

"It was Kruschtschov's favourite."

Kievskaya station, named in honour of the Ukrainian capital, was opened in 1954. Featuring columns of beige Ural marble and an arched plastered ceiling, the structure was covered in Soviet-era frescos depicting various aspects of Ukrainian life. Art, history and culture wrapped in propaganda, Cathy always thought.

Rossi nodded. "I can see why."

"Take a good look, because we're not coming back."

Their whimsical chatter abruptly ceased. Ahead stood two policemen scrutinising the faces in the thinning crowd.

"The description?" one of the policemen shouted into his walkie-talkie, as another train arrived.

"Kazakh male. Green field jacket and a Spartak Moskva cap," a barely audible voice crackled over the line.

"Keep moving. They're not looking for us," Cathy said, hurrying past, head down.

43

A cross town, Moscow's main CCTV control floor was hectic. The incident at Park Pobedy ten minutes earlier had all dispatch officers on high alert. More than half the screens on the vast video wall ran live feed from cameras placed in and around the Metro network.

The floor supervisor barked orders from the Command Room overlooking the main floor. In the adjacent CCTV monitoring suite an FSB agent had just arrived and was being briefed by the senior dispatcher.

"There. You see – the woman was pushed," the dispatcher said, motioning to one of the four screens set in a semi-circle in front of him. "It was no accident."

"Big bastard," the FSB agent said. "CIA."

"And there's your tail."

"Where's the footage of Agent Kvost entering?"

The dispatcher swivelled his chair towards the monitor on his right. The screen was already locked on the tail as he approached the Metro entrance.

"Back it up to Krotsky."

The dispatcher rewound the recording to the moment Krotsky appeared on Kutuzovsky Prospect.

"Stop – now slow forward," the FSB agent said, leaning closer to the monitor.

"There's Krotsky – now Agent Kvost – and the foreigner," the dispatcher said, pointing at each of them.

"The tall lady that comes into shot here. She seems to be involved. Have you got a shot of Krotsky on the platform? Let's check if she's there."

The dispatcher ran the footage on the third screen.

"There," the FSB agent blurted out. "That's her behind Krotsky."

The dispatcher paused the recording as the lady turned her face towards the camera. With a couple of swirls of his mouse, like magic, he expanded and enhanced the image.

"That's CIA operative Doherty," the FSB agent said, his voice gathering intensity. "The Americans just can't help themselves."

The dispatcher ran the recording again. "Look here! She's talking to someone."

The FSB agent squinted. "Nothing like his passport photo, but by association I bet you that's Rossi – the cop from the Vatican."

44

Cathy and Rossi stopped dead. Three policemen stood in the middle of the Koltsevaya platform between them and the only way out.

"In here," Cathy breathed, pulling Rossi into a small service recess near the connecting passageway.

Rossi glanced at his watch. Ten minutes since entering the Metro. "Surely they're not already looking for us?"

"If Krotsky's tail spotted us…"

"Either way, the longer we hang around here, the worse it gets."

"Here's our chance," Cathy said, as another train pulled up.

Like a flock of starlings, the arriving passengers merged and divided without colliding. Half of them moved towards the connecting passageway from where

Cathy and Rossi had just come. The rest darted towards the escalator that led to the ticketing hall and the street.

Cathy locked arms with Rossi and melded in with the swarm. "Look casual."

"Piece of cake," Rossi said, as they sailed past unnoticed.

The escalator journey to the top was agonisingly slow.

"I feel like I've got an AK-47 pointed at my head," Cathy whispered, fighting the urge to look back.

"Strange thing, adrenaline. That was almost enjoyable," Rossi said, stepping off the escalator into the ticketing hall.

"Yeah, a real hoot. But let's not do it again soon." Grabbing Rossi's hand, she pulled him towards the swinging glass doors of the street exit.

"Stop," a penetrating voice came from the side.

Cathy and Rossi kept walking.

The heavyset police sergeant, walkie-talkie crackling in hand, repeated the order in a more aggressive tone. "Stop!"

Cathy turned towards the voice with a confused expression. "Who us?"

"Move to the side," the sergeant ordered.

"Keep shuffling towards the exit," Cathy whispered, while nodding politely at the sergeant.

Rossi gave Cathy a nudge and motioned with a tip of the head towards the exit. Two responding officers had entered the ticketing hall from outside. Then as if they had walked into a trap, the three policemen from below appeared at the top of the escalator, guns raised. "Let's see you talk your way out of this."

"Lock the exits," the sergeant barked.

Cathy scanned the hall for options. Nothing. "Is there a problem, Sergeant?" she asked, with an unmistakable note of annoyance.

"Sergeant Timchenkov," he said, stepping forward and saluting. "Your documents, please."

As Cathy wasted time in her handbag, the ticketing hall filled with passengers arriving from below.

"Documents," the sergeant repeated, one eye on Rossi.

Cathy shook her head and tutted. "Now isn't that a nuisance. I'm afraid I've left them in the hotel."

"Wait here," the sergeant said, putting the walkie-talkie to his ear.

By now the ticketing hall was clogged. The throng rotated around a central point. Cathy and Rossi found themselves drifting towards the blocked exit.

"Move the crowd on," the sergeant screamed.

"Where to?" one of the officers called back. "You told us to lock the doors."

"I said nothing of the sort. Open them you imbecile."

The locks released and the two officers stepped aside. Commuters waiting outside shoved forward like a rugby scrum. The crush was unbearable. An old lady fell to the floor, then another.

"I'm suffocating," came a faint voice.

"My daughter – where's my daughter," a mother cried.

"Stop the escalators," Timchenkov yelled furiously, as the passengers arriving from below piled onto one another like bales of hay. "Are you all idiots?"

Amidst the mayhem, Cathy and Rossi rode the wave towards the exit.

"Tuck in behind me," Rossi said.

Putting his shoulder to the crowd, Rossi heaved. Crack! The swinging doors gave way. Next thing he knew, he was face down on the pavement amongst the metal and glass – with Cathy on top of him.

"Run!" Cathy yelled, shaking herself off. She led Rossi across the square to a white Subaru parked on the side of the road.

"Not quite what you were expecting," Cathy said, firing up the engine.

Rossi smiled. "Krotsky's more complicated than I thought."

Cathy hit the accelerator and fishtailed the Subaru down an icy side street. "A Russian-Jewish KGB agent. You don't get more complicated than that."

"Maybe I should drive?"

"In your dreams. This is Moscow, not Monza," Cathy said. "Besides, I haven't forgiven you for those horrible things you said to me last night."

"That's no reason to kill me."

"Isn't it?" Cathy said, tearing towards the first intersection. "Now watch and learn."

"I prefer to keep my eyes closed, if you don't mind."

Cathy turned the wheel slightly left and hit the brakes. The Subaru slid sideways, facing away from the right-hand turn. She then flicked the wheel right and went hard on the throttle, slingshotting the Subaru around the corner. At the very next intersection, she repeated the manoeuvre, only this time, to the left.

"That's not my fault," she insisted, glancing back at the wing mirror from a new BMW bouncing along the road.

"*Sì*. The parked car moved."

Cathy opened a window. The sound of police sirens built around them.

"Sounds like they're setting up a perimeter," Rossi said. "Do we have a plan?"

"The CIA always has a plan."

"Good." He paused then added, "as long as it doesn't involve the Metro."

"You worry too much, Enzo. Everything's under control."

For the next couple of blocks, Cathy drove less conspicuously. "This looks like it," she said, turning into the driveway of a disused foundry.

At the rear of the property inside a workshop, Special Agent Brodzinski jumped out of a late-model ambulance as Cathy drove in.

"*Bene!* This almost makes up for the shitty morning. I've always wanted to ride in an ambulance," Rossi said, with childish enthusiasm.

They greeted each other briskly and got straight to business.

"Inspector General," Brodzinski said. "You're the patient. So if you don't mind, jump in the back and lie on the trolley."

"What's wrong with me?"

"Ugly judging syndrome," Cathy quipped.

Rossi turned to Brodzinski and shrugged his shoulders, as if to say, 'What's with her?'

Brodzinski tossed Cathy a white coat and a stethoscope. "You're the nurse."

"Nurse?" Cathy protested. "Why not a doctor?"

45

Brodzinski stopped the ambulance at the address Cathy had provided. He had no idea it was a full kilometre past the safe house. After Rudoi's murder, Cathy was taking no chances. Only Lawrence knew Rossi's address, and that's the way it would stay.

"Mayo Clinic," Brodzinski announced in an official tone of voice. He jumped out and opened the back.

Cathy removed the white coat and tossed it on the trolley. "I'd invite you up for coffee, but we have none."

"No problem," Brodzinski said, throwing her a casual salute. "Besides, I've got to get this rig back before they realise it's missing."

Cathy and Rossi waited on the pavement until the ambulance disappeared over the rise. They then turned and headed back in the direction they had just come from.

"*Cavolo!*" Rossi said, patting his pockets. "I've dropped my gloves somewhere."

"That's silly. It's a long walk."

Rossi cringed as he buried his hands deep into the sticky pockets of his pre-owned coat. "What's this?" he said, pulling out a blue memory stick.

"The coat's last owner was a corpse."

"Krotsky?" Rossi said excitedly.

Cathy shook her head. "My money's on the corpse."

Fifteen minutes later, Cathy sat in the wing chair, booting up her laptop.

Rossi stood at her shoulder as she inserted the memory stick into the USB port. "I'll wet myself if you don't hurry."

She tutted and said, "You wouldn't notice."

"I knew it – I smell, don't I?"

"You blend in," Cathy said, not looking up. "Now let's see what we've got."

A long pause.

"Well I'll be damned. Krotsky's written you a love letter."

"*Stupendo!*" Rossi said, his eyes darting between the screen and Cathy's face as she read the Cyrillic file.

"You got to him."

"What does it say?"

"I'm still reading."

Rossi sat down on the sofa opposite. "You're going slowly on purpose."

"Would I do that?"

"*Sì,*" Rossi said emphatically.

Cathy sat up. "Good news… plus some *not* so good news."

"Hilarious."

"There's a major flaw in the Concordat."

"I knew it," Rossi said. His face seemed younger.

"But we need the original to prove it."

A dismissive shrug. "That's only to be expected."

During their absence, the apartment had become unbearably hot. Rossi went over and opened the window. "So what's Krotsky's dirty little secret? Is it black and white provable?"

Cathy smiled. "He used a relatively modern type of paper containing an additive not used in manufacturing until the early 1970s. Easily proved by conducting an elemental dispersive spectroscopy analysis – whatever that is."

"*Perfetto!*" Rossi said with a clap of his hands.

"Not so fast, Enzo."

Rossi placed a dead pot plant on the sill to hold open the casement window. "Coffee?" he said, heading for the kitchen.

Cathy followed. "Enzo, you *are* listening? Volkov will never agree. In fact, he'll never let you anywhere near the Concordat."

The kitchen was clean, but asserted an air of abandonment. The cabinets were hand-painted blue; some doors slipped on their hinges. A compact two-door fridge stood on its own opposite the cooker. There was cutlery in a ceramic jug on the breakfast table in the corner by the window. And the patterned yellow linoleum flooring was tattered along the full length of the join that ran down the middle of the room. For a safe house it was adequate. Neither Cathy nor Rossi complained.

Rossi switched on the electric kettle. "You're right. But at least we can now both agree that the only way to resolve this iniquity is to steal back the Concordat."

Cathy threw up her arms in feigned despair. "You're infuriating."

"You sound like my mother," Rossi said, lapsing into a pensive silence as he rinsed two mugs in the sink. He suddenly spoke. "Tell me. You're the expert. What is it that makes Russians so bloody pig-headed?"

"Where to start?" Cathy passed Rossi the ground coffee. "Everyone has a theory. And there's no one right answer. I like to think it's deep-rooted. A Carl Jung collective unconscious. An inherent tribalism."

Rossi nodded. "And to survive, tribes need strong leaders."

"Exactly," Cathy said, watching Rossi make the coffee. "And Volkov plays off this tribal loyalty. He feeds the common people a regular diet of anti-Western rhetoric. This, in turn, reinforces their mindless nationalism that demands a strong ruthless leader. An endless loop."

They took their coffee into the living room and sat down on the sofa. There was a long, unnatural hush before Cathy spoke. "We can't put it off for ever. We need to clear the air."

"Look, Cathy, I'm sorry," Rossi blurted out. "I didn't mean to offend you. I am so clumsy at times."

"Style is not the issue, Enzo. This is all about content and perception – is that how you see me?"

SEAN HEARY

"I was only trying to say…" Rossi found himself lost for words.

"That I'm a bike," Cathy said, gazing at him with mild disgust.

"Come on Cathy. 'Experienced' and 'bike' are two completely different beasts."

"And pray tell, how did you come up with such a flattering assessment of me?"

"Well, the way you dress…"

"Careful now," Cathy interrupted.

"I can't win, no matter what I say."

"Because you're damned wrong – and a male chauvinist pig to boot."

"Can I…"

"And who's to say the quality of my love is inferior to yours? Because you consider yourself more righteous. Well you're wrong, you stupid man."

"Cathy, I only thought…"

"That's the problem. You didn't think."

"The way you dress…"

"We're back on that one, are we? Let me tell you something about the way I dress. Firstly, I dress like this because I choose to. Comments?"

"No, no, no," Rossi stuttered, holding up his hands.

"Secondly, if I didn't I couldn't do my job. I have an IQ you could only dream of and the face and body to match."

"I can vouch for the body," Rossi said.

"Idiot."

"*Stupido.*"

"The trouble is that most guys fantasise about marrying an attractive, intelligent girl, while in reality they are intimidated by them. Being shown-up by a woman frightens the hell out of them. And their reaction is always the same – avoid at all costs. Before my mother passed away, she told me that if I wanted a boyfriend, stop being so smart. Practical advice – but why the hell should I? Men must change."

Rossi shrugged his broad shoulders.

"At Colombia it was manageable. Full of open minded people. The real problem started during intelligence training at Sherman Kent. What I was forced to endure inside *the vault* shocked me. Half my fellow recruits wanted me naked, the other half wanted me gone. I was a threat to their pathetic male egos."

Rossi's sympathetic eyes rested on Cathy for a moment, unsure whether to reach out and hold her. He didn't move.

"I was having none of it. It might sound farcical, but I discovered the best way to counter this type of discrimination was to flutter my eyelids and show a bit of leg. Dress and behave like the women they dated. My mother was right. Enzo, this is all show," Cathy said, holding up her breasts. "This is not who I am."

"Cathy, I'm so sorry."

"Sorry won't cut it. I was falling in love with you and you went and ruined everything. Why? Because I'm not the vestal virgin you dream of marrying. It's all screwed up. What was it that Voltaire said about Catholics? 'God created sex. Priests created marriage.'"

"I'm not sure he was only talking about Catholics," Rossi mumbled to himself.

"I don't get you. You're clearly attracted to me. Is it a question of faith?"

"Partly. But I'm not a prude. I'd describe myself as a practical Catholic."

"A PC – nice. Well I'm an RC."

Rossi looked surprised. "Roman Catholic?"

"A Retired Catholic," Cathy said, smirking. "I was raised a Catholic, but I lost my faith along the way. Science presents a rather compelling case. Once NASA proves we're not alone, I'm shorting the Church."

"Interesting!" Rossi said, surprised at Cathy's oversimplification.

"Are you being condescending again, Inspector General," Cathy said, playfully poking him in the ribs.

"No. Not at all. It's just that I put the decline in traditional religions down to the pace of modern life. No one seems to have time any more for spiritual contemplation. I don't see science coming into it. If people just sat down now and then and reflected upon why we exist – they couldn't help but subscribe to something more than the Big Bang theory."

"The old 'meaning of life' argument. I thought that was already settled?"

"42?"

Cathy nodded.

"Again a rabbit hole," Rossi said, taking her hand. "Cathy, I'm so, so sorry for last night. Please forgive me. It was totally unfair and wrong – what I said and assumed."

"You're forgiven," Cathy said with a smile.

Rossi moved closer. "So let's pick up from where we left off before I put my foot in it."

"I don't think so, Mr Rossi. It doesn't work like that. You broke the spell. What I saw in you before is no longer there." Cathy abruptly stood up. "Shall I make lunch?"

46

The moment Father Dominic Sullivan, the sixty-three-year-old director of the Vatican Press Office, was briefed by Commandant Waldmann on the newly discovered Concordat, he realised his usual calm, pastoral approach would not suffice. Against the current generation of journalists and editors, he knew it was an all-out war.

Father Sullivan glanced about as he entered the Vatican press hall. The room was overflowing with journalists, all eager to hear the Church's response to Volkov's most recent provocation. He sat down alone behind the long presenter's table under the large crossed keys fixed to the wall. "Thank you for coming," he said, in thick Irish. The crowd fell silent. "This evening I will read a brief statement and then take a few questions," he said, adjusting his reading glasses on the end of his nose.

"His Holiness this morning received with great sadness a letter from the President of the Russian Federation, demanding the immediate cessation of the Church's mission in Russia. The reasons for the President's actions are false and fabricated and do not merit comment.

"To the Church, the most disturbing aspect of this unholy scandal is the role being played by Patriarch Pyotr.

"The Vatican implores the Patriarch to abandon his false crusade and return to his vocation of spreading God's word in Russia.

"The Patriarch, by collaborating with President Volkov, has put the credibility of the Russian Orthodox Church at risk. How can the Russian Church provide a convincing witness to Christ if its own leader is seen to be supporting a totalitarian regime that tramples over the rights of its own citizens and commits atrocities in foreign lands?

"In these troubled times, people from all faiths should come together to fight against the evils of the modern world. We should not be jealous of one another's achievements. Instead, let us rejoice if someone does something good in the Lord's name.

"Our political leaders should not be allowed to discriminate on the basis of culture or religion. These are the seeds of nationalism and fundamentalism that have been so destructive throughout history.

"Christians must rediscover their faith and fight against the tyrants of the world that act out of self-interest and greed."

Father Sullivan removed his glasses and tucked them in his pocket.

"That's the end of the formal statement. Now, if you're up to it, I'll take a few questions," he said, glancing about the room for a friendly face. "Clifton."

"Clifton Hill from *The Tablet*. The Russian Orthodox Church has long accused the Catholics of proselytising in Russia. Is this what lies behind the Patriarch's support for Volkov?"

"The Russian Patriarch has refused the Vatican's calls," Father Sullivan shrugged. "So we can only speculate. But if it is as you suggest, the Vatican considers this view misguided."

"Why does the Catholic Church feel it necessary to expand its mission in countries traditionally considered Orthodox?" a hostile voice yelled out from the back of the hall. "Is it because the Vatican considers its version of Christianity superior?"

Father Sullivan could not ignore the uninvited question from Angyalka Callas, *The Radical* correspondent. "The Pope has articulated on a number of occasions that he does not wish to grow the Church in Orthodox regions. You are acutely aware of this, Mrs Callas. Now, Dr Andretti."

"Yes, thank you, Father. What do you think the Russian Patriarch expects in return for supporting Volkov?"

"To me, it's obvious. But I'd prefer not to be accused of second-guessing the Patriarch."

A journalist from *The Sun* cried out from the side, "In today's secular society, where even the Catholic Church emphasises the respect of other religions and cultures, the Vatican continues to enforce existing concordats. When will this practice cease?"

"The Church is not a political organisation," Father Sullivan said with a sincere, but stern expression. "She exists to do God's work on Earth. When she negotiates a concordat with a sovereign state, she does so to set out the Church's rights…"

Father Sullivan stopped. In the rear of the press room, bedlam had broken out. Five Ukrainian feminists had removed their tops, revealing anti-Church slogans painted across their bare breasts. Fists high in the air, they chanted, 'Christmas is cancelled', and 'Abortion is a woman's right'.

Photojournalists, who had been expecting a dull evening, snapped wildly as security dragged the women away.

The din died down. Father Sullivan cleared his throat, signalling his readiness to continue. "A little something for those amongst you who prefer scandal to real news," Father Sullivan said with a wink. Polite laughter rippled through the room. "Now where were we – the lady from CNN."

"Russian news sources claim Inspector General Rossi is currently in Moscow. Can you please comment?"

"The Inspector General is on leave," Father Sullivan said, looking away. "Hugo, you had a question?"

47

evealing Light – the words repeated in Archbishop Esposito's head as he sat outside Cardinal Capelli's office waiting for His Eminence to finish his phone call with Senator Carrick Maloney.

What did he say? the archbishop thought, fiddling with his ecclesiastical ring. *We will clear the way, expose the endemic corruption and profligacy that runs through the upper echelons of the Russian Church, sacrifice the charlatan who wears the white koukoulion.*

Last night, in the narthex of Moscow's Cathedral of the Immaculate Conception, Archbishop Esposito was confronted by a young bearded man wearing the black cassock of an Orthodox priest.

The man identified himself as a loyal servant of the real Russian Church. "I'm here to ask for your patience and cooperation in the name of Christianity," he said, lowering his gaze as a gesture of reverence.

Although the wrought iron gate to the cathedral grounds had been locked for some time, the archbishop felt no fear. He beckoned his mysterious visitor to follow as he descended a narrow stone staircase to a small chapel in the crypt.

"We won't be interrupted in here," he said, lighting a candle as he entered and placing it on the altar.

The priest sat next to the archbishop in the front pew. The warm glow from the candle illuminated his handsome face. Seemingly in no hurry, he turned towards the archbishop and motioned his readiness.

"My son, you ask for the Church's patience. Whom do you represent?"

"Revealing Light."

"Daniel 2:22 – now how does that go?" the archbishop said, casting a slow traversing eye over his visitor, looking for any sign of deceit. "Ah, yes. He revealeth deep and hidden things and knoweth what is in darkness: and light is with him."

"The Revealing Light I serve is a little more earthly," the priest said with a hint of a smile. "It's a secret society whose primary purpose is to free the Russian Church from state control, although today we spend most of our time exposing the endemic corruption and profligacy that runs through the Church's upper echelon. The Patriarch and his accomplices are vaguely aware of our existence, but they do not know our strength or the identities of our members."

The archbishop nodded as he listened. He had heard rumours of such a society since arriving in Russia, but had paid little attention to what seemed to be a myth or a folktale. "Assuming the society does exist and you represent it, what do you want?"

"In the past, the power of Christ's message and the strength of our clergy sufficed to ensure the spiritual integrity of the Russian Church. But today in modern Russia it's different. Seventy years of communism has weakened her. There was a time when the KGB infiltrated our ranks and influenced the appointments of the Church's leaders. Now we are vulnerable. We are walking blindfolded to the edge of the precipice, while the Patriarch stands shoulder to shoulder with Volkov's coterie of crooks and thieves."

"Yes, but what *is it* you want?" Archbishop Esposito repeated.

"Time."

The answer took the archbishop by surprise. "Is this about the Concordat?"

"Yes," the priest nodded. "Revealing Light wishes to resolve this evil injustice on its own. It is not in the interest of Christianity if the Concordat leads to a war of creeds. This is what the Kremlin wants."

"But it's not my decision to make."

A period of silence. "This evening the President and the Patriarch will release a joint statement, announcing the immediate expulsion of the Roman Catholic Church from the territories of the Russian Federation."

Archbishop Esposito's frail frame straightened. "This must not be allowed to happen," he said defiantly.

"They also plan to arrest you."

"Arrest me?" the archbishop said, raising his voice ever so slightly. "Whatever for?"

"To be used as a bargaining chip in the event the West retaliates."

"How do you know all this?"

"Does it matter?"

"Of course it matters," the archbishop said, loosening his collar. "What do you suggest I do?"

The priest laid his hand on the archbishop's shoulder. "Leave Russia tonight."

"Abandon my flock?"

"Your Excellency, as a hostage you will be of no use to anyone."

The archbishop blew out a long stressful breath and nodded as if conceding.

"Let Revealing Light clear the way," the priest said calmly, like a father counselling a child. "We will sacrifice the charlatan who wears the white koukoulion. Those who put our Church at risk will be made accountable here on Earth, as well as in Heaven."

"Speaking metaphorically, I assume?"

"Sometimes war needs to be waged to allow good to re-establish itself and grow."

Archbishop Esposito frowned, but said nothing.

The priest glanced at his watch. "I must go."

The archbishop led him back up to the narthex. "How can I contact you?"

"Only through your prayers, Your Excellency."

"But there will be questions."

"Please, for Christianity's sake, convince the Vatican

to hold off. Soon, with God's help, the Russian Church will be free from the repugnant imposters that lurk within her walls. And communion between the Catholic and Orthodox Churches will be restored."

"I'll pray for you my son," the archbishop called out as the stranger descended into the darkness and the heavy wooden doors closed behind him.

Monsignor Polak picked up the phone on the second ring. "*Sì, Vostra Eminenza.*"

Archbishop Esposito's ears pricked up.

"Cardinal Capelli will see you now, Your Excellency," the Monsignor said, moving to the door and opening it.

The cardinal was already standing as the archbishop entered. He moved from behind his desk and embraced his long-time friend. "Sorry to keep you waiting. I can only imagine how tired you are. I've been playing politics with the Americans. We are in need of their technical assistance."

"They agreed?"

"It's what they do," the cardinal said with a wink.

"God knows Inspector General Rossi needs help."

They sat down at the cardinal's mahogany desk; Archbishop Esposito's parched frame stooped over more than usual.

"What have you found out about Revealing Light?" the archbishop asked.

"Most of what was known has been long forgotten. I barely recollected the name when you called. My staff are still searching the Vatican archives. So far they've found only a handful of references." Cardinal Capelli leant forward and handed the archbishop a few pages of typed notes.

"So it exists? That's encouraging."

"Well at least it did. Revealing Light was established early in the eighteenth century in response to the annexing of the Russian Church by Peter I. The most recent reference we've found dates back to the 1890s." Cardinal Capelli pointed to the relevant paragraph on the second page. "The assumption was that Tsar Nicholas II's secret police, the Okhrana, infiltrated the society's ranks disguised as priests. Then once inside they rounded up its members and jailed or executed them. That's the last they were heard of."

Archbishop Esposito sat forward. "But it *is* possible that some of their number survived to continue the work… or maybe a new secret society was established, spiritually inspired by the original Revealing Light?"

"Anything's possible."

"It could even be a Kremlin ploy to entrap the Church."

"I've thought of that too," Cardinal Capelli nodded. "Either way, whether or not they exist – they're no match for the Kremlin and its security apparatus. So waiting for Revealing Light to sort out this mess is not an option."

"No, that would be unwise."

"Even so, we should try to locate your mystery visitor." The cardinal wrung his small pale hands. "Squeeze a little more information out of him."

"That's in hand. I've already arranged for the CCTV footage from inside the cathedral to be sent to the US Embassy in Moscow as requested by Commandant Waldmann. If the priest is active in the Russian Church we should be able to identify him."

"That's if he is a priest."

"The way he carried himself, I sense he is." There was an awkward silence as Archbishop Esposito chose his words. "Your Eminence, it's possible Revealing Light intends to harm Patriarch Pyotr. Should we be concerned?"

The cardinal stared into the middle distance as though he hadn't heard the question.

"Cardinal Capelli, should we be concerned?"

Silence.

48

The key turned in the lock. Rossi grabbed his handgun and positioned himself hard against the wall. The door flung open and rebounded off his big toe onto a large paper bag full of groceries.

"It's me," Cathy called out. "I've got brunch."

"Whatever happened to three slow rings," Rossi said, stepping from behind the door.

Cathy peeked over the groceries. "Get with the programme, Enzo. That was before Lawrence organised the spare key."

Rossi shrugged his shoulders and smiled.

"How do you want it?"

"Interesting question," Rossi said, acting surprised.

"Denver, Spanish, Greek…" Cathy said, emptying the groceries onto the breakfast table.

"You know your omelettes."

"It's the only thing I know how to cook." No hint that Cathy was anything but serious. "I'm an eat-out sort of girl."

"Mediterranean?"

"Black olives, feta and spring onions?" Cathy said, setting aside the ingredients. "Can do."

An astonished look. "You certainly came ready to play."

"By the way, the boys identified the archbishop's mystery visitor."

Rossi shot Cathy a glance. "Why didn't you say?"

"I just did." Smirk. "His name is Father Grigori. He's the parish priest at the Church of Saints Cosmas and Damian. You have a meeting with him this afternoon."

"I thought he made it clear to Archbishop Esposito that he wanted no further contact."

"He did."

"Is he expecting me?"

Cathy laughed. "Not exactly."

Resting his backside against the sink, Rossi skimmed through the report from Commandant Waldmann that Cathy had just handed him. "You've read this?"

"Sure," Cathy said, whisking the eggs.

"Father Grigori seems to know an awful lot about what's going on; must have friends in high places."

"That's the Commandant's conclusion too. So there's a chance that someone in Revealing Light knows where the Concordat's buried."

"That's cause for celebration," Rossi said, beaming with optimism.

"Double cheese?"

49

The fifteenth-century Church of Saints Cosmas and Damian, located in the central Moscow district of Kitay Gorod, appeared strangely out of place; dwarfed on three sides by multi-storey pre-revolutionary buildings.

An Orthodox priest hurried towards the small, plain, Indian-red brick church from the south-west. On the narrow pavement, in front of the entrance, a porcine old woman wrapped in shabby rags stepped out in front of him.

"Please, kind father, a few roubles to buy medicine for my dying daughter," she said, holding out her gloved hand. An unpleasant vodka-laden mist swelled in the frozen air as she spoke.

Unmoved, the priest sidestepped around her and entered the church. It was not a typical orthodox house of prayer. The white plastered walls and vaulted ceiling

266

were cracked and water-stained. If not for the wooden iconostasis that covered the wall to the right of the entrance, the building could have been mistaken for an abandoned ruin.

The priest stood in the centre of the empty nave and listened. The whistle of a steam kettle could be heard from behind the iconostasis. He pushed opened the 'beautiful gates' and reverently entered the sanctuary. Opposite was an open door. He moved towards the sound; the floorboards creaked with every step. In a well-lit room at the end of a short, windowless passageway, the priest saw the shadow of someone moving about inside.

"*Kto tam?*" Father Grigori called out, spooning tea into a pot.

"My name is Inspector General Rossi of the Vatican Corpo della Gendarmeria," Rossi said, already standing in the doorway.

Father Grigori stood stone-faced, gazing at Rossi in disbelief. "How did you find me?"

"No one knows I'm here," Rossi said reassuringly.

"If you can find me, so can the FSB," Father Grigori said, peeking out of the window.

Slight smirk. "I had a little help."

"What do you want? I explained everything to the archbishop."

"The Concordat."

"Do not trouble yourself with the Concordat," Father Grigori said dismissively. "When the wrath of God falls upon my Church's leaders, all else will pale into insignificance."

More riddles. "I'm not sure I understand you, Father Grigori, but I do need to find the Concordat – now. And I think you can help me."

"Be patient, Inspector General."

"That's not possible. There is no time and there's too much at stake."

"Isn't that a rather selfish view?" Father Grigori said, again checking the window. "The future of the Russian Church depends on the success of Revealing Light's mission. Is your concern greater than our need?"

"Our battles may be different, but the war is the same. We both have the best interest of Christianity at heart."

"But you consider the Russian Church's cause less worthy?"

"The Vatican considers the Russian Orthodox Church an absolute equal, and her flock no less Christian," Rossi continued. "It is the symbiotic relationship between your Church and the Kremlin that is the source of all our difficulties."

"And that is why Revealing Light must be given time to complete its holy mission."

"If I'm going to convince the Vatican to be patient, it would help if I had some idea what your holy mission is," Rossi said.

"My dear Inspector General, Revealing Light has survived for over three hundred years by maintaining the utmost secrecy over all its activities and by being obscure and abstract. Disclosing details of the mission to the Vatican could only serve to compromise everything we've worked for."

Half a kilometre away, Cathy sat behind the wheel of her Escalade, binoculars focused on two men who had just climbed out of a black saloon in front of the church. *That doesn't look right*, she thought, feeling for her phone.

Abruptly, one of the men swung around and pointed towards her. Cathy slid low in the seat. *He couldn't have seen me*, she thought, frantically dialling. The sound of a heavy vehicle approaching from behind lifted her gaze. Her heart raced as a police bus packed with OMON Special Forces passed, heading towards Rossi.

"Come on Enzo, pick up," she pleaded.

Decked in blue urban camouflage fatigues and body armour and carrying AKS assault rifles, the troopers stealthily took up positions around the church and waited for instructions.

"Special Forces are here," Cathy screamed into her phone the instant she heard Rossi's voice. "You're surrounded. Ten, maybe more. Heavily armed."

Rossi pulled Father Grigori away from the window. "The police are here. Is there another way out?"

The priest was preparing to berate Rossi, but there seemed no point. "Grab an end."

Together they dragged the pantry cabinet away from the wall. Concealed behind it was a one-metre-tall solid wood door.

"They'll find us in there," Rossi protested.

"It's a tunnel that leads to the street."

Rossi grabbed the torch from above the cooker. Then, on all fours, he followed the priest through the tiny door onto a small landing above a flight of stairs. He couldn't help but think there was something very *Alice in Wonderland* about it.

Father Grigori slammed the door shut and pulled across the huge bolt. "That'll keep them busy."

They descended the stone steps to a subterranean passageway. The tunnel was damp and the air foul. Putrid brown water lay in the dips and hallows, and splashed up onto their cassocks as they ran.

"How long's the tunnel?" Rossi asked, noticing how the beam of the torch faded into a misty nothingness.

"Not quite two hundred metres. It leads to an old church building on the next block."

"That's great if the door holds. If not, we're sitting ducks."

"It'll hold," Father Grigori said, wheezing.

"Are you okay?" Rossi called back.

Father Grigori had slowed to a walk. "Asthma," the priest said, spraying a bronchodilator inhaler into his mouth.

Rossi threw Father Grigori's arm over his shoulder. "We can't stop."

From behind came the sound of boots striking the tunnel door.

"How old's the portal?" Rossi asked.

"It's the original."

"Let's pray that that's a good thing."

Rossi shone the light into the distance. This time he could just make out the stairs. *That's got to be another hundred metres,* he thought, taking more of the priest's weight.

"I should never have gone to the cathedral," Father Grigori said, regaining his breath.

"What are the chances they're waiting for us at the other end?"

"The tunnel's hundreds of years old. It's not on any city map. They couldn't possibly know it exists. At this moment they think we're contained in the cellar."

"Keep moving, we're almost there," Rossi said, glancing behind, wondering why the hammering had stopped. *Maybe they're searching the church.*

Moments later, a bright flash of light, followed by the sound of a breaching charge blowing off the tunnel door.

"Go, go, go," came the order from behind.

Rossi smashed the torch against the wall. Pitch black.

"I guess that's one way of turning it off," Father Grigori said, now moving under his own steam.

"Where's the goddamned light?" a voice barked in the distance.

"We must be close," Rossi said.

Father Grigori inched forward, feeling for the first step with his foot. "A torch would come in handy."

At that moment, multiple beams of light illuminated the tunnel.

"God answers all prayers," Rossi said.

"Sometimes too well."

A shot rang out. Rossi felt the bullet whizz past his ear and ricochet off the stone wall. For the second time in a week, Rossi was sure he was about to die.

Then from behind, a voice rang out barely discernible above the stomping of half a dozen pairs of boots. "Don't shoot. We need the priest alive."

"Which one?" came a trooper's voice.

This made Rossi think. He had assumed that they were after him. But now he wasn't so sure. *They said the priest. It's possible they have no idea I'm here. The irony of it all,* he thought, ascending the stairs.

"There's a key hanging on the wall," the priest said, confidently, as though he had seen it only yesterday.

Rossi fumbled as he removed it from the hook, and inserted it into the keyhole. Smiles of relief as the lock turned and the hand-forged wrought iron door swung open.

Rossi glanced about; a maze of ceiling-high metal shelving. "Which way?"

"Left," Father Grigori said, pointing to a slither of dull winter light seeping in from under an external door.

"Someone's here," Rossi said in a tense whisper. Eyes scanning the darkness he reached down and pulled his pistol from his ankle holster.

They listened. Silence. Then Rossi let out a low chuckle. "Angels." The shelves were stacked high with crumbling church statues, all gazing down upon them. *An icon's graveyard.*

Rossi turned the lock and opened the external door. Anxiously he poked his head out into the daylight. The pavement was empty; traffic thin. "It's clear," he called back to the priest who was still securing the tunnel. A quick call to Cathy. Rendezvous point agreed. "Let's go."

"The tunnel's straight as an arrow," Father Grigori said, now at Rossi's shoulder. "It won't take them long to figure out where it leads."

"Then we'd better hurry."

The priest grabbed Rossi by the arm. "I can't be taken alive. They have ways of making you talk."

Rossi half nodded, half shrugged. But said nothing.

"You don't understand," Father Grigori persisted. "You must shoot me if we're captured."

Rossi gave him a sideways glance and broke into an awkward smile. *Sure, I'm bound to do that.*

"Promise!"

"Let's pray it doesn't come to that." Rossi stepped onto the pavement. Stealing a final look up and down the street, he hitched up his cassock ready to run.

"Wait," Father Grigori wheezed. "We'll have a better chance if we split up. Besides, it's me they're after, not you."

"If we split up, how am I going to shoot you," Rossi said, pulling him by the arm.

"They're behind us," Father Grigori said, struggling for oxygen. He had stopped dead and his face had taken on a purple tinge.

Rossi glanced back. Over the priest's shoulder, half a dozen troopers poured onto the street. "Come on. We're almost there."

"You go on alone," he said in a squeaky whisper.

Rossi was tempted, but he had no choice. He needed the priest, or at least the information he could provide. "Lean on me."

Father Grigori glanced back at the troopers, and then up at Rossi's desperate face. "Let's go."

A few metres short of the intersection, a sharp crack from a marksman's rifle rang out. Rossi's knees buckled, but he kept his feet.

"This has turned into a real mess," Father Grigori said, falling limp on Rossi's broad shoulders.

"You damned fool," a voice screamed out. "We need him alive."

Rossi dragged Father Grigori to the corner and propped him up against the wall. He unbuttoned the top of the priest's cassock and checked his wound. He was dying.

"At least I got my wish. Revealing Light's secrets will go with me to the grave."

Rossi wanted to scream. He didn't know what to do or say. He needed the priest alive. Failing that, he would settle for a name. "Father Grigori," Rossi said in a cold, desperate tone, "is there anyone else who can help me locate the Concordat?"

Father Grigori, anaemic and barely alive, closed his eyes and prayed as blood drained from his body.

"Stay with me," Rossi pleaded, pulling his pistol and discharging two rounds into the air, temporarily halting the troopers' advance.

"Find Father Arkady, the Patriarch's private secretary," the priest said in a faint murmur, without opening his eyes. "Give me your gun. I'll hold them off as long as I can."

Rossi thought it wrong to go, but the priest was dying. "Christianity will for always honour you as a martyr," he said, placing the firearm in the priest's open hand and closing his index finger around the trigger.

Father Grigori groaned in pain as Rossi rolled him onto his stomach. "God be with you in your quest, Inspector General," he said, firing indiscriminately down the street.

Rossi took his chance and bolted towards the Escalade.

As the SUV screamed away, a barrage of automatic gunfire reverberated between buildings. "They're getting nothing out of him," Rossi said, glancing back over his shoulder.

"What the hell happened back there?" Cathy asked.

"Poor timing, I guess. We both came looking for Father Grigori at the same time."

"You mean they were after him, not you?"

"Seems that way," Rossi said, his voice straining as he removed the cassock. "They must have staked out the cathedral."

"Unlucky that," Cathy said, grinning, thrilled to have her man back alive. "So did he tell you where to find the Concordat?"

"More or less."

50

Rossi was not a big fan of the internet. In fact, he despised it. Social media addictions, sexual predators, cyberbullying, fake news, the deep web, cyberterrorism, his list went on and on. Of course he used it when he needed to, but believed far more evil came from it than good.

Tonight not a word of complaint. Sitting on the arm of the wing chair at Cathy's shoulder, Rossi watched in awe as she retrieved enough material on Father Arkady to write his unauthorised biography. Most of the information was sourced from the mainstream press, targeting the casual reader. Other postings had a more malevolent purpose; to discredit him and the Russian Church.

"I think we might have something here," Cathy said, reading an interview he'd recently done with an

Ekaterinburg newspaper. "He's a fitness fanatic. Wakes up at five. Runs endless laps around Patriarch's Pond." She scoffed. "The more extreme the weather the better."

"You hot?" Rossi asked, rising from the chair.

A slight grin. "Always."

Rossi went over and opened the window. "Where's the Patriarch this week? I assume they travel together."

Cathy keyed in a new search string. "We're in luck. Tomorrow he's celebrating mass at Christ the Saviour. Then on Saturday he's attending the opening ceremony of the World Judo Championships."

"*Fantastico,*" Rossi said, placing the dead pot plant on the sill. "We go jogging tomorrow at five."

Cathy closed her laptop and went over to Rossi. "Let's hope it turns out better than this afternoon."

"The whole week hasn't been particularly special."

"You met me this week," Cathy said, punching Rossi in the arm.

"That's true," Rossi smiled. "Patriarch's Pond; are you familiar with it?"

"It's close to the Patriarch's working residence where, incidentally, Father Arkady lives. There's not much to it. A rectangular pond surrounded by a path and lots of trees. At one end there's a lovely children's playground and at the other end a ratty-looking pavilion.

"Where's the best place to ambush a fitness fanatic?"

Cathy giggled like a schoolgirl. "The pavilion."

"What's so funny?"

"Patriarch's Pond figures prominently in Bulgokov's *The Master and Margarita.*"

"And?"

"The devil appears before an atheist editor there and predicts his beheading. Minutes later he's decapitated by a tram when leaving the park." A short silence. "Rather ominous don't you think?"

"You trying to scare me?" Rossi said, wrapping his arms around her from behind.

As they wrestled, Cathy's gaze was drawn to the muted television. "This should be good," she said, breaking free and turning up the volume.

President Volkov, dressed in a judogi, was about to face off against an opponent twice his size and half his age at the final training session of the Russian national judo team.

"You're joking. Does anyone believe this nonsense?" Rossi said, staring at the screen.

In a stage-managed manoeuvre reminiscent of the Three Stooges, Volkov grabbed the sleeves of his adversary and effortlessly tossed him over his shoulder. The giant lay writhing on the mat until he was helped to his feet by the apologetic President.

"Looks like the Russian team is in trouble," Rossi quipped.

"That's the cult of personality in a totalitarian state. No one wants to tell the narcissistic emperor that his crown jewels are on display."

"Particularly when those closest to him are paid well not to."

Cathy glanced at her watch. It was already past six. "Be a dear and open the red in the kitchen while I phone

Lawrence. I need him to buy me something sporty for tomorrow."

"You mean clothes?" Rossi asked, thinking it odd.

"Yeah. He's got excellent taste."

By the time Rossi returned with the wine, and some cheese and grapes, Cathy was already sitting on the sofa reading.

"Lawrence will be here in an hour," she said, glancing up.

"How do you think Father Arkady will react tomorrow?"

"Pissed off… but dead keen to find out what you're up to."

"So I'll have to be forceful."

"Persuasive."

"That's what I said."

An hour and a half later, the click-clicking of high heels on concrete drew Rossi's gaze to the door. Then three slow rings.

"That's Lawrence," Cathy said, not moving.

"Shall I get it?"

Rossi peeked through the spy hole and did a double-take. "It's not Lawrence," Rossi said, baffled by the strangely familiar face.

"It's Lawrence," Cathy said emphatically.

"It's most definitely not him," Rossi insisted, standing aside. "Who else knows we're here?"

Cathy put her eye to the spy hole and opened the door. A tall lady in heels stood in the doorway holding out several designer label shopping bags.

"Come in," Cathy said.

"No time. Got to dash. We ladies are clubbing tonight," the woman said, turning and leaving.

Rossi stood aghast. "Was that Lawrence?"

"Yes. Didn't he look lovely? Now let's see what he's bought for me," Cathy said, heading to her bedroom.

Rossi picked up his glass and sat back down on the sofa. After a short moment he called out, "Is that considered normal behaviour in the CIA?"

"It's not unusual," Cathy said, standing in the doorway wearing a pink lace bra and panties set.

For the second time in ten minutes Rossi was awestruck. But this time he liked what he saw. "Does this mean I've been rehabilitated?" he said, moving towards her.

"Stay right where you are, Inspector General," she said, holding up her hand. "I only wanted to prove to you I always wear something pink. You doubted me back in the apple orchard."

"Come on, that's not fair, Cathy."

"You do the crime, you do the time," she said, turning sideways to show off her firm pear-shaped backside.

"How can you be so cruel?"

"It's for your own good. It'll make you a better man – now sit down and read your book."

"I don't have a book."

"Then read mine," Cathy said, closing the bedroom door.

51

There was an eerie stillness and all God's creatures fell to their knees. The universe had stopped expanding and was turning back on itself – imploding in a violent ball of white and blue light. The code had been broken. Order had been made of the chaos. It was in the numbers. The end – decreed by God. Six days was all it took. Everything was back to nothingness – darkness. Judgement Day was upon the billions of souls – past and present. Screams, mirth, agony, ecstasy, sorrow, joy, terror, anticipation – they all waited to be judged. The space was dark and light; it was everything at the same time. Souls were wrenched and torn to the right or the left. Black, red, orange heat, then to ashes swirling to dust. Light, stardust, peacefulness, the Kingdom. No questions allowed. One way or the other, and sometimes back to the end – purgatory for you. But there can be no purgatory now. It all depends on the worth of your soul, and the worth of your soul depended on you.

Father Arkady's alarm clock rang. He reached for his diary next to his bed and recorded what he could remember. It was a dream he had had more than once. The scene was familiar, but the meaning not. The end of the world, or perhaps his own life? Today was not the time; he had other things on his mind.

Father Arkady made his way to the bathroom at the end of the hallway. He shaved his face and combed his straight brown hair before returning to his small modest room and layering up in black for his run.

Descending the stairs without his usual spring, he donned his beanie and gloves, his mood still sombre from yesterday's news of Father Grigori's violent death.

He greeted the guards as he passed through the gate onto the deserted street. The sky was clear and the overnight snow lay fresh on the ground. *The run will clear my head*, he thought, setting off east towards the pond.

Ahead, in front of a construction site, the pavement was barricaded off. As Father Arkady attentively crossed the road, Cathy stepped out unnoticed from an alleyway fifty metres in front of him.

Dressed in pink polka dot thermal tights and a grey jacket, Cathy looked every bit the college athlete she once was. As she glided along she could hear the priest's footsteps drawing closer with every stride. With a squeal, she threw herself forward onto the pavement.

Father Arkady glanced up, concerned. "Are you all right?" he called out, as he approached.

Cathy sat up grimacing, holding her ankle.

"Are you hurt?" he asked again, crouching down next to her.

Cathy glanced about, checking they were alone. "I think I've torn my peroneal tendon."

"Can I call someone for you?"

"There's no need, Father Arkady," Cathy said reassuringly.

"I'm sorry, are you from the parish?"

"The Vatican," Cathy declared, having already decided that those two words would suffice.

The Good Samaritan did a double-take, realising Cathy was a foreigner. "How did you get my name?"

"From Father Grigori, as he lay dying in the street." Cathy paused, expecting to be interrupted. Silence, so she continued. "Inspector General Rossi of the Vatican Police is waiting for you inside Patriarch's Pond, behind the stone wall to the right of the pavilion."

Father Arkady's hazel eyes were fierce and appraising, but his voice calm. "You're putting everything at risk."

"Not if you do as I say," Cathy said, her eyes watering from the icy wind.

"This town has ears," he said, looking over his shoulder. "Little goes unnoticed."

Cathy wanted to argue, but there seemed no point. "Inspector General Rossi is expecting you."

"And if I refuse?" Father Arkady said, helping Cathy to her feet.

"Would you prefer we visit you at Chisty Pereulok?"

Patriarch's Pond was bleak and foreboding. A ribbon of yellow light from the cast-iron street lamps lit the crushed-stone path that encircled the frozen pond. Father Arkady stood momentarily at the western entrance and glanced about. Even with the early hour, he was not alone. Two middle-aged women greeted him as they walked past with their dogs. To his left, an old man shuffled along in a race against death. And on the far side of the pond a group of five young athletes, all regulars, moved at a brisk pace. Nothing unusual. He made a sign of the cross and set off.

In front of the pavilion, Father Arkady slowed, but kept running. It took another fifteen minutes before the priest persuaded himself that he had no choice. He needed to know what Father Grigori had disclosed to Rossi, and whether Revealing Light's sacred mission had been compromised.

He glanced about as he approached the pavilion. The group of five had just passed. And the ladies with the dogs were down the far end. "Not again," Father Arkady cried out, skipping a step, then hobbling to the stone wall.

"Father Arkady?" came a shivering voice from the other side.

The priest stepped closer and rested both hands high on the wall. "What do you want?" he asked in an angry whisper.

"Volkov's Concordat."

"Who killed Father Grigori?" Father Arkady demanded, putting his weight on his pseudo-cramped leg and bending his knee forward.

"Enemies of Christianity."

"How do I know it wasn't you?"

"Because Father Grigori entrusted me with your name. Besides, do you really think a representative of the Vatican is capable of such evil?"

He scoffed.

Ask a silly question. "I plan to recover the Concordat with or without your help. By cooperating you reduce the risk I unwittingly draw attention to your mission."

A long silence. "Don't misunderstand me, Inspector General," he said, testing his calf. "I know the Concordat is forged, and it is my intention to help you prove it. It's not in Christianity's interest we appear divided. The truth is the Patriarch and his inner circle do not represent the values and beliefs of the Russian Orthodox Church. They are parasites attached to a healthy host. Revealing Light has worked for three hundred years to cleanse the Church of this unholy spirit. And now we are within hours of eradicating those who stand between the Russian Church and God. That's why I sent Father Grigori to speak to Archbishop Esposito."

"He requested patience, but his message was too vague. When waging war with Volkov, long delays are not advisable. How much time do you need?"

"Until tomorrow."

"One day I can wait, provided you tell me where I can find the Concordat. Father Grigori said you would know."

"If I tell you, you must agree not to act on the information before eight o'clock tomorrow night."

"You have my word."

"I pray it's enough," Father Arkady said, pausing. "The Concordat is kept at the Patriarch's Chisty Pereulok working residence – where I live. It was given to him by President Volkov, no doubt to draw him further into this treachery."

Elation swept through Rossi's veins, leaving him lost for words. Something that had seemed so far away was suddenly within his grasp.

"But be warned – you will need to recover it on your own. I cannot risk being caught helping you. Before the ruling elite are finally defeated, they will retaliate – with or without Volkov. If there is any doubt about my loyalty, I will lose my influence, and with it access to privileged information."

Rossi could only guess what the priest had hinted at, but this was not the time or place for questions. "I need a detailed sketch of the residence, pinpointing the precise location of the Concordat."

"I warn you it won't be easy. In fact it is impossible. There is only one way in and that's through the front gate. It's manned around the clock by two armed policemen, supported by CCTV cameras that monitor the street and the grounds. There are no cameras inside, but FSB audio surveillance is likely in some rooms. We keep sweeping them and they keep replacing them. I'm not too sure on the current score. Wait, someone is coming." The two ladies with the dog approached and then passed.

"How soon can you get me the sketch?" Rossi asked, as the ladies' voices faded.

"Tomorrow. Every Saturday morning at ten I take my niece to the playground at the opposite end of the park. I'll drop a newspaper into one of the bins. The map will be inside."

"You are a true Christian," Rossi said, his voice full of emotion.

"The best time to recover the Concordat is tomorrow night at eight-thirty. The residence will be empty, as the Patriarch is blessing the athletes at the Judo Championships. Under no circumstances approach the residence before eight."

Father Arkady tested his cramped calf muscle one more time, then jogged off towards the park's exit.

52

Femme fatale – CIA station chief William James knew his Achilles heel. It was his inner thief. He was married once, twenty-five years ago, a marriage so short he often forgot it had ever happened. It had taken only two short weeks for his trusting bride to catch him in bed with their plain-looking neighbour. While James had loved his wife deeply, the bitter experience had taught him that his irrepressible libido was not compatible with family life. With that realisation, James adopted the lifestyle of a Don Juan, which he has maintained to this day.

"Wow! I could just lie here for ever," Albina gushed, running a hand through the chief's wiry faded red hair.

"I do my best," he grinned, satisfied with his chemically enhanced performance.

Stretching over the chief's barrel chest, Albina took a cigarette from the packet on the bedside table. "What about breakfast? We can walk down to Coffee Mania."

The chief glanced at his wristwatch. "Sure, but not before eight. I'm expecting a call." His eyes followed Albina as she climbed naked from the bed and sauntered to the en-suite. *I hope it's not her,* he thought, ogling her soft round backside as she bent over the basin, splashing water onto her flushed face.

The sound of roaring elephants. The chief grabbed his phone and squinted to read the display. "It's the call I've been expecting."

"Don't be long."

"Hey buddy, what's up?" Silence as James listened to Lawrence's account of yesterday's high drama at the Church of Saints Cosmas and Damian. "So where are they now? What do you mean it's classified? Don't give me that crap. If something goes wrong, it's my neck on the block."

The chief scribbled down the address and ended the call.

"The shower's free," Albina said, standing naked in the doorway with a towel wrapped around her head and a toothbrush protruding from her mouth.

"Albina, I'm sorry but I need to go to the office. Let's do dinner instead."

53

It was still early morning. Cathy sat at the breakfast table arguing with Rossi as he made coffee.

"Enzo, we need to involve the office."

Rossi shook his head. "It needs to be kept tight."

"You know we'll only get one crack at this," Cathy protested.

"We won't even get that if the FSB get wind of the fact we know where the forgery is kept," Rossi said. "It'll disappear into some impenetrable vault, with a note attached: only to be opened on the death of the Catholic Church."

"Enzo, what you're proposing is safe but sorry. I know we've deliberately avoided the subject, but it's obvious to both of us that Revealing Light plan to assassinate Patriarch Pyotr tomorrow night. Whether they fail or succeed, it will trigger a purge. The security alert level will

SEAN HEARY

be raised to burning-red hot, and any chance you had of recovering the Concordat will go up in smoke. So this is no time for pussyfooting around."

Rossi smiled. "Burning-red hot. Very *Spinal Tap.*"

"But it's what will happen."

Rossi sensed that the fear of failure had clouded his judgement. After a pause, then a nod, he said, "Okay, let's do it your way. What do you have in mind?"

"Something that requires the Patriarch's residence and guardhouse to be evacuated."

Rossi's eyes lit up. "A bomb threat?"

"Rarely taken seriously in Moscow. At best they would send a couple of rookies to investigate."

"Then what?"

Cathy shrugged. "The real thing."

"Are you crazy?"

"Tomorrow evening we park a truck loaded with ANFO in front of the Patriarch's residence. Then just before eight we call it in. Simple really."

Rossi gazed at Cathy, waiting for her to burst into laughter. But she didn't. *She means it,* he thought, wondering whether such an operation was routine in the shadowy world of espionage.

"Won't we look a little suspicious, walking into the residence when everyone else is running for their lives?"

"Not if we're dressed as explosives ordnance engineers."

"Now why didn't I think of that?"

"Or would you prefer to go as an Orthodox priest again? It did suit you."

"Very funny," Rossi said. "So where do we get a truck packed with explosives at such short notice?"

Cathy gazed at him smugly. "That's why we need the office. I'll contact the chief."

54

When FSB Major Andrei Bardin, received a tip-off as to the whereabouts of Inspector General Rossi, he swore to himself that he would not repeat the mistakes of the last few days. Trying to take Rossi alive had made him the laughing stock of the division. "Deadly force," he growled, bundling fourteen of his best agents into four armoured Mercedes-Benz G-Wagons.

As the convoy drove west through heavy traffic, the agents readied themselves for a full-out assault. For the average Muscovite, the journey from FSB headquarters in Lubyanka to Oktyabrskoye Pole would normally take forty-five minutes. Today Major Bardin and his men covered the distance in half that time.

They turned off Marshal Zhukova and headed north along Narodnogo Opolcheniya. A kilometre from the address provided, Major Bardin ordered all sirens and flashing lights off.

The G-Wagons pulled up fifty metres short of the fugitive's last known address. The squad piled out and moved stealthily to their designated positions.

Next to the entrance, Major Bardin and his three-man entry team stood pumped, waiting for the snipers to take up positions on the rooftops of the neighbouring buildings.

"We're good to go," Major Bardin said, as the last sniper signalled his readiness.

Bardin pushed a random button on the intercom. No answer. He tried another.

"Boris?" a woman asked.

"Da," Bardin answered, muffling his deep voice behind his massive hand.

The moment the magnetic door lock released, the team raised their weapons and followed the point man into the foyer. They took up positions against the entry point wall, facing the open stairway.

With the area secure, the team moved rapidly in file formation up the stairs. Major Bardin, carrying a ballistics shield, brought up the rear. Just before the snake reached the fourth-floor landing, the point man slowed the ascent and signalled to the team to tighten formation.

On his signal, the entry team moved silently onto the landing and took up positions hard against the wall next to apartment number eight. The explosive breacher attached charges to the heavy metal door and then retreated to a safe distance.

Major Bardin passed the ballistics shield forward to the point man, who held it in position to protect the men behind.

"Clear to fire," the point man mouthed to the breacher. He counted down from three with his fingers. A violent burst of heat and gas sent the door hurling inwards. For a hostage rescue situation the charge was excessive, but Major Bardin wasn't concerned. He'd prefer to deal with the fallout from killing the Vatican's top cop than to have Rossi escape again.

Before the door had hit the floor, the team lobbed two stun grenades deep into the room to incapacitate anybody still standing. "Go, go, go," the point man yelled as he led the men into the smoke-filled room.

The team panned out as they entered – each covering their assigned area. The bloody, lifeless body of a half-naked woman lay on the floor in the middle of the room.

To the left was an open door to what appeared to be a child's bedroom. Dust-covered toys were scattered on the floor. The point man held up his hand. He had heard a cupboard door close.

As the apartment fell silent, Major Bardin heard the sobbing of a small child. "We've been set up," the major screamed, grabbing the ballistics shield and hurling it violently out of the shattered windows.

Down below on the street, a group of teenagers emerged from behind a skip where they had taken shelter from the falling debris. In front of them, a blue Ford SUV with dark tinted windows drove past slowly.

At the wheel a grim-faced Chief James gazed up indignantly at the ballistics shield as it fell. "Damn you, Albina."

55

Cathy lay back on the sofa and swung her freshly pedicured feet onto Rossi's lap. "What a day."

"Two hours and that's all you've got to show for it?" Rossi said, massaging her soft feet, as if it was something he always did.

Cathy held out her fingers. "I did my nails too."

"I like the colour."

"First crush pink."

"It matches perfectly with the lingerie you unwittingly showed me yesterday."

An alluring smile and a forward tilt of the head. "Only a romantic would notice that."

"Or a maniac."

"That was the other possibility."

Rossi laid his hand on Cathy's knee. "So tomorrow's all set?"

"With the office. But we still need Father Arkady's map."

"Well, let's pray he's a man of his word."

"He's a priest for God's sake. They're not allowed to lie."

"Right."

A long silence; lost in their own thoughts. Rossi worried about losing the Concordat. Cathy worried about losing Rossi.

Cathy suddenly withdrew her feet and sat up. "Enzo. Aren't you afraid?"

"About tomorrow?"

"What if you're killed?" Cathy said dolefully.

"Good Lord – what brought this on?"

Cathy slid closer. "Love."

Rossi stayed silent for a moment, not sure whether she was referring to him. "Love?"

"I hate love. It brings nothing but pain."

"Love brings joy. Pain comes from not being loved by the person you love."

"Damn it, Enzo. That's not what I wanted to hear."

Rossi smiled awkwardly. "But…"

"Shut up," she said, slapping him on the wrist. "Say something nice."

For Rossi, words never came easily. He always felt clumsy when it came to matters of the heart. A romantic mute. Yet as a man he loved more deeply than most.

Instead of awkward words, Rossi turned to Cathy and gazed soulfully into her beautiful honey eyes. He slid his hand under her chestnut hair and cradled the back of her neck. Cathy's head rolled back and her mouth opened in anticipation as he pulled her towards him. His yearning lips brushed against her silky skin as he kissed her neck. The sound of her breathing excited him. He wanted to take her at that moment, but he resisted. Rossi lifted his head and allowed his lips to linger over her open mouth. Then he kissed her.

"I think I've stopped hating you," Cathy said after a short while, still in Rossi's arms.

"Did you really hate me?"

"As a man – yes. But not as a person."

"So now you like me as a person and don't hate me as a man?"

"Yes."

"What precisely does that mean, because I've grown rather fond of you?" Rossi said with an awkward smile.

"It means if you asked me to marry you I would say no."

"And if I invited you to my bed?"

"Also no. That privilege is reserved for love."

"Complicated, isn't it?" Rossi said, kissing her again.

56

The wind raced through the lime trees and across the frozen pond escaping down Ermolaevsky Pereulok towards the Garden Ring. Rossi didn't like their chances. A blizzard was blowing; the park deserted.

"Children don't go out in weather like this," Rossi said, pacing about to keep warm.

Cathy glanced at her watch. It was well past the agreed time. But there was no alternative other than to wait. Without the sketch, locating the Concordat inside the Patriarch's grand residence was unimaginable.

"He could have been lying," Rossi said.

Cathy pursed her lips and shook her head. "Doubt it."

"He was under extreme duress."

"He's not stupid. Keeping his word is the only way he can ensure we don't gatecrash his little party."

"Then where the hell is he?" Rossi said, glancing about – more for theatrics than purpose.

"When he woke this morning, he would have immediately realised the play day was off. So presumably he came up with another plan that fitted his regime – like dropping it off during his morning run."

"That's if he ran. Even priests are prone to exaggerate."

The icy wind stung Cathy's cheeks as she glanced about. "It's here somewhere."

"A rubbish bin in the playground. That's what he said."

Fearlessly, they scrounged through yesterday's waste. Nothing.

"Do we keep going?" Rossi asked. "There's got to be at least fifty bins in this park."

Cathy thought for a moment. "Father Arkady wouldn't have done anything conspicuous in case he was being observed."

"Like deviating from the running track."

"Correct. And probably there was no newspaper either. No one runs with a newspaper – do they?"

"I've got shit up to my armpits and you're telling me this now."

"It enhances your look."

Rossi shook his head and smiled. "So where?"

Cathy stood in silence for a long moment. Then suddenly the answer popped into her head. "You idiot."

"Me again?"

"I know where it is," Cathy said, pausing for dramatic effect. "The stone wall. The last place he saw you."

With renewed optimism they hurried to the pavilion

at the other end of the park. Rossi glanced up nervously, scanning the rows of windows looking down at them. "Let's pray this isn't a set-up."

"For someone from the Vatican, you have an unhealthy mistrust of priests."

"That wasn't there yesterday," Rossi said, pointing excitedly at a cobblestone on top of the wall.

Cathy rushed over and grabbed it. Underneath, a plastic sleeve. Inside, folded into quarters, was the sketch of the Patriarch's residence.

"O ye of little faith," Rossi said, grinning with relief.

57

Patriarch Pyotr stepped majestically out onto the front porch of his Chisty Pereulok residence and gazed up at the heavens. The morning blizzard had passed, and the evening was calm.

Father Arkady motioned to the chauffeur to open the rear door of the white limousine. "It's time, Your Holiness," he said, holding the Patriarch's black ceremonial cassock off the ground as they descended the steps.

Father Arkady removed the Patriarch's white koukoulion and passed it to the driver while he helped His Holiness into the back. He then signalled their readiness to the security escort before climbing into the front next to the driver.

In the distance, above the hum of the traffic, the bells of Christ the Saviour struck six. The Patriarch was not scheduled to bless the athletes at the opening ceremony of the World Judo Championships until eight, but he had agreed with President Volkov to arrive early to discuss strategies for undermining the Patriarch of Constantinople who had come out in support of the Vatican.

"When we arrive, I will take Your Holiness directly to the Presidential Box for your meeting with the President. At seven, along with the other dignitaries, Your Holiness will watch the athletes enter the arena. At seven forty-five, Your Holiness and President Volkov will be taken down to the events area. After the blessing of the athletes, Your Holiness will be shown to the limousine and escorted to the official residence at Danilov Monastery."

"Thank you," the Patriarch said in a soft voice, seemingly distracted.

The luxurious Mercedes 600 Pullman was joined by three security vehicles as it pulled out of the driveway.

Moments later, a grey windowless Ford Transit cargo van entered Chisty Pereulok from a side street. It rolled to a stop opposite the Patriarch's residence and backed into a parking space between two saloons. The driver reached back and tore down a temporary curtain, covering the bulkhead window. Now visible through the cabin were forty 25 kilogram bags of ANFO, all bearing the unmistakable orange hazard pictogram for explosives. Upon closer inspection, it was possible to see the timer-controlled firing device attached to a cartridge of nitroglycerine. Even to the untrained eye, the vehicle was recognisable as a truck bomb.

The CIA agent glanced over at the guardhouse as he

locked the van. He could see the guards inside drinking tea and playing backgammon. They didn't even turn their heads as he hurried off and vanished into the night.

***

To the west of the city, Rossi and Cathy, dressed in thirty-kilogram EOD suits, climbed into the back of a KAMAZ Typhoon-K 4x4 armoured vehicle. Freshly painted on the side were the words 'Ministry of Internal Affairs, Department of Sapper Engineers.'

"The van is in place," Agent Lawrence said, firing up the engine.

Cathy laid her hand on Rossi's knee. "Now it's all up to us."

"I'll be following your every move. I've done nothing like this before."

"And I have?"

Lawrence glanced back over his shoulder at Cathy. "The chief identified the source of the leak."

"Who?" Cathy said, playing dumb.

"He didn't say."

"That's because it was his saggy-arse prostitute girlfriend."

"Prostitute maybe. But from what I've seen, no saggy-arse."

Rossi blew out a breath of Catholic disgust. "A honey trap? I thought that sort of thing only happened in old Greta Garbo films."

"After what happened to Rudoi, the chief got

suspicious. So he fed the tart a random fictitious address – and she took the bait," Cathy explained.

"Wasn't it obvious?" Rossi asked. "Old man, pretty girl."

"In Russia, more often than not they're harmless," Cathy said. "As a rule they're after a rich husband or a passport. Rarely are they working for the FSB."

"But they're after something?"

"Oh yeah," Lawrence teased. "They're always after something. After all, they *are* women. It's in their DNA."

Cathy yawned. "Agent Lawrence ate too much testosterone for lunch."

"True. But I'm cutting back."

So you can fit into your dress, Rossi thought, laughing along.

***

7.15 pm. Inside the Presidential Box, all but one of Volkov's guests had arrived. Down below on the stage, a troupe of artists from the Moscow Circus entertained the capacity crowd.

"Ladies and gentlemen, please welcome the athletes from the 138 participating nations," came the announcement over the public address system.

"Thirty minutes, sir," Anastasia whispered in Volkov's ear.

The crowd stood. A mighty roar went up as the first team marched in. Pavel Greshnechov was also on his feet. But his gaze was fixed on the Presidential Box.

It was the first time he and Oleg had been back to

Olympisky since planting the IED. Everything looked different.

"They've done a good job," Pavel said, removing a pair of binoculars from his pocket. He trained them on the events area at first and then casually panned up to the *real* event of the night.

The Patriarch, wearing his koukoulion, was easy to spot. The vertically challenged President was more difficult. Pavel counted them off one by one.

"It's already seven-thirty," Oleg said.

"The Prime Minister's missing."

***

"112 Emergency Services. Your name please," the operator said in a dull monotone voice.

"Hello, I have a dog," a woman blurted out.

"Name?"

"Druzhok."

"*Your* name," the operator said calmly, immune to the stupidity of her callers.

"Tishkova, Gulnara."

"What's the emergency?"

"As I was saying, I have a dog…"

"Then you need the city pound."

"My dog's sitting next to me – why would I need the pound?"

"Lady, this line is for emergencies only…"

"He's a retired Army bomb-sniffing dog," the caller interrupted, sensing she was about to get cut off.

SEAN HEARY

"And," the operator said.

"I took him for toilettes – along Chisty Pereulok, as I do every night.

"Lady."

"He sat on the pavement in front of this van, barking. Wouldn't move. He's never done that before."

"What's the point?" the operator asked.

"I sneaked a look inside."

"Well done."

"It was a bomb."

"Chisty Pereulok. There are a lot of police in that area. Did you inform them?" the operator asked, her tone sceptical.

"No," the caller answered bluntly. "I don't like to get involved with the police. They can't be trusted."

***

Back inside the Presidential Box, a boisterous good-natured argument had broken out about caviar and champagne. It was quickly and unanimously agreed that the light grey Beluga caviar from the Caspian Sea was the crème de la crème. But consensus could not be reached with regard to champagne.

"Fantastic, our local expert has arrived. He can settle this," the President said, as Kalinin entered the room. "My dear Prime Minister, the best champagne in the world – what is it?"

"That's easy, Mr President. Louis Roederer Cristal."

"Of course," the Patriarch said. "He's absolutely right."

"Did you know Louis Roederer was once the official

307

wine supplier to the Imperial Court of Russia?" Kalinin added, playing to the crowd. "The first cuvée de prestige was created in 1876 for Tsar Alexander II."

On the opposite side of the arena, Pavel's heart raced. "Full house."

Oleg fished a mobile phone from his pocket and speed-dialled the IED's remote detonation trigger. "Something's wrong."

"They're getting ready to move off," Pavel said, his face darkening. "Check the number."

"The number's correct."

Pavel snatched the phone from Oleg and dialled. Same result.

Across the arena, Father Arkady lowered his opera glasses in disbelief. He checked his watch. They were out of time. Live pictures of Volkov and Patriarch Pyotr preparing to leave the Presidential Box flashed up on the four-sided HD video board suspended above the stage.

There were only two possibilities in his mind. Either the security services had discovered the IED, and removed it, or there was a problem with the signal amplifier device inside the box. He took a few deep, calming breaths as he worked through the options.

"That's it," he murmured, grabbing his mobile phone. Frantically he dialled Anastasia Lebedova, whom he had just seen on the big screen standing behind Volkov. *Her phone is never off.*

No connection.

58

Heads turned as the KAMAZ Typhoon rumbled past the Cathedral of Christ the Saviour with blue lights flashing. Lawrence sounded the air horn as he sped through the intersection onto Prechistenka Ulitsa. "This doesn't look good," he said, as the road straightened. The traffic was backed up in both directions.

Cathy leant forward. "Someone's called it in early."

"You can't account for bad luck," Lawrence said, zigzagging the KAMAZ through the long line of red tail lights.

"What happens if the real EOD technicians are already there?" Rossi asked.

Cathy blew out a dismissive breath. "They'll be too busy defusing the truck bomb to notice us."

Rossi suddenly felt hot and claustrophobic.

"Make way – bomb disposal," Lawrence repeated over

the KAMAZ's PA system as they approached the police barriers.

"Absolute chaos," Rossi said, tugging at the sleeves of his bomb suit.

Cathy put a reassuring hand on Rossi's thigh. "That's exactly what we need. We could say we're from Mars and there would be no one with the balls to bet against it."

"Evacuate the area… imminent danger," could scarcely be deciphered from the warning being broadcast from one of the fire engines already on the scene.

Nosy residents drifted out onto the street, then hurried back to collect their valuables as the gravity of the situation became apparent. In the back of the KAMAZ, Rossi and Cathy shifted about trying to catch a glimpse of the truck bomb.

"Damn! They're here," Cathy said, pointing between emergency vehicles. In the distance they could see two men dressed in khaki blast suits peering into the front of the van.

"Now what? Abort?" Lawrence asked, glancing over his shoulder at Cathy.

Cathy shook her head. "No. We stay on plan."

"Two actors playing the same role on the one stage. Bound to be a disaster."

"Two stages," Cathy smirked.

"I'm not following," Rossi said, sweat collecting on his brow.

"If anybody asks, we're here to defuse a second bomb."

"I can see that working," Lawrence quipped.

"Why not?"

Lawrence wasn't buying it. "I say we abort."

"As long as we're here…" Rossi said. There would be no second chance.

The stream of residents quickly turned into a torrent as word spread. They hurried to the police cordons at either end of the street but refused to go any further for fear of looting.

A busload of fresh-faced recruits pulled up behind the KAMAZ. Orders were given to conduct a door-to-door search and to assist the elderly. "Move it," yelled the police captain, as the rookies pushed their way through the congestion.

"This is as good a time as any," Cathy said.

After helping them down from the vehicle, Lawrence continued to protest as he fitted them with blast suit collars and helmets.

"This is nuts," Rossi said.

Cathy chuckled. "Welcome to the CIA."

"You're good to go," Lawrence said, handing Cathy a rucksack containing clothes. "And try to walk like a man."

"I think he means you, Enzo."

"I'll do my best."

"Let's go do this," Cathy said, lowering her visor.

Rossi picked up a brown duffel bag full of tools and followed Cathy through the crowd.

"Look Mama, a cosmonaut," a small child called out, as Cathy pushed aside the interlocking steel barriers.

"Where the hell are you going?" came the call from the police captain standing off to the left.

Rossi and Cathy didn't hear through their helmets and kept walking.

"Stop," he insisted.

"What's your problem, Captain?" Lawrence, standing on the KAMAZ's running board, called out. His father had taught him a thing or two about the Russian psyche. He knew position was everything. And from where the captain stood, Lawrence outranked him.

"Lieutenant Colonel. I didn't notice you drive up," the captain said, half apologising.

"Stick to crowd control," Lawrence barked, enjoying his new-found authority.

The police captain saluted then rejoined the conversation with his colleagues.

59

The steel door to Box 7 was cloaked in the shadow of two massive bodyguards from the Presidential Security Services. The taller, Agent Velikano, had a disfigured face from a stint as a professional no-rules fighter. The broader, Agent Ustinov, had weird beady eyes and scaloppini squash ears. No one could enter the Presidential Box without their express consent – not even the Patriarch's private secretary.

Only the best of the best were ever assigned to protect the President. Still, their numbers were too great for Father Arkady to know them all personally. Tonight, he didn't recognise either of them.

"Good evening," he said as he approached, handing Ustinov his identification. "Patriarch Pyotr has called for me."

"Wait here," Ustinov mumbled, as if he was sucking on two large gobstoppers. "I'll need to phone."

Velikano approached the priest casually; a Kalashnikov AK-400 slung over his shoulder and a security wand by his side. "Arms out, legs apart," he said, without a hint of diplomacy.

Father Arkady complied. He knew enough not to argue.

"What's this?" Velikano asked, as the security wand went crazy against the priest's right ankle.

Father Arkady wanted to scream. *Game over,* he thought, lifting his inner cassock. A compact small calibre handgun in an ankle holster.

The bodyguard dropped the wand and trained his rifle on the priest. "Hands in the air."

Ustinov aborted his call. "What are you doing with a pistol inside the stadium?"

"You guys haven't done your homework, have you?" Father Arkady shook his head, disappointment on his face. "In addition to being the Patriarch's assistant, I double as his personal bodyguard. I suggest you phone General Dengov before you make fools of yourselves in front of the President."

Dengov was the head of the Presidential Security Services – not a guy to mess with. His subordinates did their best to avoid him for fear of being noticed and put under scrutiny. Father Arkady knew phoning the general was something agents didn't do.

Whether through inexperience or stupidity, Agent Ustinov called. "Patch me through to General Dengov – we have a situation at Olympisky," Ustinov said, his voice lacking conviction.

From the look on his face, it was clear to Father Arkady that the conversation started poorly and deteriorated from there.

"Yes, sir... that's clear, sir... right away, sir," the guard answered in a loud soldier's voice, standing to attention as if the general was right there in front of him.

"Three bags full, sir," Father Arkady murmured to himself.

The look on Ustinov's furrowed face said it all. "He checks out."

"Now can I see the Patriarch?"

"Wait there," Ustinov said, pointing to a spot on the ground. He redialled. A short silence. "Strange. No signal."

I could've told you that, you doltish thug, the priest thought. "Can't you just open the door?"

"Follow procedures or you'll get yourself shot."

Father Arkady coloured. "Then what do you suggest? Patriarch Pyotr was expecting me ten minutes ago."

"It's probably the connection to the mobile phone signal booster," Ustinov grinned. "Someone nicked it last night."

"That's the temporary fix." Velikano tapped the toe of his size 50 shoe on the cable running from the Presidential Box to a wall plate on the other side of the corridor.

"Was it working earlier today?"

The two agents looked at each other and shrugged.

Father Arkady bent over and lifted up the grey cord cover. The coax cable underneath showed no sign of damage. He then checked the wall plate. It fell to the floor. "You've got to be kidding me."

"That should be attached to something," Ustinov said, looking stupidly at his partner.

Down on all fours, Father Arkady closed one eye and gazed into the drill hole where the wall plate had been. "I can see it," he said, sticking his little finger into the hole.

"Just leave it, for God's sake," Ustinov said, as politely as he knew how. "They'll be out in a minute."

"Quick, I need a piece of pliable wire," Father Arkady said, glancing up at Ustinov and then Velikano.

Both grunted in agreement, but didn't move.

Think, Father Arkady told himself, looking around for something remotely useful. "Your pen," he demanded. "Give me your pen."

Ustinov, who was taught to follow orders, did what he was told.

Father Arkady furiously unscrewed the Parker and removed the front spring.

"What the hell…?" Ustinov protested, but it was too late.

Father Arkady had already stretched the spring out of shape and inserted it into the end of the connection. "Got it," he cried, snagging the cable on the first attempt.

"Congratulations. But you owe me a pen."

Father Arkady glanced at his watch. Three minutes to the top of the hour. From below he could hear boos and jeers as the stadium announcer introduced Team USA. *They're running late.*

Behind Father Arkady, the steel door opened a few centimetres and Velikano spoke briefly to the guard inside. The door then quickly closed.

"You'll have to move away from there," Ustinov said, marching menacingly towards the priest.

"One second," Father Arkady said, without looking up.

"Now."

"Done," Father Arkady declared, jumping to his feet.

"Your pistol, until the President leaves."

"I'm responsible for the Patriarch's safety," the priest argued, playing for time. "I need my weapon."

"Not around the President you don't," Ustinov said, in no mood to argue.

Father Arkady took his time unclipping his pistol; furious with himself for not knowing the mobile number for triggering the IED. *An unforgivable oversight.*

"Now move aside," Ustinov ordered, pointing down the corridor.

Father Arkady's heart sank as the door opened for a second time and Anastasia Lebedova appeared in the doorway; whereupon, for want of a better idea, he dropped to his knees and chanted like a madman.

Ustinov swung around and trained his weapon on the priest. "What are you doing?" he barked, rushing over to tackle him.

Then, as if through divine intervention, three mobsters stepped into the corridor from an adjoining VIP box.

"He's got a gun," Father Arkady called out.

From the mobsters' vantage point, set back along the curved corridor, the only thing they could see was a priest being body-slammed by a crazed gorilla. Instinctively they drew their weapons.

"Back inside," Velikano yelled, pulling the blast proof door closed.

The moment the mobsters spotted Velikano they instantly recognised their mistake. "We're with the Governor of Magadan," one of them said apologetically, raising his hands high in the air.

"Now we've got the fishing mafia – what's going on tonight?" said Velikano, collecting their weapons.

"How the hell were we to know," the dumbest of the three goons said. "All we could see from here was that mad monk saying mass…"

"Shut up, you moron and get the hell out of here."

"But my gun…"

"Fuck your gun," Velikano screamed, leaving them in no doubt that the conversation was over.

Still in place on the opposite side of the arena, Oleg watched through his binoculars as security manhandled Volkov and the Patriarch back into the Presidential Box and the door slammed shut. "Something weird just happened. Try calling again."

Pavel redialled.

A blinding flash and a thunderous crack. Oleg and Pavel dived behind the flimsy plastic seating as thick panels of laminated glass shot from their metal frames and twirled across the arena like giant lawnmower blades.

Oleg rose to his knees and trained the binoculars back on Box 7. Inside was nothing – only raw human flesh plastered against the pockmarked concrete walls.

"What have we done?" Oleg murmured, gazing down

at the bloody wounded, stumbling about like zombies over the headless and limbless corpses lying at their feet. "Is this not murder?"

Pavel showed no emotion. "Not murder, but a righteous rebirth."

60

Rossi and Cathy strode purposely towards ground zero. Ahead, on the left, the Patriarch's residence, lit up like Buckingham Palace. Opposite, on the right, the truck bomb.

"You've got to wonder about people who do that for a living," Cathy said, motioning towards the two sappers who were scrutinising the underside of the Transit van for booby traps.

"That's rich coming from you."

Rossi's gait softened as they drew level with the van. As Cathy predicted, the sappers were too preoccupied to look over as they passed.

"I hope you haven't got the dates mixed up," Cathy quipped. "We'd look silly turning up at one of the Patriarch's posh parties dressed like this."

"If you believe Father Arkady, the Patriarch's no more – *finito*."

"Until I hear bells toll the death knell, I'm going to assume he's still alive."

The high wrought iron gate at the front of the yellow-walled building was locked and the guardhouse abandoned.

Cathy grabbed the gate and shook it. The antique didn't even rattle. "I'm not dressed for climbing."

Rossi poked around in the duffel bag and pulled out a crowbar. He speared it in between the lock and the gate frame. Planting a foot on a fence pale, he pulled back hard. The old brittle lock ruptured, and the gate swung open under its own weight. "After you, *signora*."

"Such a gentleman."

Rossi felt strangely in control as they climbed the porch steps. It was as though the worst was behind them. Or perhaps he never truly believed they would make it this far. He pressed hard on the doorbell. The building was silent at first. Then a slow tapping on the floor.

Cathy put her ear to the grand wooden door. "Hello, is anyone there?" she called out.

The tapping grew louder, then stopped.

Cathy glanced up at the CCTV camera above the door. "We're being watched," she mouthed, motioning with her eyes.

Rossi removed his gloves and retrieved his police EOD identification from the duffel bag. He held it up to the camera and smiled. It did the trick. The entrance hall light came on and the door opened.

An old woman in her eighties resting on a walking stick appeared in the doorway. Despite her years, Cathy observed a sharpness in her demeanour that spelt trouble.

"Good evening," the housekeeper said with a puzzled look on her face.

"Sorry to disturb you, ma'am," Cathy said in a kindly voice, "but there's a large, unstable explosive device just outside the gate."

The housekeeper opened the door wider. "Yes. I know."

"Then why are you still here?" Cathy said, gently manoeuvring the old lady back inside. "Let's get your hat and coat."

"I can't abandon the house. Security has fled."

"But there are police and emergency services everywhere," Cathy said smiling. "The residence is secure."

"It's the police and emergency services I'm worried about. They have a certain reputation."

"I don't understand."

The housekeeper leant forward, cupped one hand around her mouth and whispered. "They're all light-fingered larcenists."

"Maybe – but you can't stay here," Cathy said, in a firmer tone.

The old lady moved deeper into the house. "I'm not going anywhere."

With the entrance free, Rossi stepped inside and closed the door. He then helped Cathy off with her helmet and blast collar.

The housekeeper gazed suspiciously at Rossi as Cathy reciprocated. "You're not Russian."

"This is Captain Fuccinetto, ma'am. He's part of a joint EU-Russian anti-terrorist unit," Cathy explained.

The housekeeper pulled a mobile phone from her pocket. Walking stick hanging from her wrist, she dialled.

"What are you doing?" Cathy said, snatching the phone from her pale hand.

"I have my rights," the old woman protested, cracking the walking stick against Cathy's ankle.

"Hold her while I get out of this damned suit."

"You won't get away with this, I've already called the police," the housekeeper warned Rossi in English. "I recognised you before I even opened the door."

"Like my colleague told you – I'm from an EU anti-terrorist unit."

"Liar."

"That's not nice," Cathy said, throwing the housekeeper over her shoulder and carrying her kicking and screaming towards the back of the house.

Rossi discarded his EOD suit then hurried down the unlit southern hallway to the second door on the right. He listened for a moment and entered. The décor confirmed it was the Patriarch's sitting room. Rossi glanced at Father Arkady's map. Opposite a door, through it the study. Moving across the room, his gaze was inexplicably drawn to *The Last Judgement* hanging over the fireplace. The ghost of Patriarch Pyotr kneeling before God flashed through his mind. Rossi pushed open the door and switched on the light.

It was much larger than expected. The room resembled a stately library trapped inside a private chapel. The walls were deep red and the soaring ceiling covered in hand-painted images of God in His Heaven surrounded by angels and saints. Endless shelves of books ran along the windowless wall on the left. The room was divided into two functional areas with the placement end-to-end of three double-sided display cabinets. In the front half of the room – from where he had just entered – stood two cabriole sofas, separated by a large ornate rectangular coffee table. A flat screen television hung on the wall. At the far end, in front of an imposing panelled window, an oak desk and a high back leather chair. Probably the Patriarch's working area.

Rossi turned the map to match what was in front of him. The sketch showed the bookshelves, represented by a dotted line along the left wall, the display cabinets that divided the room and the fireplace on the right. A red X was drawn halfway along the bookshelves, marking the location of the safe. There were also two arrows pointing to the fireplace opposite. Written underneath were the words 'key' and 'painting'.

Despite its simplicity, Rossi was certain he had what he needed. He made a beeline to the point marked on the map. Running his eyes over the leather-bound tomes, he felt for a faux book panel. At first nothing seemed unusual. Then a block of English language books with the oddest titles. He pushed on *Amazing Facts about Badgers* and the panel popped open. Rossi's face lit up at the sight of the small black safe.

Now for the key. Rossi glanced over at the large portrait of St Tikhon hanging above the unlit red marble fireplace.

He grabbed the library stepladder and dragged it across the room. Placing the ladder's front legs on the hearth, he climbed up. The steps wobbled, but this would not take long. He gently pulled on the base of the large gilded frame and ran his fingers along its rough wooden back.

"It's got to be here somewhere," Rossi murmured to himself, working his hand further up. Still no key.

Time for finessing was over. Rossi took a deep breath and heaved the portrait off its hook. The weight of the massive wood and moulded plaster frame took him by surprise. He let out a yelp as the ladder tilted backwards. To his immense relief, he flung the painting forward onto the cluttered mantelpiece as he fell. But there the portrait stood for only a brief moment. Prostrate on his back, Rossi looked up helplessly as the portrait toppled forward onto the metre-long brass hand-support of the steps – spearing the 11th Patriarch of the Russian Church through the heart.

The Bolsheviks would've loved that, Rossi thought, struggling to his feet. He cringed as he inspected the damage. Antique ceramic objects lay smashed on the floor. Then joy. In the broken base of a priceless Athenian black figure vase he spotted what he was looking for. *I would have drawn a vase.*

Rossi swooped on the key and bustled to the safe. Heart pounding, he opened the door. He could hardly contain his excitement as he peered inside. Under a treasure trove of precious stones and gold coins, Rossi found his salvation.

With trembling hands he removed the document from the plastic sleeve, then ran his fingers reverently over the cover. "*Grazie a Dio!*" he murmured, looking up to the heavens.

Rossi's moment of ecstasy was short-lived. Cathy burst into the study in a panic. "We've got to go. She really did call the police."

Startled, Rossi looked over confused, not sure what she had said.

"I checked her mobile phone."

"No harm. We're done here anyway," Rossi said, following her into the hallway. "Where is she?"

"Tied to a chair in the kitchen."

"How'd you manage that?"

"With great difficulty," she said, pointing to the scratches on her face.

In the entrance hall, Cathy emptied the rucksack onto the round Persian rug. Changing into their civilian garb, an unwelcome interruption: the sickening chimes of the front doorbell. Gazes shot in unison to the CCTV monitor mounted on the wall next to the front door.

"This could get messy," Cathy whispered, eyeing two baby-faced rookies standing on the front porch.

"Messy all right. They're about to shit themselves," Rossi said, his voice hardly audible over the wail of sirens that filled the neighbourhood.

Officer Shevchenko, a pimply-faced kid with an only child look, stepped forward and rang the bell for a second time. "Police," he shouted, rapping on the door with his baton.

"Let's go," his partner, Officer Moiseev, said, turning to leave. "It's a prank."

"Are you crazy? We at least need to check the perimeter."

"Okay, but let's be quick about it. I'm not planning on being anywhere near the truck bomb when it goes off."

As the rookies headed for the east side of the residence, the noise from the kitchen grew louder.

"Keep an eye on the debutants and I'll quieten the old lady," Rossi said, scurrying away.

Cathy removed her boots and tiptoed from one doorway to the next, following the rookies' progress around the well-lit grounds.

By the time they reached the north-east corner, where the kitchen was located, their enthusiasm had waned. The bellowing had stopped, and the tapping of batons against the window frames had become sporadic.

Hidden away in the darkest corner of the large open kitchen, Rossi stood anxiously behind the old lady, waiting for the rookies to pass. Suddenly a shadow appeared on one of the white lace curtains. Rossi wrapped a hand around the housekeeper's mouth.

Putting his head to the window, Shevchenko peered in. Although the kitchen was partly illuminated by the external landscape lighting, Rossi was sure they couldn't be seen.

Slowly the rookies' voices grew fainter and merged with the noises on the street. "They've gone," Rossi said, removing his hand.

"Enzo, we have a problem," Cathy said, rushing into the kitchen. "Listen!" The distinct sound of an external door closing.

"Whatever happened to locking the door," Cathy said, glancing accusingly at the old lady. "This is Moscow for God's sake."

"Police," Shevchenko called out. "Anyone home?"

"Stay here and keep her quiet," Cathy said, drawing her pistol, and moving stealthily out into the hallway.

Following her lead, Rossi removed his pistol from inside his jacket and unclipped the safety. In that moment of distraction the housekeeper stretched out a thin bony leg and connected with a broom leaning against the wall. Rossi instantly recognised his mistake. But it was too late. The broom fell beyond his reach and struck the wooden floor like a drum.

At the other end of the residence, Shevchenko held up his hand. The laundry fell silent just in time to hear the sound reverberating down the northern hallway.

"There's someone here," Shevchenko whispered, unclipping his pistol.

"I heard nothing," Moiseev said in a cowardly tone.

Shevchenko shone his torch down the long, dark passage. "It came from there."

Moiseev took a step backwards towards the external door. "Let's call it in."

Shevchenko moved dauntlessly towards the noise. The rug-covered wooden floor creaked and moaned with every step he took.

In the kitchen, the housekeeper continued to struggle, even as Rossi held her high in the air. Her shifting weight in the wooden chair gave off a sound no louder than the squeaking of a mouse. But it was enough to keep

Shevchenko moving in the right direction.

Cathy took advantage of his slow, hesitant pace. Timing her every step with his, she retreated into the dining room.

"Moiseev, get your lily-livered arse down here," Shevchenko said in a breathy whisper, realising his partner was still cowering in the laundry.

"I'm telling you, there's no one here," Moiseev called out, refusing to budge.

"Move it or I'll report you to the captain."

"You can't report me for being right. And if I'm wrong, you can't report me either – because you'll be dead," Moiseev said.

"Then piss off home to Mummy. I'll do this myself." Shevchenko continued alone towards the kitchen.

In the dining room, Cathy froze; listening. Someone had moved behind her. She swung around. Her eyes, already adjusted to the light, scanned the room. There it is again. She trained her pistol at the heavy velvet curtains that were swaying. The sight of a huge Russian Blue sauntering towards her with its tail high in the air brought a smile to her face. And an idea.

Shevchenko stopped short of the kitchen door and listened. Silence. With pistol raised and torch held high, he pushed open the ajar door with the tip of his soggy boot. Holding his breath, he stepped into the darkness and ran the torch beam from one side of the kitchen to the other. Face coloured, he exhaled with relief. The kitchen was empty. And there was absolutely nowhere to hide.

"I told you there's no one here," Moiseev said, reaching in and switching on the light.

"Thanks for the back-up, you gutless turd," Shevchenko said, lighting up a cigarette to calm his nerves.

"I'm here aren't I?"

"Go to hell."

"That's what you heard," Moiseev said, pointing to the broom lying on the floor.

"And it fell by itself?"

In the adjoining room Cathy took her cue, shoving the Russian Blue out into the hallway and steering it towards the light in the kitchen.

"Ghosts – it's an old house," Moiseev said, as the cat wandered in unnoticed.

Shevchenko moved to the window over the sink and stared pensively out into the snow-covered garden. "Something's not right," he said, dragging hard on his cigarette.

"You're not really going to report me, are you?"

"There's that noise again," Shevchenko said, swinging around.

This time Moiseev heard it too. He moved over and lifted the tablecloth. "There's your culprit," Moiseev said, crouching down and stroking the Russian Blue, who had its nose buried in a bowl of cat biscuits.

"Let's go," Shevchenko grumbled.

As soon as the laundry door clicked closed, Cathy rushed into the kitchen bursting with nervous curiosity. She gazed dumbfounded at the spot where she had last seen Rossi, but he wasn't there. "He'll turn up," she said with a smile, scurrying off to check that the rookies had left the premises.

By the time Cathy returned with their getaway gear, Rossi had reappeared. He was standing next to an open window. "Damn it Enzo, how did you do that – and where's the housekeeper?"

The mystery was solved when Rossi leant out of the window and lifted the old lady back inside. "I took advantage of their rather noisy and unprofessional altercation," he smirked.

Cathy tossed the clothes onto the table. "Let's get out of here before someone else turns up."

"Christ, is she okay? She looks dead."

Cathy crouched down and removed her gag, then gently slapped her pale cheeks.

"It takes more than a little fresh air to do me in, young lady."

"As soon as we're safe, I'll have someone contact the police about your predicament," Cathy said in a slow, clear voice. "So remain calm until you're rescued."

"I'm neither deaf nor senile, you lawless marauder," the old lady said, spitting in Cathy's face.

"Now why do that?" Cathy said, spitting back.

As they hurried through the back garden towards the rose bush lattice that covered the three-metre-high perimeter wall, Cathy called Brodzinski. "We're on our way."

Rossi, nimble for his size, scaled the wall first. "Give me your hand," he said, reaching down from the top.

"In your dreams," Cathy said, clambering up unassisted.

"Entirely right. You're far too heavy."

61

Rossi and Cathy sighed with relief when the door of the blacked-out Escalade slammed closed.

"How'd it go?" Special Agent Brodzinski asked, planting his foot on the accelerator pedal.

"Nothing we couldn't handle."

"Did you find what you were looking for?"

Cathy's eyes were on Rossi. "We did."

"Congratulations, Inspector General. Now all that's left is to get you safely back to Rome."

"God knows I'm ready."

Cathy punched Rossi in the arm. "And your tour of the Metro?"

"Gone right off that."

"But why? We had so much fun."

Brodzinski grabbed the small canvas backpack lying on the passenger seat and tossed it back to Cathy. "From the chief."

"Has Volkov gone mad?" Cathy said, gazing at a long column of T-14 Armata tanks passing them in the opposite direction.

"It wasn't Volkov – he's dead."

Cathy turned to Rossi with wide disbelieving eyes. "No friggin' way."

"Information's thin on the ground. But from what we've found out so far, there was a detonated explosion inside the Presidential Box at Olympisky."

Cathy removed her beanie and shook out her hair. "That would've been ugly."

"Volkov, Kalinin and Chernik – all gone to meet Lucifer."

Rossi felt a strange sense of remorse. "And Patriarch Pyotr?"

"I suspect so, though no official word. Russia's cut itself off from the rest of the world. The internet is dead and all radio and television stations are playing Tchaikovsky."

"*Ai mali estremi, mali rimedi.*"

"Enzo, this is not the time."

"An old Italian saying. 'For severe ills, severe remedies.'"

Cathy rested her hand on Rossi's thigh. "Getting you out has just got a lot more complicated."

Brodzinski shot Cathy an impish look over his shoulder. "You're going with him."

Cathy's jaw dropped. "You're joking?"

"After the Metro debacle, and *High Noon* at Kitay Gorod, I'm afraid you're *persona non grata.*"

"Who decided this?" Cathy growled.

"Ask the chief."

Not listening to a word of Cathy's conversation, Rossi grumbled to himself, "They'll blame the Vatican."

A long silence, then Brodzinski spoke first. "Cathy, who's behind this?"

"Not Revealing Light, that's for sure. They don't have the skill sets for such an operation. More into saving souls than toasting them."

"With a little luck, and plotters close enough to the throne – it's possible," Rossi countered. "Besides, it's what we assumed Father Arkady was up to. So why the surprised look?"

"The Patriarch, sure. But not the whole ruling class. It's got to be a coincidence."

"A bloody big one," Rossi said.

Cathy removed the small bottle of water from the seat pouch and took a mouthful while she thought. "Maybe the real assassins piggybacked onto Revealing Light's operation – unbeknown to Father Arkady."

"It would help if we knew who the target was," Brodzinski joined in. "The Patriarch or Volkov?"

Cathy nodded. "If they're smart, it would've been everyone in the box. The Russian ruling class is like crab grass. You've got to remove every last trace, if you want to stop the scum returning."

"*Ai mali estremi, mali rimedi,*" Rossi repeated.

"Unfortunately the ruling class is deeper and wider than those that died tonight," Cathy said. "Communism taught them how to survive and reinvent themselves.

They'll quickly pick a new leader, redistribute the wealth, and carry on as though nothing has happened."

"Who do you think will replace Volkov?" Brodzinski asked. "With Chernik and Kalinin dead, there's no one obvious."

"They will most likely pluck someone out of obscurity, like they did with Volkov. But this time someone weaker. Someone they can control."

"You keep saying 'they'. Who the hell are 'they'?" Rossi asked.

"The Gatekeepers," Cathy said, in a mysterious tone. "They used to be the real power behind the throne – until Volkov outmanoeuvred them. They're like the Freemasons on steroids."

"I'm hearing this for the first time. Did I sleep through something or did you forget to mention it before?" Rossi said, with a look of astonishment.

"They're a group of nameless, faceless individuals that choose the preferred candidate for President," Cathy said.

Brodzinski scoffed. "And we all know the preferred candidate wins the general election."

"No one knows who they are?" Rossi asked. "Sounds fanciful. Do they have a secret handshake too?"

"Well at least no one knows for sure – not even the CIA or the FSB. But the Gatekeepers do exist. If you follow the capital flows, you can guess the identity of a few. Others you can eliminate by what they do."

"For instance?"

"If you're paying the multimillion-dollar salary of the Russian national football coach, or buying Fabergé eggs to donate to the Hermitage – it's likely you're a beneficiary of the Russian system, but not a Gatekeeper."

"Is it conceivable the Gatekeepers are the assassins?" Rossi asked without waiting for a response. "Or perhaps they teamed up with Revealing Light. If Volkov usurped their authority and influence, they'd have a good reason for wanting Volkov dead."

"Yeah, but if they did, Revealing Light didn't know about it. The Gatekeepers and Revealing Light are anchored at opposite ends of the ideological spectrum. In fact, as long as the Gatekeepers exist, the crab grass keeps growing."

"And the Russian Orthodox Church remains an appendage of the Kremlin," Brodzinski added.

62

Not since the height of the Cuban Missile Crisis had the US Embassy in Moscow seen such frantic activity.

Chief James sat at his desk with Agent Lawrence. Between them an empty pot of coffee. They'd called every contact they had, trying to piece together what had happened at Olympisky forty-five minutes ago. The story was anything but clear.

"We seemed to have underestimated Revealing Light," Lawrence said, smoking his first cigarette in ten years.

"I refuse to believe it," the chief said, shaking his head. "It's hard to imagine men of the cloth doing something like this. Technically and morally it doesn't fit."

"Technically? Father Arkady had an exhaustive knowledge of the whole shooting match. He only needed to find a chummy ordnance guy and sit back and wait."

Chief James glanced over at the television mounted on the wall. A smile. In the midst of the chaos the Russkies had failed to jam the satellite signal. Breaking news flashed across the screen. He turned up the volume.

'Good afternoon, I'm Cecil Jones reporting. We have breaking news from Moscow. CNN has received unconfirmed reports that the Russian President, Alexander Volkov, has been killed along with several high-ranking officials in an explosion at a sporting event in Moscow city centre.

'A Kremlin spokesman has described the claim as baseless and mischievous and part of a broader US plot to destabilise the country before upcoming regional elections.

'The spokesman conceded that there had been a minor incident at the Olympisky Stadium where the President was scheduled to open the World Judo Championships. However, the spokesman insisted that President Volkov was not in attendance at the time due to a bout of influenza.

'There are also reports coming in that troops and heavy equipment have been deployed in and around Moscow, and that all airports and border crossings are closed.

'The White House said that the President was monitoring the situation. As a precautionary measure, the US Navy is stationing five warships in the Black Sea to promote peace and stability in the region.

'The NATO Secretary General, Knut Soltenberg, subsequently announced that NATO forces in Eastern Europe and the Baltics have been put on heightened alert.

'CNN will continue to follow this story and bring you updates as soon as they come to hand.'

"Hasn't anyone told the Russians that blanket denials don't work any more," Lawrence said, turning down the volume.

The chief might not have heard. He searched his cluttered desk for the memory stick his PA had brought in while he was speaking on the phone. He found it in his pocket.

"Look at this," Chief James said, swinging his monitor around to face Lawrence. "The bullpen downloaded it from social media just before the internet was brought down." The video taken on a mobile device was grainy and faded, but of sufficient quality to identify faces in the Presidential Box.

"Volkov, Chernik, Petrov," Lawrence said, writing their names on a scrap of paper, "Sokolov, Patriarch Pyotr…"

"Kalinin's missing," the chief said, excitedly, already at Lawrence's shoulder. "Ah, he's there… these pricks stole Russia."

Lawrence seemed pleased. "And they're leaving with nothing."

Suddenly a flash of bright light; the screen went white. Silence as they waited.

"That's fairly conclusive," the chief said, as the camera refocused.

Through the smoke and dust they could make out the Presidential Box. It was empty, no windows, no furniture, nothing, just colour.

"And a power vacuum of unprecedented proportions – I hope you've got a good plan for getting Rossi and Cathy out."

63

Rossi was surprised. "Leave now? Wouldn't it be safer to lie low for a couple of days?"

"Just the opposite," Brodzinski said, searching for Rossi's eyes in the rear-view mirror. "We need to take advantage of the chaos."

"Makes sense," Cathy said, examining the contents of the rucksack. There was an escape plan, two Australian passports, a handheld GPS device, a satphone, a topographical map, a large torch and a stack of cash: US dollars in large denominations.

Brodzinski sat upright, his eyes straight ahead, as a convoy of canvas-covered troop trucks passed going the other way.

"Who's the enemy?" Rossi asked, looking straight ahead. "Rogue generals?"

Brodzinski scoffed. "There's no such thing. In the

Russian Army, by the time you make colonel you are so thoroughly brainwashed the mere thought of opposing the state would cause your brain to explode."

"Maybe that's what happened at Olympisky?"

"Exploding brains?" Brodzinski said. Laughter.

"A distinct possibility but I don't think I'll include that in the official report," Cathy said, continuing the joke.

Rossi turned to Cathy. "So what's the plan?"

"We drive to Orsk in the Southern Urals."

"That's a hell of a long time to be out in the open."

"The plan was devised before Volkov's assassination," Brodzinski said. "But it's still good. In fact, with all airports and border crossings closed, I can't think of an alternative."

"Why Orsk?"

"Your destination's the Kazakh border, a few kilometres south of Orsk. It's circled there," Brodzinski said, throwing his arm back, pointing indiscriminately at the map opened on Cathy's lap. "You'll cross by foot and rendezvous with one of our agents who'll drive you to Aktobe where we've got a jet waiting to fly you home."

A look of concern crossed Rossi's face. "I'm not sure I'm up to that?"

"Cathy's going too. She's no longer welcome here."

"Great."

Cathy frowned. "How kind of you."

"I meant, um – I'm glad you're coming with me," Rossi said apologetically.

"I'm teasing you, Enzo."

A half smile. "Are the Kazakhs in on this?"

"Why complicate things?" Brodzinski said, over his shoulder.

"You make it sound so simple. Is it?"

Cathy shook her head. Her expression serious. "But what choice do we have?"

Ahead, a squad of soldiers were unloading a truck. A makeshift checkpoint they figured. Brodzinski drove slowly past, unchallenged.

"I don't want to be the perpetual black hat," Rossi said, "but won't we look a little conspicuous criss-crossing the countryside in a blacked-out SUV while Russia's on high alert?"

"You're right. That would be obvious," Cathy smirked. "That's why we're travelling incognito."

"As?"

"The Georgian bandit."

"Stalin?" Rossi said, nodding his head, playing along. "So where do we find a ZiL limousine at this late hour?"

"We won't need one. Brodzinski's been contracted to deliver two bronze statues of the man himself to Orenburg."

"Let me guess. We're travelling inside them?"

Cathy nodded.

Nervous smile. "I thought the CIA was more high tech than that."

"They're hollow with concealed hinges and hydraulic gas strut lift supports," Brodzinski said, glancing again in the rear-view mirror.

"Hollow's good."

"If I spot something suspicious, I'll bang on the bulkhead. That'll be your signal to climb in. When it's all clear, you climb out again."

"It's not as dumb as it seems. Volkov was rebadging the psychopath," Cathy said, "so no one will think the story odd. A Stalin statue for every town square – to be erected next to the great political theorist Vladimir Ilyich Ulyanov."

"Who?"

"Lenin."

"Who dreams up this stuff?"

"A group of highly intelligent misfits."

"Agent Lawrence," Rossi mouthed.

Cathy smiled and nodded.

"And how long's the drive?"

"Twenty-five hours, if we're not delayed at one of the police checkpoints," Brodzinski said.

"And if we're stopped and detained while we're still inside the statues?"

"What does the chief say?" Brodzinski asked.

Cathy rechecked the escape plan. "He doesn't mention it."

"That's excellent," Brodzinski said. "That means you're free to improvise."

Rossi rolled his eyes. "A half-baked plan is better than no plan, right?"

Cathy laid her hand again on Rossi's thigh. "Come on, Enzo, don't be like that. It'll be fun. While you're saving the Catholic Church, we'll get to see some of the Russian countryside."

"Now you've put it like that, I don't see how I can refuse."

Fifteen minutes later, the Escalade pulled into a small warehouse on the outskirts of Moscow. Inside, a Volvo 4x2 box truck was fuelled and ready to go.

"We leave in five minutes – so if you need a pee, it's out the back," Brodzinski said, climbing in and firing up the engine.

Despite being behind the wheel of a nondescript vehicle, Brodzinski felt no less conspicuous. The normally congested Moscow streets were quiet, making it difficult to blend in.

In the back, it was cold and uncomfortable. The truck was not designed for transporting passengers halfway across Russia, especially during the height of winter. But neither Cathy nor Rossi complained. They were happy in each other's company. And after all that had happened, they were grateful for the respite.

"You know it's far from over, Enzo?" Cathy said, cuddling up next to him. "Even after you've presented the evidence, there's nothing to stop the Kremlin from turning round and producing another original, claiming the Vatican's version is a fake."

"That's good for Krotsky. He gets to stay alive," Rossi said, with a tired smile.

"And it goes without saying they'll blame the Olympisky attack on you."

"But isn't it equally possible that the surviving ruling class turn on each other? Surely Volkov's dream of a Holy Russian Empire is dead in the water for now?"

A loud thump on the bulkhead. "Police checkpoint," Brodzinski screamed through a piece of piping he had crudely installed through to the cargo area.

"I hope I don't turn claustrophobic suddenly," Rossi said, helping Cathy to her feet.

Cathy opened her Stalin first. "Good God!"

"Lawrence?"

The interior of the statue was lined with purple quilted velour fabric, fitted tightly over a moulded polyurethane foam base. It was difficult not to associate it with death.

"Handy in the event that something goes wrong. Just dig a hole and bury us."

"Smart that," Rossi said, climbing in.

"See you on the other side." Cathy lowered the lid.

Brodzinski approached the DPS control station slowly. He realised this was only the first of many such stops, but given what was at stake he was anxious all the same.

The responsibility of the DPS police was the enforcement of the road traffic regulations. But Brodzinski knew, in reality, each checkpoint was a thriving enterprise – operated for the benefit of the robber police who ran the stations. Their main undertaking was the collection of bribes from vulnerable motorists for minor breaches of the deliberately vague traffic code.

Out of the hundreds of vehicles that passed each hour, only high potential customers were ever stopped. This evening, with so few vehicles on the road, Brodzinski's brand new Volvo was flagged down in a desperate attempt to make up for a slow night.

"Junior Sergeant Grasny, papers please," a haggard-looking policeman said, a hand-rolled cigarette hanging from the side of his mouth.

Brodzinski presented his freshly printed documents in silence. Grasny examined them showing no expression of concern.

"What are you carrying?"

Brodzinski told his story. Not unexpectedly, he was ordered to get down and open the back.

"Two bronze statues of the Motherland's newest hero," he said, as the cargo doors swung open.

Seemingly unimpressed by the soles of Stalin's large bronze feet, the policeman turned his attention to the truck. Brodzinski followed him as he strolled around the vehicle, shining his torch up and down the bodywork as he went.

"The truck's three months old. You won't find anything wrong with it."

"Your side mirror's broken," Grasny said, shattering the glass with his patrol baton. "Park over there. I'll need to conduct a full inspection."

Brodzinski, familiar with such tactics responded appropriately. "How much?" After a short, cordial negotiation, Brodzinski handed over two hundred dollars and continued on his way.

Two kilometres down the road, Brodzinski pulled off onto the hard shoulder and jumped down. He opened the back and signalled the all clear. Cathy and Rossi wasted no time in climbing out. Cathy looked pale, but insisted she was all right.

This process repeated itself twice more before they reached the outskirts of Orsk.

"Let's hope this is the last time," Brodzinski bellowed, sending his two passengers scurrying back into their sarcophagi.

Brodzinski pulled into the siding as ordered by one of the four policemen who were standing in front of the office like roadside whores waiting for a customer. Opening his door, he handed down his documents.

"This is the fourth time I've been stopped since Moscow," he said, appearing annoyed. "Why can't you guys coordinate yourselves? This costs me time."

"Officer Salko," the policeman said, saluting. "Get out of your vehicle."

"What's the problem this time?"

"You've got a broken side mirror."

"I do now."

"Open the back."

Retelling his well-drilled story, Brodzinski sensed that Salko was after more than the usual fee. His intuition was quickly confirmed.

"Offload the statues," Salko ordered. "We'll take them from here."

Brodzinski's jaw dropped. "What do you mean?"

"You're already in Orenburg. Consider them delivered."

Brodzinski did his best to laugh it off, but the policeman was serious. "It doesn't work that way."

"I'll make sure they get to the right address," Salko said, waving the submachine gun slung over his shoulder in Brodzinski's general direction.

"Look! I understand how the game's played. I've been at this for twenty-three years. The statues have no aesthetic value to you. You plan to sell them as scrap. So let's do the maths. Two tons of bronze at four thousand dollars a ton – they can't be worth more than eight thousand dollars."

The officer nodded. "It's good we understand each other."

"So how much do you need to let me do my job?"

"Half their value would be a win-win."

"Four thousand dollars? That's absurd," Brodzinski said, his tone now distinctively aggressive.

"Welcome to the new reality."

"Why would I ever agree to such an amount?"

"Because you get to keep the statues."

Brodzinski lit a cigarette and drew deeply as he thought. Then against his better judgement, he agreed. The policeman's greedy round eyes twitched. Brodzinski sensed he had made a stupid mistake.

Salko tapped his baton on Stalin's feet. "Doesn't sound hollow."

"Should it?"

"No one agrees to such an amount unless they're smuggling contraband."

"These statues are a work of art. They're worth much more than their weight in bronze," Brodzinski said in a loud voice, trying to warn Cathy and Rossi of the impending danger.

The policeman ignored Brodzinski's plea. Instead he craned his neck around the corner of the truck and motioned to one of his colleagues to join him.

"Officer Tankov, my friend here has just offered me four thousand dollars to look the other way."

"What's he carrying – gold?"

"Two bronze statues of Stalin," Salko said, laughing as if it were a joke.

"You're the fourth truck with Stalin statues this month. Not very inventive, are you?"

Salko climbed up onto the truck tray and banged his baton along the full length of Cathy's hideaway. A betraying dull thud reverberated through the cargo area.

"That doesn't sound right," Tankov said. "I was expecting something more like church bells?"

"They're filled with polyurethane foam to stop water collecting inside."

"And you're full of shit," Tankov scoffed.

"Keep an eye on him while I grab the cutting torch," Salko said, jumping down from the tray, then heading towards the workshop.

Brodzinski turned to Tankov. "Touch the statues and you'll have the Ministry of Culture to answer to."

The policeman burst into laughter. "I suspect Moscow has higher priorities right now. Besides, our next President might revert to the previous view that Stalin was a stain on Russian history. So we would be doing everyone a favour."

"This is total anarchy."

"Yes it is. So grab what you can."

"Then just take the money," Brodzinski said, reaching into his pocket.

"I'm afraid curiosity has taken hold."

Brodzinski moved to the side of the truck and lit a cigarette. "You're wasting your time."

"Out here we have plenty of time."

On the path from the workshop, the oxyacetylene welding rig was bogged deep in snow. "Give me a hand," Salko bellowed.

Through Stalin's moustache, Rossi had heard enough to know it was time to go. Unclipping the internal latch, he rolled out. Cathy followed – her face a ghostly white. "I need a holiday," she said.

"Me too. Let's go to Rome."

Rossi jumped down and peered between the wheels. He saw the two policemen pulling and pushing at the cutting rig. Brodzinski stood nearby doing everything possible to impede their progress.

Without a sound, Cathy lowered the statue lids then dropped down to join Rossi. They edged along the driver's side of the Volvo unseen. Rossi held up his hand, stopping short at the front wheel. To his right he spotted a third policeman strolling back to the office counting his plunder.

Ten metres in front of them, the policeman's victim climbed behind the wheel of his vehicle transporter and fired up the engine. His cargo of eight wrecked SUVs looked to Rossi like the perfect place to hide.

As the truck moved off, they sneaked up from behind and clambered onto the trailer. The transporter bucked and rolled as it built up speed. Balanced precariously on the narrow icy frame, Cathy glanced back at Brodzinski, who threw her a reassuring wink.

"We seem to have got away with it," Cathy said.

"Will Brodzinski be okay?"

"He's a big boy. He knows how to take care of himself. Besides, he's still got a bag full of cash to buy his way out."

64

"Commandant Waldmann has arrived, Your Eminence," Monsignor Polak said, standing in the doorway of Cardinal Capelli's office.

The cardinal, who hadn't slept since President Volkov's letter, glanced up. "Show him in."

"Good news," Waldmann said, sitting down in front of the cardinal's desk. "The US Ambassador has confirmed that Inspector General Rossi has recovered the forged Concordat."

"Thank God," the cardinal said, clapping his hands together once. "And where is he?"

"At this moment, no one's sure."

"How's that?"

"Russia has lapsed into complete chaos – as Your Eminence could imagine. So the CIA decided to smuggle him out before things are brought back under control."

"Quite right."

"And along the way," Waldmann cleared his throat, "they sort of lost him."

"Lost him? With all their surveillance satellites, drones and goodness knows what else, how on God's earth could they lose him?"

"Russia's a big place, Your Eminence," the Commandant said, instantly regretting his choice of words.

"I don't need a geography lesson, Commandant."

"Your Eminence, I meant to say there was an incident close to the Kazakh border. It required Rossi and his partner to abandon their CIA escort and to carry on alone."

"By partner, you mean the young lady he's been spending an awful lot of time with lately?"

"Well yes. Agent Catherine Doherty. By all accounts her help has been invaluable. The Vatican should consider honouring her once this matter is resolved."

"You mean make her a saint?" the cardinal said, looking at Waldmann, expressionless.

"I beg your pardon, Your Eminence."

Cardinal Capelli broke into a broad smile at the sight of Waldmann's confused face.

"Very good, Your Eminence," Waldmann said, discovering for the first time that the cardinal had a sense of humour.

"So what are they doing about it? We can't have Rossi wandering about in the wilderness."

"They're waiting, Your Eminence. As far as the CIA is concerned, Inspector General Rossi and Agent Doherty are on plan."

"Then we should pray for their safe return."

"We all are, Your Eminence."

"I assume the CIA escort is okay?"

"More or less," the Commandant said.

65

The driver shifted down gears. Rossi kicked open the door of the smashed Cayenne and looked out. "He's turning into a transport café."

Cathy checked the GPS device. "We're eleven kilometres from the rendezvous point."

"Close enough?"

"On this ride anyway."

They climbed out onto the icy frame, and one perilous step after another shuffled to the back. On the unlit country road they were invisible to the tired driver. The air brakes hissed, and the twin-deck trailer groaned as the driver swung his truck into the driveway and pulled up next to a refrigerated van.

Hand in hand they jumped down. No one seemed to pay them any attention as they appeared from between the two soaring trucks.

"Supper, or is it breakfast?" Cathy glanced at her watch. One in the morning. They hadn't eaten since leaving Moscow twenty-eight hours ago.

"Both. I'm starving."

As they entered the café, Rossi glanced about. Several heads rose indifferently at the sound of the bell hanging above the door, but nobody appeared to give them a second look.

They took a table at the end of the long, narrow café and sat facing one another. Rossi, the more infamous of the two, sat with his back to the door.

"Did anyone reach for their mobile phone?" Rossi asked.

"Not a soul. Thanks to my handiwork, you bear little resemblance to that scrumptious guy in the mugshot the police are circulating. As long as you keep your mouth shut we'll be okay."

"Again."

Rossi fell silent as the waitress approached with a pot of coffee. Cathy ordered scrambled eggs and sausage for both of them, then waited until she was out of earshot before speaking.

"That wasn't so difficult, was it?"

Rossi smiled. "So what are our options?"

Cathy grabbed the GPS and studied it for a moment. "It's too far to walk. Besides, we'd stick out like sore thumbs."

"We could hop another truck."

"There's a major junction up ahead," Cathy said, shaking her head. "We could end up anywhere."

"Steal a couple of pushbikes?" Rossi smirked. "I'm quite an accomplished cyclist I'll have you know."

Cathy sat forward. An idea had popped into her head. "Look around. We're invisible. No one's looking for us this far from Moscow. I'll get the waitress to call us a cab."

Fifteen minutes later the taxi pulled up in front of the café entrance. Cathy paid the bill, and they exited without fuss.

"You Hannah?" the clean-cut young driver asked, looking Cathy up and down.

"*V aeroport, pozhaluysta.*" Cathy jumped in the back and slid over, making room for Rossi directly behind the driver; hidden and out of sight.

The driver swung the taxi around and drove south.

"The airport?" Rossi mouthed.

Cathy nodded. "Trust me," she whispered.

"Where are you flying to?"

"Home," Cathy answered coldly, not wanting to get caught up in a chatty conversation.

"Where's that?" the driver persisted, eyeing Cathy closely in the rear-view mirror.

"Stockholm."

"I thought I detected a slight accent," the driver said. "What on earth are you doing in Orsk? Not everyone's first choice of travel destination."

"Shooting a film."

The driver stretched over and removed something from the glove compartment. "You're an actress then? I thought I recognised your face."

"I'm not that famous. It's a small part," Cathy said, following his gaze in the rear-view mirror.

"What's it called? I might go see it."

"It's an English language film. The studio's not planning to release it in Russian – you speak English?"

"Not a word, unfortunately. If I could, I'd be in Moscow working for one of those greedy multinationals earning the big *mani*."

"Pity – the producer's looking for extras."

The driver nodded as he adjusted his rear-view mirror onto Rossi's face. He immediately fell silent. For the next couple of kilometres he drove noticeably slower.

Cathy watched suspiciously as the driver glanced down several times at the empty passenger seat and then in the mirror at Rossi. She craned her neck to check what he was looking at, but without success.

66

"I don't care what the Ministry says. Get me on a plane out of here," Chief James screamed at his personal assistant.

"It's almost midnight, Chief. Everyone's gone home," the PA said.

"Bullshit. After what happened last night, no one's sleeping."

Chief James was furious. He'd been summoned to CIA headquarters in Langley, Virginia to brief the top brass, but with the country on total lockdown, he couldn't secure approval to fly. To further raise his angst, the only two people with full knowledge of the circumstances leading up to the Olympisky assassinations were missing in action.

Lawrence entered the chief's office as his PA left. "I've spoken with the US Ambassador. She said she'd try to speak to the Russian Foreign Minister – but there were no guarantees."

"Tell her to tell Foreign Minister Potapov that if I don't get clearance within the hour, then Washington will destroy every Russian city between St Petersburg and Vladivostok with a barrage of intercontinental nuclear missiles."

"I'm not sure that's a proportional response, Chief," Lawrence said, the corner of his mouth twitching. "And besides, I doubt whether the ambassador would be willing to say that."

"Then what the hell do you suggest?"

"Excluding the nuclear option, we can ask Langley to contact the Secretary of State for help."

"You're right. I'll try to contact Langley now."

Lawrence walked out of the door with a grin on his face.

67

The lights of the airport now visible across the dark, windswept steppes, Rossi wondered what on earth Cathy was thinking. *Every airport in the country would be crawling with armed police. Why walk into a hornet's nest?*

Turning onto the deserted airport approach road, Cathy discerned fear in the driver's prying eyes. She realised this could mean only one thing. "Stop the car," she said, holding her pistol to his head.

Rossi stared at Cathy in stunned disbelief. *What the hell is she doing?*

Without protest, the driver pulled onto the hard shoulder. It was almost as though he had been expecting it.

Cathy leant forward and grabbed the clipboard that was lying face down on the front passenger seat. She turned it towards Rossi. "He knows who we are."

Rossi recoiled in horror at the sight of their faces on the FSB wanted poster. "Christ. What do we do now?"

"Send the FSB a new photo. I look terrible."

"I'm serious."

Holding her pistol to the back of his head, Cathy persuaded the driver to unlock his phone and hand it over. "Damn," she said. "He texted taxi dispatch five minutes ago."

"We need to turn around. Find somewhere else to cross," Rossi said, gazing out of the back window, as if he was expecting the police to arrive any moment.

"Everything's set up for Orsk. If we abort now, we could end up stranded. So unless we absolutely have to, we stay on plan."

"But why play chicken at the airport?"

"We're not. The airport's a reference point. Chosen because the north-south runway runs right up to the Kazakh border. By following the peripheral fence south, we can't help but find Billy. It's dumb-proof."

"For me?"

Cathy smiled.

"Incidentally, what do we do with the driver?"

"We kill him," Cathy said in Russian.

Rossi guessed what Cathy had said by the driver's reaction. Masking a smile, he pulled the Russian from behind the wheel and dragged him round the back.

"I'll freeze to death in here," the driver protested, as Rossi manhandled him into the boot.

"Easily fixed," Cathy said, training her gun at his head.

Without further grievance he lay down and Rossi slammed the boot shut.

The driver's phone beeped in Cathy's hand. "I bet you that's not his mother," Rossi said.

"You're right. It's a response from the dispatcher. It tells him not to do anything stupid..."

"Too late for that."

"And to drive as slowly as possible to the terminal while he contacts the police."

"Now, Plan B?"

"No," Cathy said decisively. "We stay on plan."

"Are you crazy? We'll be driving straight into an ambush."

"We still have time. You know how these things work. Right now the dispatcher will be trying to connect to the airport. And after he gets through, the airport security, the local police, OMON Special Forces and the Russian Air Force will all argue amongst themselves about who's in charge."

"So how much time do we have?"

"At least fifteen minutes," Cathy said, with a confident nod of the head.

"Is that enough?"

"If we run. But first let me finish sending a response." Thumb typing, Cathy informed the dispatcher that the whole thing had been an unfortunate case of mistaken identity. "Done."

"That should buy us a few more minutes," Rossi said, jumping in behind the wheel and hitting the accelerator. "By the way, what's Plan B?"

"Have you ever seen *Butch Cassidy and the Sundance Kid*?"

"Of course, it's a classic."

"Do you remember the ending?"

"Butch and Sundance were surrounded by the entire Bolivian Army and instead of surrendering they went out all guns blazing?"

"That's Plan B."

"What sort of plan is that?"

"That's why Plan A is better," Cathy said.

"I think I'm getting the hang of this CIA spy stuff. Mission success is directly correlated with selecting the least worst option."

"Pure mathematics," Cathy said. "Now let's check whether my old friend Billy's waiting for me as promised. The Kazakh steppes are not the best place to be stuck without a ride." Cathy grabbed the satphone and dialled.

Airport car park now visible, Rossi slammed his foot on the brake. Cathy looked up startled thinking something was wrong.

"Let's not make it too easy for them," Rossi said. He crunched the gear stick into reverse and backed up twenty metres. To their right was a derelict pump station. He swung left down a barely visible driveway and pulled up behind the crumbling cream brick building and killed the lights.

"ETA twenty-five minutes," Cathy said, waiting for confirmation before ending the call.

Rossi grabbed the torch from the backpack and jumped out. "I love it when a plan comes together," he said.

Cathy threaded her arm through Rossi's as they followed the driveway back to the approach road. An Arctic wind swept in from the north across the steppes carrying ice crystals that stung their eyes.

"I wish I had packed my sable," Cathy said.

"You would've never got it through customs."

"Yeah, I hear they're strict out here."

Rossi shone the torch beam across the frozen steppes, parallel to the faint silhouette of the airfield's peripheral fence. "How far is it from here?"

"About three k's. Twenty-five minutes at a reasonable clip."

"That's if we don't break an ankle," Rossi said.

"Didn't you do cross-country at school?"

"Sure, but the conditions were a little more Mediterranean. And rarely at night."

"A pampered childhood," Cathy quipped, jogging off in the direction marked by the torch's beam.

They covered the first two kilometres in no time flat, pushed on by adrenaline and the thought of being together in Rome.

"We're out of range, Enzo. Give me a minute to check our bearings. I don't want us ending up in Mongolia."

While Cathy checked the GPS, Rossi glanced back towards the road.

"If this device can be trusted, we've got less than a kilometre to go."

Rossi switched off the torch. "Let's hope it's not a kilometre too far."

Cathy followed Rossi's gaze back across the steppes.

Police vehicles converged from both directions in front of the old pump station.

"I guess they found the taxi."

"I told the driver not to worry," Cathy said, checking the GPS one more time. "We need to veer left."

"Well let's keep moving. There's no sense in giving them a sniff."

68

Captain Igor Blokov fired up the powerful gas turbine engines and engaged the coaxial rotors of his 2-seat Ka-52 Alligator attack helicopter. As he taxied out to the runway at Orsk airport, co-pilot Lieutenant Chayka rechecked the weapons systems. Mounted to the fuselage was a 240-round, 30mm cannon, and under each wing were six Vikhr AT-16 laser-guided beam-rider anti-tank missiles.

This was no training exercise. Their mission was to make an unauthorised incursion into Kazakhstan, and with deadly force eliminate two foreign agents who had just crossed over from Russia.

"Let's go barbecue ourselves some American imperialists," Blokov said, opening the throttle and pulling up on the collective lever. The Alligator launched forward and climbed effortlessly into the dark, overcast sky.

Away from the airport, the steppes were sparsely populated. The absence of town lights and surrounding features required Blokov to fly at an altitude higher than he would've liked. But tonight it was to his advantage, as the rolling terrain gave the fugitives few places to hide. And with the Alligator's state-of-the-art night vision systems, and the pilot's in-helmet rangefinder and night vision eyepieces, target acquisition would be routine.

"Nothing better than fresh meat," Chayka said, as the Alligator banked right and headed west towards the point Rossi and Cathy were thought to have crossed.

***

Down below, Rossi and Cathy entered Kazakhstan without a shot being fired. The chasing pack had given up and were heading back to the road. Rossi allowed himself to relax as he followed Cathy towards the coordinates shown on the GPS device.

"Darn cold out," a man's voice came from out of the darkness.

"Billy," Cathy shrieked, rushing forward and throwing her arms around her compatriot. "Am I glad to see you!"

"Y'all got yourselves in a bit of a pickle I hear."

"You could say that."

Rossi thrust out his hand and introduced himself. They then stood around chatting while Billy smoked a cigarette.

"We should get going," Rossi said suddenly, as though he had just remembered a dental appointment.

"Don't get your cows runnin', Sheriff," Billy said, winking at Cathy.

Rossi stood perplexed.

"Billy's from Texas," Cathy said, as though it explained everything. "He means to say let's wait a few minutes to see how the Russians respond. We don't want to go running into trouble."

"Look yonder," Billy said, pointing across the steppes to the retreating policemen. "If the foot soldiers ain't comin', it means they're sendin' in the fly-boys. There's positively no navy in these parts."

"Would the Russians do that?" Rossi asked.

Cathy nodded. "It would be categorised as an accidental air incursion. You appreciate how inventive the Kremlin is with the truth."

Billy held up his hand, motioning for silence. "That there's a Ka-52 Alligator," Billy said.

Billy, whose duties included intelligence gathering on Russian military technology, prided himself on being able to identify a helicopter type based solely on its sound. A unique feature of the Alligator is its coaxial rotor design in which the two main rotors contra-rotate one above the other, which eliminates the need for a tail rotor – the source of much of the noise in conventional helicopters. Billy recognised the Ka-52's distinctive soft noise profile immediately.

"We need to hightail outta here before they make Texas barbecue outta us."

Rossi stood for a moment longer, gazing towards the dark, distant sound. The thought of the Russians hunting him for the rest of his life popped into his mind.

"This way," Billy cried, bounding towards a rocky outcrop that separated them from the Orsk-Aktobe highway – the only road out.

Rossi and Cathy scampered after Billy, all the time wondering if the Alligator had them lined up in its sights.

"In here," Billy yelled, vaulting over a large boulder. On hands and knees he led them into a small natural grotto in which he had been sheltering for the last five hours.

The foreigners held their breath as the Alligator approached and hovered nearby, searching for evidence of their crossing. Rossi stared into Cathy's tired eyes and gave her a reassuring smile.

"Won't they spot your vehicle?" Cathy asked, after a nervous silence.

"This ain't my first rodeo, good-looking," Billy winked. "My ride's been under a camo tarp for the last five hours. It's as cold as a Texas beer."

"No thermal image," Cathy translated.

Before long the Alligator approached, then flew in an ever-expanding square pattern around the grotto. Ten minutes later the sky above them was once more silent.

***

"They can't be this far west," Captain Blokov said, flying low over the deserted Orsk-Aktobe highway.

"They must be hiding in the rocks."

Blokov banked the Alligator hard left, and in a narrow creeping line pattern, flew slowly east over the rock formation.

"Target at four o'clock," Chayka said, glancing at the video feed from the Gator's nose-mounted camera. The monitor showed the thermal image of an idling SUV and three people. One at the wheel, another two standing behind the vehicle; one possibly armed.

"That's strange! Why would they do that?" Blokov said. "They must have known we would double back."

"The head count's correct."

"If it's not them, who else could it be out here at this hour?" Blokov said, still wavering. "But it's not a mistake you'd expect from a CIA operative."

On the ground, the taller of the two men aimed his weapon towards the sound coming from behind the clouds. He mimicked a shot with an exaggerated recoil, then threw the rifle into the back of the SUV.

"He's taunting us," Chayka said.

"It makes little sense. Do they really think they're safe just because they're in Kazakhstan?"

Suddenly the quarry scrambled into their vehicle. The clouds had rolled back, revealing the Alligator silhouetted against a full moon.

"They're on the move," Chayka said, urgently.

Lurching forward, the SUV plunged down a shallow gully and took off west towards the highway. Blokov glanced at his co-pilot and nodded.

"Target confirmed," Chayka said, his tone intense.

Blokov glanced at the screen. "A compact Subaru. Not exactly the CIA's vehicle of choice," he said. But there was no other explanation, and he wasn't prepared to blow the mission on a hunch.

"Target designated."

Blokov's lips moved, but nothing came out.

"Weapon launched," Chayka said. An evil smirk on his face as the Vikhr AT-16 missile, with its High-Explosive Anti-Tank (HEAT) warhead, corkscrewed its way to the target.

In an instant, the Subaru was consumed in a ball of fire and light. Metal and dust filled the air.

"I may have overcooked it," Chayka said, laughing.

Blokov turned the Alligator for home.

69

Five hundred metres to the west, Rossi and the two Americans were showered with debris from the grotto's ceiling as the blast impact shook the ground.

"What the hell was that?" Cathy cried.

"That there's a case of mistaken identity," Billy said, blessing himself with the sign of the cross.

"Maybe they're trying to flush us out," Rossi suggested, puzzled by what Billy meant.

Cathy grabbed Rossi's arm as the Alligator approached for a second time and then hovered overhead. "They've spotted us," she whispered, bracing for the worst.

***

Above the grotto, Captain Blokov was not convinced they'd liquidated the right target. So he made one final pass.

"The kill was good," Chayka insisted, surprised that Blokov had doubts. "Besides, if we've messed up no one will be the wiser."

Blokov laughed dismissively. "If we've messed up and our targets make it out alive, I'm sure the entire world will know."

"But we haven't messed up."

"Let's hope," Blokov said.

With an uncomfortable sensation in his gut, Blokov tilted the cyclic control forward, opened the throttle and headed back towards the Orsk airfield for clearance to land.

***

When the sky fell silent, Billy ushered his charges out of the grotto and bustled them towards his nearby silver Ford.

Rossi folded up the camouflage tarpaulin while Billy warmed the engine. Cathy, still shaking from the notion of being buried alive, climbed in the front and turned on the radio in search of news.

"Let's get out of here," Rossi yelled, jumping in the back.

"What y'all do to get the Russkies so rattled?" Billy said, hitting the accelerator.

"Long story, Billy."

"Hell, you weren't involved in Volkov's death, I hope?"

"Guilty as charged."

"Shit, no," Billy said, scanning the horizon for a way out. "You Yankees fixin' to start a war?"

"I'm messing with you Billy. The CIA would never involve itself in the affairs of another foreign state."

"Shit, it's great to see ya again, Cathy. I've missed your sassy sense of humour – not to mention your short skirts."

"How long's it been, Billy?"

"Too long."

In the back of the vehicle, Rossi gazed up at the clearing sky.

"They're not comin' back, Inspector General," Billy said, glancing in the rear-view mirror at Rossi's tired face.

"What makes you so confident?"

"Because you're already dead," Billy said, pointing to a smouldering tyre, caught in the SUV's headlights.

"I'm sorry," Rossi said.

"The explosion you heard earlier. That was a Russian Vikhr AT-16 laser-guided missile hittin' the wrong target."

"You mean…"

"Uh huh. They think you've already gone to visit Elvis."

"But how – who?" Cathy asked, surprised that in such a godforsaken place an alternative target was even possible.

"Lady Luck," Billy said, kissing the horseshoe ring on his little finger. "When I arrived, I did me some recon – lookin' for alternative ways out in case there was a chase. I stumbled across a small group of Russian geologists over yonder. I listened for a while. They were packin' up to go home after a week in the field. Then at the last minute one of them produced a large bottle of vodka. Likely they got themselves drunk as a fiddler's bitch, then woke up at precisely the wrong time."

"That's ghastly," Cathy said.

Billy chuckled. "One man's loss is another man's gain."

Cathy and Rossi tossed from side to side as Billy manoeuvred the SUV down a rocky embankment onto the frozen creek bed that led to the only road out. "Shaken but not stirred," Billy said, glancing at Cathy, who was almost asleep.

Fifteen minutes later they were on the Aktobe-Orsk highway heading south-east. Rossi, alone in the back and exhausted beyond caring, felt an upsurge of relief and delight so powerful that tears welled up in his eyes. *God's in His Heaven – all's right with the world.*

70

Having slept most of the 170-kilometre drive from the Kazakh border, Rossi and Cathy felt relatively fresh as they boarded their covert flight to Rome.

"Inspector General, there's a master stateroom with a shower at the rear if you would like to freshen up," the flight attendant whispered in his ear. "We have another hour before take-off."

"Yes, of course," Rossi said. As he rose, he glimpsed his reflection in the silver champagne bucket on the table in front of him. *I hope I don't smell as bad as I look.*

"We also carry spare designer clothes for emergencies," the flight attendant added. "Please help yourself. I'm sure you'll find something in your size."

The customised Boeing 737 business jet was like nothing Rossi had ever seen. The interior was configured to carry a mere eighteen passengers. It included a plush living room and a high-tech boardroom. There was even a fully equipped kitchen with a centre island for preparing gourmet meals for the most discerning palate. *Looks more like an upmarket Manhattan apartment than a plane*, Rossi thought as he moved towards the back.

"We also have a range of ladies wear, Agent Doherty," the stewardess said, her tone flat. "I'll let you know when the stateroom is free."

Cathy sat for ten minutes stewing before ringing the call button. The flight attendant appeared promptly with a fresh bottle of champagne.

"You called, Ms Doherty."

"Ah, you read my mind," Cathy said, holding out her glass.

As the stewardess removed the foil from around the cork, Cathy rose abruptly. "On second thoughts, I should really go and help the Inspector General wash his back," she said with a wink as she strutted off.

***

Cathy opened the stateroom door and entered. She stood listening to Rossi sing in the shower. Something in Italian. Bocelli, she thought. Through the partly opened en-suite door she saw a disposable razor lying on the vanity unit and imagined his soft skin against hers.

She undressed, tossing her dirty clothes on top of his. In the full-length mirror she gazed at her perfect body, wondering how Rossi would react. *He couldn't help but want me*, she thought, placing her hands over her warm, heavy breasts and running them sensually down to her thighs.

For the first time in many years Cathy felt nervous. She pushed open the door and stood in silence, watching the shampoo foam run down Rossi's back and flow over his buttocks. Her breathing grew deeper and she could feel her heart pounding in her chest.

"Cathy, is that you?" Rossi said, frantically wiping the shampoo from his eyes. He turned towards the sound and instinctively dropped his hands over his genitals.

"Yes," Cathy said, searching for just the right words.

"You're naked."

"Nice of you to notice."

"What are you doing here?"

She frowned. "What sort of question is that?"

"Sorry," Rossi said, sliding open the shower door.

"Would you like me to leave?"

"Why would I?"

"Well you don't seem too pleased to see me."

"Do you think so?" Rossi said removing his hands.

"I take that back," Cathy said, staring.

"You'd better get in then, before we run out of water."

"You sure there's enough room?" Still staring.

***

Forty-five minutes later, the flight attendant knocked softly on the locked stateroom door. "Inspector General, we are ready for departure."

Rossi opened the door. "Give us a minute."

"I see you found something in your size," the flight attendant said, casting an admiring eye over him. "If I may be so bold – black's your colour."

"Yes it is," Cathy said, stepping between them; irked by the intruder's forwardness and Rossi's naivety.

"Very stylish," the stewardess said, now admiring Cathy. "Hugo Boss, if I'm not mistaken."

"It was the only thing in my size," Cathy answered, in a more amicable tone. "I feel a little like a secretary."

"Not at all," the flight attendant said.

Cathy unfastened one more button of her black blouse and straightened her grey pencil skirt over her pear-shaped backside. *A damned sexy secretary.*

"Smutty hussy," the flight attendant mumbled to herself as she headed back towards the lounge.

"Wrinkly bitch," Cathy said, slipping on a pair of high heel shoes.

Rossi, oblivious to the cat fight, grabbed the Concordat from amongst the dirty clothes and waved it in the air. "Ironic, isn't it? After all the trouble we've gone to, we haven't even opened it."

"That's because in your possession the document is only ink on paper," Cathy said, following him to the door.

Rossi stopped and took Cathy in his arms. Looking deep into her eyes he said in a soft, wistful voice. "Thank you for everything."

"For what?" Cathy yearned to hear more.

"For everything you've done – but above all, for your love – I love you, Cathy."

Tears welled up in Cathy's eyes as Rossi held her tight. She wished the moment would last for ever. "I love you too, Enzo," she whispered, tears now unashamedly running down her flushed cheeks.

As they walked dreamily back to the lounge, Cathy spotted a familiar face sitting in front of an upturned champagne bottle.

"Chief," she called out, feeling the weight of responsibility lift from her shoulders. "You're the last person I expected to see on this flight."

Chief James sprung to his feet and gave Cathy a heartfelt hug. "We thought we'd lost you."

"You can't get rid of me that easily," she said, turning to Rossi. "Enzo, this is the infamous Moscow bureau chief – William James. Chief, let me introduce you to Inspector General Lorenzo Rossi of the Vatican Police."

"Pleasure to meet you, Inspector General," the chief said, holding out his fat hand. "I trust you've been taking good care of my Cathy."

"The truth be known, she's been taking good care of me," Rossi said with a genial smile.

71

By the time the jet levelled off, the chief had finished explaining the reason behind his surprise visit.

"Can I offer you some breakfast?" the stewardess asked, reappearing from the front of the aircraft wearing an apron. "Unfortunately, we didn't have time to organise one of our gourmet chefs for the flight. But we have a fully stocked kitchen and I would be only too happy to prepare something for you."

"Sure," the chief said, unbuckling his seat belt. "We'll take it in the boardroom."

"Is this how the CIA normally flies?" Rossi quipped, following the chief to the adjoining room.

"I wish," the chief said, with a breathy laugh. "It's the property of a very nervous oil trader. He's hedging his bets on what will happen next."

"The mega-rich are a pragmatic lot," Cathy said. "No

matter what crisis befalls the planet, they somehow end up better off."

"Mind you, the crew's ours. And the TSCM boys have swept the interior from nose to tail just in case. So we can speak freely."

"Good decision," Cathy said, shooting Rossi a nervous glance; motioning with her eyes towards the stateroom. "We wouldn't want anybody listening in, would we?"

A weary smile crept over the chief's face as he sat down at the head of the eight-seat conference table. Cathy sat on the chief's right; Rossi on his left – opposite Cathy.

The flight attendant, who had followed them in, suggested a buffet of Russian pancakes, smoked salmon, Beluga caviar, fresh fruits, assorted cheeses and coffee.

"Perfect," Cathy said, trying to hurry her along.

The moment the door closed, the chief cleared his throat and began, "Well now, Cathy, I trust you have a good handle on what happened?"

Cathy stayed silent, assuming the question rhetorical.

"Please tell me you had nothing to do with Volkov's assassination. Because if you did, we're talking World War III and nuclear Armageddon," the chief said in a soft, uncertain voice as if he feared the answer.

Cathy took a deep breath and chose her words. "There were crossed paths and common characters within several related and unrelated plots, but it's true to say we weren't directly involved."

The chief shot Cathy a disapproving look. "Was that a no, or a yes?"

"Chief, I don't know where to begin."

The chief removed a notebook and pen from his briefcase. "From the beginning."

"Then it is best if Inspector General Rossi starts as it all began in Berlin long before the Agency got involved."

Rossi's demeanour stiffened as he explained how he had been entrusted by Cardinal Capelli to acquire the Concordat. "It was discovered by a young German man in his deceased father's apartment in Berlin. Although it was a counterfeit, Cardinal Capelli thought it best to pay the ransom. It was the only way of ensuring the document didn't fall into the hands of the Church's enemies.

"Such as Volkov's Russia," the chief said.

Rossi's expression grew grim as he described the bloody scene that confronted him in the presbytery of the Bonner Münster Basilica. And his subsequent encounter with Bishop Muellenbach's killer in Paris.

"It was through Oksana Koroleva that I established the Moscow connection," Rossi said, pausing as a knock came at the door.

The flight attendant entered pushing the breakfast trolley. She quickly set the table and poured the coffee. "If there's anything else you require please press the call button."

"We most certainly will," Cathy said, in a haughty tone.

As they filled their plates, Rossi resumed. "With Rudoi's defection, we confirmed most of what we had already deduced."

"But Rudoi didn't know whether the Concordat was forged," Cathy added for clarity.

"He didn't have to," Rossi insisted. "The Vatican would never enter into such an agreement. So we knew from the beginning the document was a fake."

The chief rolled his eyes. "Inspector General, unfortunately or otherwise, faith-based answers don't cut it in Washington any more."

"Well, maybe in Alabama," Cathy joked, in a bid to avert a show of primate chest-beating.

"That's because America has lost its spirituality," Rossi fired back. "Run by the rich for the benefit of the few. Godless capitalism taken to its evil extreme. I'm sure it's not what your founding fathers had in mind?"

"I see, you're now an expert on…"

"It was a reasonable assumption to make," Cathy said, speaking over the chief until he relented. "So we went hunting for the counterfeiter. And we got lucky early. Our man inside the FSB supplied the name of a person of interest. David Krotsky. We snatched him off the street. And under interrogation he acknowledged that he was the forger. Well, to be more precise, he didn't deny it."

"Initially he refused to cooperate," Rossi added.

The chief huffed. "What did you expect? A marriage proposal?"

Rossi glanced at Cathy wondering whether the chief was always this disagreeable. Her face gave nothing away.

"Then, the morning after Volkov announced the expulsion of the Catholic Church from Russia, we followed Krotsky onto the Moscow Metro," Cathy said with satisfaction. "We wanted one final crack at him before the noose tightened around his neck."

Rossi poured himself another coffee, then topped up Cathy's cup when she pushed it towards him.

"From what Lawrence told me, it could have gone better."

Cathy laughed. "From an execution point of view, a complete disaster. But the outcome exceeded expectations. Krotsky informed us he had deliberately used paper not available until the 1970s."

"But to prove it to the world, you needed the original?"

"Correct. That's where Revealing Light came in. One of their members paid a visit to Archbishop Esposito."

"Remind me again who they are."

"A secret society of Russian Orthodox priests." Cathy hesitated, as if wondering what the chief was playing at. "Established during the time of Peter the Great to liberate the Church from state control."

"Three hundred years and nothing to show for it," the chief scoffed. "Hell of a record."

"Until now," Rossi said softly, as if speaking to himself.

The chief turned his head towards Cathy and rolled his eyes. "A goddamned leap of faith."

At that moment it occurred to Rossi that the source of the chief's unpleasantness was good old-fashioned jealousy. Or perhaps fatherly concern for his daughter's welfare. Either way, it didn't bother him. The chief was no match.

"What was the purpose of his surreptitious visit?"

Rossi trailed his fingers through his hair. Now short and functional. "To petition the Pope to delay his response to Volkov's provocation."

"The reason for the request wasn't made clear," Cathy said, glancing at Rossi for support. "Other than some cryptic gibberish that made no sense."

"And this mysterious priest was Father Grigori – murdered by the OMON in Kitay Gorod?"

Cathy's expression turned sombre at the mention of the priest's name.

"He pointed us towards Father Arkady – the Patriarch's private secretary – who supplied us with the map of the Patriarch's residence."

"That's another thing I don't understand. Why on earth did Father Arkady cooperate? Secret societies aren't known for their openness."

"He was terrified we might jeopardise Revealing Light's mission," Rossi said.

"How could you, if you didn't know what the mission was?"

"It didn't seem to matter," Rossi shrugged. "As long as we swore up and down to stay away from Chisty Perevlok until eight on the night of the massacre, he was happy."

The chief threw Cathy an accusing glance. "Why didn't you connect the dots? You knew Volkov and the Patriarch would be together at Olympisky about that time."

"Chief, we had no way of knowing what was planned."

"Then why the leap of logic? Other than a request to defer the Vatican's response and a time embargo on your little burglary – nothing links Revealing Light to the incident?"

Rossi, deaf to the blame game being played, recited Father Grigori's words to Archbishop Esposito. "We will clear the way – expose the endemic corruption and profligacy that runs through the upper echelons of the Russian Church. We will sacrifice the charlatan who wears the white koukoulion."

"What!" the chief barked, glaring at Cathy. "Did you know about this?"

Cathy bit her tongue, knowing Lawrence had informed the chief of the threat. "Yes, but at the time it had no meaning. I interpreted it as histrionics."

"Well it wasn't, was it?"

"Chief, we don't know who's responsible. Let's not jump to conclusions," Cathy said, defensively.

"*Quel ch'è fatto, è fatto,*" Rossi said, trying to defuse the situation. "What's done is done," he repeated in English.

"I'm sorry, Cathy," the chief said, softening his tone. "You're right. I'm just tired and grumpy. Maybe I'm getting too old for all this."

"We're all tired, Chief."

"Either way, we'd better get on top of this quickly. It happened right under our noses. And on my watch. Careers are on the line."

Cathy let out a soft grunt of frustration. "Maybe someone's already claimed responsibility. I can check with the captain."

"Fine, but let's not over-science things," Rossi said. "All evidence points to Revealing Light."

The chief was standing behind his seat, stretching his legs. "Inspector General, you keep assuming the Patriarch was the target. But I doubt very much he was. It's inconceivable to think Volkov was nothing more than collateral damage."

"If it *was* Revealing Light, then they were all targets," Cathy said. "We know the death of Patriarch Pyotr wouldn't have brought the Church independence. The Kremlin would've simply replaced the Patriarch and carried on."

"But it's a real stretch of the imagination to believe that a couple of men in frocks pulled off the greatest act of political treason since Brutus and his cohorts assassinated Julius Caesar."

"It only takes an opportunity, and the means to execute," Rossi persisted.

"They didn't have the means to execute. That's the point. From what I've seen, it was a professional job. High explosives planted under the floor of the Presidential Box and remotely detonated. How many priests do you know capable of pulling off something like that?"

"Is it possible they had outside help?" Rossi asked, half-heartedly.

"Big risk to involve anyone not ideologically aligned; especially for a mission that must have been months, if not years, in the making."

"The Gatekeepers," Cathy suggested.

The chief took a deep breath and exhaled. "Don't know about you, but I need a strong drink."

"It's late evening in Washington," Cathy quipped, already moving towards the well-stocked bar. She poured a double bourbon for the chief and a Laphroaig for Rossi and herself.

"The two of you are damned lucky to be alive," the chief said, taking his drink.

Cathy raised her glass. "To our good fortune."

"And the grace of God," Rossi added.

The chief checked his watch. "Shall we continue?"

Cathy and Rossi sat patiently while the chief flipped through the last few pages of his notes.

"The Gatekeepers. That's an interesting idea. But how feasible is it?"

"Revealing Light rids itself of Patriarch Pyotr and the Gatekeepers take back control of the Presidency," Rossi said.

The chief shook his head. "The Gatekeepers would never surrender control of the Russian Orthodox Church. Besides, from what we've been able to determine, a number of the Gatekeepers were amongst the dead."

72

"Another drink, gentlemen?" Cathy asked. The chief and Rossi nodded. But before she rose, a short rap on the door. A serious-looking man in uniform entered.

"Good evening. I'm First Lieutenant Phillips, the co-pilot for your flight to Rome," he said in an official tone, shaking each of their hands. "I'm afraid I have troubling news. Two fighter jets from a Russian aircraft carrier anchored off the Syrian coast are approaching from the south."

The chief sprung from his seat and opened the window blinds. "Have they made contact?"

"Affirmative. They have requested that we switch off our transponder and divert the aircraft to Belbek."

"The Russian military airfield in the Crimea," Cathy said, staring at the co-pilot in utter disbelief. "What's been our response?"

"Three US fighter jets have been scrambled from the Incirlik Air Base in Turkey to intercept. US ground command has requested we maintain course over the Black Sea."

The chief squinted into the morning sun, scanning the horizon for the approaching jets. "Have the Russians gone completely mad? They can't go snatching a civilian aircraft over Turkish airspace simply because they feel aggrieved. There are rules, you know."

"That's what happens after bloody revolutions. The power vacuum is filled by extremists who do crazy, violent things. Don't underestimate the scale of their stupidity," Cathy said to the co-pilot.

First Lieutenant Phillips reassured Cathy that he had no intention of doing anything other than following US Air Force orders. He then excused himself and returned to the cockpit to prepare for their Russian escort.

"So what do you make of that?" the chief asked Cathy, returning to his seat.

"I'm not sure you can read much into it at this point. But it opens the door to other possibilities."

"For instance, a military coup?" the chief said.

"Again, we're grasping at straws," Rossi said, wondering why his American cousins insist on overcomplicating the obvious. "I suspect the jets have more to do with Russian domestic politics than anything else. The common thread through this whole misadventure is Revealing Light. So let's focus on *them* for a while."

Cathy and the chief glanced at one another, then nodded in agreement.

"You said the forged Concordat and the explosion at Olympisky Stadium are unrelated," the chief said, flicking back through his notes. "One designed to expand Volkov's empire, and the other to bring it down."

"That's one way of looking at it, Chief," Cathy said, smiling.

The chief tapped his middle finger rapidly on the table. "To date, we've assumed the incident went according to plan."

Cathy screwed up her face. "You mean an unintended victim?"

"Why not?" the chief said excitedly, resting his forearms on the table and leaning forward. "If the programme had run to schedule, Volkov and the Patriarch would have been down with the athletes when it all went bang – not inside the box."

"Another nice theory, but highly unlikely," Rossi said, frustration in his voice. "You said it yourself. This was a professional job. Remotely detonated high explosives. The killer would have had a clear line of sight to the Presidential Box. Missing the target was not possible."

Without warning, the Boeing rocked as the Russian fighter jets screamed past on both sides. Rossi and Cathy rushed to the windows and peered out. The more seasoned Chief James grabbed his iPhone and snapped pictures.

"Holy shit, what was that?" Rossi asked.

"Wake turbulence from two Russian MiG-29K jets," the chief said evenly. "Nothing to worry about. They're announcing their arrival."

Rossi looked troubled. "What happens next?"

THE CONCORDAT

"The fighter jets continue to intimidate us – and we play for time until the cavalry arrives," Cathy said. "You nervous?"

Before Rossi could reply, the fighter jets reappeared from behind and took up positions off each of the Boeing's long, flexing wings.

"That doesn't appear safe," Rossi said, thinking he'd prefer a thunderstorm.

"Look! He's waving," Cathy joked, gazing out of the port window at the MiG's pilot, who was signalling for them to bank right.

At the controls in the Boeing cockpit, Captain Powell eyeballed the Russian pilot and flashed him the middle finger. Next to Powell, First Lieutenant Phillips frantically tried to contact the US fighter jets en route from Incirlik Air Base.

"Back off, Natasha," Powell said through clenched teeth as the MiG drew within metres of his port wing tip.

In the boardroom, Rossi stared transfixed at a red and white dogfight missile attached to the MiG's starboard wing.

Next to him, the chief continued to take pictures. "These photos will give me bragging rights at the club for years."

"That's if we make it through this alive," Rossi said, watching as the wing tips of the two aircraft overlapped.

"Please return to your seats and fasten your seat belts," Captain Powell announced.

"Seat belts?" Cathy said, looking pale. "Parachutes would be more appropriate."

Rossi chuckled nervously as he buckled up. "Our oil trader guy's going to be peeved if we bring the Boeing back minus a wing."

"Enzo, don't."

"I'm trying to relax you."

"Well it's not working."

At that moment, the aircraft lurched and shook violently as it flew into clear-air turbulence. With the MiG in such close proximity, Captain Powell took immediate evasive action. He banked hard right.

The MiG hit the turbulence a split second later. In the cockpit the Russian pilot struggled desperately to control the bucking beast. He didn't stand a chance. Too close. Eyes wide open, he watched in horror as the Boeing's enormous wing swept up from below and snapped off his trailing edge flap.

Rossi and Cathy unclipped their belts for a better view while the chief scurried over to the starboard side to see what the second Russian jet was up to.

"Can you see him?" Rossi asked.

"There," Cathy said, glimpsing the pilot ejecting as the MiG tumbled towards the Black Sea thirty thousand feet below.

"How's the wing looking?" the chief called over to Cathy.

"There doesn't appear to be any damage, but it's impossible to be sure," Cathy said, holding on tight as she moved from window to window.

On the starboard side, the chief kept an eye on the second Russian jet. The pilot appeared to be flicking switches and readying something in the cockpit.

"What's he doing?" the chief said, as Cathy and Rossi joined him.

"Hope he's trying to flush," Cathy said.

Then their faces lit up as they watched the MiG peeled off to the north and disappeared.

"Run, you commie bastard," the chief yelled, as three US Air Force jets flew alongside.

Cathy wrapped her arms around Rossi. "Never leave me," she whispered, bursting into tears.

The chief gazed on with a kind of sad envy. A ladykiller way past his prime.

From the cockpit came an announcement. "This is Captain Powell speaking. I hope everyone's okay back there. I'm delighted to advise we've replaced our escort service. The US Air Force have now joined us for the remainder of the flight to Rome."

Cathy, Rossi and the chief roared and punched the air in celebration.

"And some good news regarding the port wing. We don't appear to have sustained any damage. One of the Air Force pilots is presently conducting a visual and if he gives us the all clear, we'll continue directly on to Rome."

The stewardess then burst into the boardroom, drying her tears. "Would anyone like something to drink?" she asked, trying her best to stay professional.

"Champagne," Cathy said, also wiping her eyes. "It's not every day you live through something like that."

The stewardess opened a fresh bottle of vintage Moët and poured it with trembling hands. She then moved to the bar and discreetly poured herself a double Scotch and knocked it back. "If you need anything else, please call," she said, wiping her lips with a napkin as she left the boardroom to convalesce on her own.

"Let's take a seat and finish the debriefing. Otherwise I'll have to hound you in Rome after we arrive. And I'm guessing you don't want that," the chief said, winking at Cathy.

"But first I insist on seeing the goddamned Concordat," Cathy said, sliding the plastic sleeve across the table to Rossi. "After what I've been through, I've earned the right."

"A quick peek won't hurt anyone?" Rossi said, removing the forgery from its cover. "Just don't tell the Pope."

"What's this?" Cathy picked up a handwritten note that had dropped onto the table. She read the page, mumbling and shaking her head.

"Are you planning on sharing that with us?" Rossi said, wondering, after all they've been through, what could be so startling as to render Cathy speechless.

"It's from Father Arkady," Cathy said, reading it out loud.

Dear Friend, if you are reading my note, then you have succeeded in your quest and I wish you a safe journey home.

God willing, I have been equally blessed and have purged the Church of corruption and profligacy and freed her from the tyranny of the Russian state.

But, as you know, God works in mysterious ways and sometimes the best-laid plans go awry.

To mitigate this risk, I took the precaution of having the Patriarch sign a letter (which I presented amongst other routine correspondence that His Holiness never reads) addressed to the Patriarchate of Constantinople, the first among equals. The letter states that after due consideration, and further scientific analysis, the recently discovered Concordat has been determined to be a vicious and sinful forgery, designed to divide the Christian faith. In his letter, Patriarch Pyotr beseeches Patriarch Gregory to help right the wrong by spreading the message of this wicked injustice.

I arranged for the letter to be sent in a diplomatic bag on the morning of Revealing Light's glorious triumph. This way, if I am called to God, I can go knowing that an unholy war between Christian faiths has been averted.

God Bless you,

A fellow Christian.

Rossi took a deep breath as he rose from the table in silence. His head was spinning in disbelief. *How could it all be so suddenly over?*

Cathy rushed over and threw her arms around him. "Enzo, we've done it."

"Well I'll be buggered. It was the nuns after all," the chief said, already standing at the bar pouring himself another double bourbon.

"We make a great team, Ms Doherty," Rossi said, looking into her watery eyes, certain he had found his soulmate. "Marry me?"

"Yes," Cathy screamed, causing the chief to gasp and choke on his drink.

EPILOGUE

Rossi held open the door. "Set it up next to the bed, please."

"The newspaper you requested, sir," the room service waitress said, handing Rossi a copy of *Il Tempo*.

Two hours earlier, as the Boeing business jet taxied to its parking position at Rome's Fiumicino Airport, Rossi had phoned Cardinal Capelli's office. He was informed by Monsignor Polak the cardinal was out of town and would not return until evening. Grateful for the reprieve, Rossi took a room at the Hotel Raphael off Plaza Navona to freshen up, and to order his thoughts.

Rossi opened the bathroom door a few centimetres. "You got any change?"

"What I had left was in my coat pocket which I left on the plane," Cathy called out from under the shower.

"*Mi dispiace.* We've just arrived from Kazakhstan."

"*Non è necessario, signore,*" the waitress said, closing the door behind her.

Rossi poured himself a cup of coffee then sat down on the edge of the bed and scanned the newspaper. The front page was awash with news of President Volkov's assassination and the threat of nuclear war. An image of the world in flames and Judgement Day popped into his mind. He shook his head to clear the thought and turned the page, continuing to search for news on the Concordat.

"That's better," Cathy said, tying her white hotel bathrobe around her waist. "Where's my coffee?"

"You've got to be joking!"

"If we're getting married, you must learn to share," Cathy said, kissing him on the top of his head.

"A single column on page seven with a three-word headline." It was exactly as he had predicted. Repairing the damage done to the Church's reputation would be nigh on impossible.

"What does it say?"

"Concordat Declared Sham."

"In more detail?"

"It refers to the letter mentioned in Father Arkady's note – from the Russian Patriarch to the Patriarchate of Constantinople. In a matter-of-fact way it says the Concordat is a forgery. It doesn't even attribute blame. It's unbelievable. There's no condemnation or commentary. Where's the outrage?"

"I guess compared to what's going on in Moscow,

the Concordat's yesterday's news – especially given it's a fake."

"Who on earth will read it back here?"

"Calm down, Enzo. I'm sure the Vatican's press office will organise a more appropriate level of coverage once the world refocuses. Right now, the world leaders have higher priorities. Your justice can wait."

"You're right. I only hope Cardinal Capelli sees it the same way."

"Stuff him."

Rossi continued to read. "*Fantastico*. Father Arkady's alive."

Cathy grabbed the newspaper and read the article herself. "He's now the spokesman for the Patriarchal Locum Tenens, Metropolitan Paul. You heard of him?"

"No. But I know what it means. Metropolitan Paul is one of them. Revealing Light has won," Rossi said.

"But at what cost?"

"Someone once said 'peace at any price is no peace at all'. Volkov needed to be stopped before he became too strong. And Revealing Light stopped him. For that we should be grateful."

"I suppose so. But this chapter of history will be decades in the writing."

Rossi walked over to the window and drew open the curtains. The low winter sun streamed onto his face and he closed his eyes. To him it was incomprehensible that the most hellish days of his life had turned out so triumphantly. He knew Revealing Light still had way to go before it found true freedom, but the first major battle had been won. And although it was unlikely that Cardinal Capelli would agree, he felt that the trouble caused by the Concordat was a small price to pay.

Then his thoughts turned to Cathy Doherty, and the chance to finally make his mama happy.